KILLER
ROUTINE

ALSO BY ALAN ORLOFF

Diamonds for the Dead

KILLER

A LAST LAFF MYSTERY ————————

ROUTINE

ALAN ORLOFF

MIDNIGHT INK
WOODBURY, MINNESOTA

FIRST EDITION
First Printing, 2011

Book design by Donna Burch
Cover design by Ellen Lawson
Cover illustration © Kelly Dyson/The Bright Agency

Midnight Ink, an imprint of Llewellyn Worldwide Ltd.

Library of Congress Cataloging-in-Publication Data (Pending)

Orloff, Alan, 1960–
  Killer routine : a Last Laff mystery / Alan Orloff. — 1st ed.
     p. cm.
  ISBN 978-0-7387-2310-5
  1. Comedians—Fiction. 2. Traffic accident victims—Fiction. 3. Stand-up comedy—Fiction. 4. Murder—Investigation—Fiction. I. Title.
  PS3615.R557K56   2011
  813'.6—dc22   2010047991

This is a work of fiction. Names, characters, places, and incidents are either the product of the author's imagination or are used fictitiously, and any resemblance to actual persons, living or dead, business establishments, events, or locales is entirely coincidental.

Midnight Ink
Llewellyn Worldwide Ltd.
2143 Wooddale Drive
Woodbury, MN 55125-2989
www.midnightinkbooks.com

Printed in the United States of America

DEDICATION

To Janet, Mark, Stuart, and the rest of my family,
who laugh at my jokes, no matter how lame.

ACKNOWLEDGEMENTS

Many very talented and generous people had a hand in getting this book published. My sincere gratitude goes to:

My readers, booksellers, and librarians. You rock!

My critique group partners, Dan Phythyon and Ayesha Court, for their terrific comments and suggestions. And for calling it like they see it.

My faithful and insightful early readers: Sam Feigeles, Sue Ousterhout, Mike White. Megan Plyler and Dorothy Patton. Mark Skehan and Doug Bell. John Stevenson, Jill Balboni, Kim Stevenson, and Samantha Stevenson.

Those who provided me with inspiration along the way: Elaine Raco Chase, Ann McLaughlin, and the P.J. Parrish sisters (Kris Montee and Kelly Nichols). Donna Andrews, Ellen Crosby, and Art Taylor. And John Gilstrap and Noreen Wald, in spades.

Reed Farrel Coleman and David Bickel for their generosity and kind words.

Basil White for telling me what a comic's life is really like. Stand-up comics everywhere.

All my friends in Mystery Writers of America and International Thriller Writers for their advice and support. All my cyberpals on Facebook, Twitter, and throughout the blogosphere.

My superb agent Kathy Green for her astute guidance (and her persistence).

All the great people at Midnight Ink: Bill Krause, Terri Bischoff, Brian Farrey, Connie Hill, Steven Pomije, Courtney Colton, Donna Burch, Ellen Lawson, and the entire—super—sales staff. GO TEAM!

The best (and most enthusiastic) family a guy could have: Ruth; Karen, Jamie, and Emma; David and Wendy; Susan, Becca, and Phillip; and Lisa, Paul, Samantha, and Malon.

My mom, Bev, and my late father, Leonard, for instilling in me a love of books.

My children, Mark and Stuart, and my wife, Janet. Without you by my side, this wondrous trip wouldn't be worth taking.

Thanks!

ONE

I LURKED IN THE wings watching the man *kill*.

He cut them with quips, slayed them with stories. Plunged his razor-sharp wit into their guts and twisted, twisted, twisted until tears streamed down their faces.

The stand-up comic on stage had the audience on a string; his feelings of power and control and exhilaration were like no others. I knew what it felt like, but unless you'd been on stage before, it was hard to fathom the intensity of the moment. The indescribable rush was what comics lived for, killed for.

For me, it had been five long months since I'd felt it, five months since the name *Channing Hayes* had graced the marquee out front. Five months since the accident. I missed the rush daily, almost as much as I missed Lauren.

The comedian continued his onslaught, and the violent lingo describing his goal echoed in my head. *Destroy. Slay. Kill.* Make the audience *die* laughing. Before the accident, I wouldn't have thought twice about it—words, just words. Now, I had trouble getting past their real meanings. In my life, the line between comedy and tragedy had dissolved one horrific night five months ago.

A tug on my sleeve caught my attention and I spun around to face Heather, Lauren's younger sister. She'd been in the crash, too, and had escaped with little lasting physical injury. I wasn't so sure about her emotional stability, but you had to give her props. At least *she* was prepared to resume her career.

I leaned over and whispered in her ear. "Ready to go?" Even if I shouted, the comic on stage probably wouldn't hear me over the crowd's riotous laughter, but I wanted to set a good example. It didn't look right if the co-owner of The Last Laff Comedy Club dissed the talent by drowning out their punchlines.

With a jerk of her head, Heather motioned me to follow. She led me down the hall toward the back, past the restrooms and the "green room" and the swinging door on the right that served the kitchen. Past the storage closet and the shoebox-sized office Artie and I shared. She pushed through the service entrance into the cool Northern Virginia spring night, while I hustled to keep up. Behind the club, the smell of ripening garbage in the Dumpster assaulted my nostrils, and the faint sound of satiated rats scurrying away raised a few hairs on my neck. *There's no place like home…*

Heather stopped short and leaned one shoulder against the filthy cinder block wall. Pulled her Dumbo the Flying Elephant towel from her pocket and began wringing it. Her good luck charm. If only she'd had it with her that night.

"You okay?"

Heather's eyes were the size of hubcaps and her lower lip quivered. "I don't know, Channing. I'm a little freaked out."

A little? I rested my hand on her shaking shoulder. "Relax. You're supposed to be nervous. If you weren't, I'd think something was wrong with you." Tonight was Heather's first time soloing in front of a crowd, not counting a few open-mic nights. Her first big test since the accident.

"It's more than that. I don't think I can do it," she said. "It's—"

"You've been working on this for a long time. Working hard. You've earned it," I said. "You'll do great." I'd been helping her with her act. Encouraging her, serving as her sounding board. Fine-tuning it. Going solo was a lot different than the improv sister act she'd been doing with Lauren, though she'd adapted well. Lauren had been a grinder, but Heather had that one-in-a-thousand natural comedic talent. Just needed focus and a dose or three of discipline.

Heather twisted Dumbo into a tighter knot. "I'm not ready. I'm not. I don't think I can do this." Her words spilled out faster, higher pitched. She stared at me with deep dark chocolate eyes, the same eyes her sister used to peel me open with. My heart *ka-chunked* in my empty chest.

I glanced down at the two remaining digits on my left hand. Thumb and forefinger. I'd lost the other three fingers in the crash, and my mangled hand would forever haunt me. I raised my head and caught Heather transfixed by my hand, too. I swallowed before I spoke. "Heather. Listen to me. Lauren would be so proud of you. She knew you were the one with the star on her back. The 'supreme crowd pleaser'—her words, not mine. More than anyone, she would want you to go out there tonight. This is the first step back. Do it for her."

Heather's head sagged. I reached out and gently lifted her chin. "You know I'm right. Remember, Channing Hayes is *always* right. Even if your sister said otherwise."

A slip of a smile appeared but vanished in an instant. "I'm scared," she said in a small voice.

"We're all scared on stage. But think of the audience. How amazed they'll be after you blow them away. Come on. You know I'm right." I gave her arm a reassuring squeeze.

Heather nodded, still wringing her towel. There was something in her face, something I hadn't seen before. Not nerves, exactly. Something deeper. "Channing?" Her voice trembled.

"Yeah?"

"No matter what happens tonight, I want to thank you for everything you've done. For helping me cope. For helping me with my act. For…" She choked up and her big eyes filled. "Just for everything. Okay?"

"Sure, sure. But don't worry, it will all—"

The back door swung open, and Artie Worsham, my mentor and partner in the club, stuck his head out. "Goddamnit Hayes, there you are. Get your tush back in here. We've got a club to run. Don't have time for girltalk. Let's go. Chop, chop." He gave Heather a parting glare and ducked his head back inside. The door *whooshed* closed on its pneumatic piston.

I tried to buck Heather up with a final round of encouragement. "You can do it. I know it. You know it. And Lauren knew it. Go out and kill for her, okay?"

She nodded, and I've never seen anyone look so pitiful, so forlorn. I could only do so much. At some point it was up to her to leave the nest and fly on her own, and that point was fast approaching. I tapped my watch. "You're on in twenty. And please, don't worry. You'll do great. Really."

———

A party of three had walked out on their bill, and Donna McKenzie, the "mother hen" of The Last Laff—head server, ticket seller, business manager—steamed. "I can *not* believe that happened. Little dipshits."

Donna and I stood behind the bar as Skip Gold, the bartender, hovered nearby, listening in while pretending not to. "Don't worry about it. Just a few bucks," I said, winking at her. "Want I should chase them down and beat it out of them? It'd be my pleasure."

Donna frowned at me, hands on hips. "Don't make me laugh. You couldn't swipe the lunch money from my little Seanie." Her asthmatic seven-year-old.

From behind us, Skip chimed in. "Why don't you just overcharge the next few parties? Like I do when that shit happens to me." He wiggled his eyebrows, first the left one, then the right one. Then both together.

"I didn't realize you even knew how to make change," Donna said. "You know, all those different coins can be confusing."

Skip made a face. "Learned it in high school. Along with how to mix drinks."

"I bet you aced that course. I mean, look at the great job you do here. You're our number one bartender."

"I'm your only bartender," Skip said. Another face, more twisted than the first. "At least no one hosed *moi* tonight."

Donna gave him the finger as she returned to her tables. Skip sidled up to me. "What's with Artie this evening? He seems kinda prickly."

"How can you tell? He's always like that," I said, scanning the room for the old guy. The comic on stage had almost finished his set, and it was Artie's job to introduce the next one. Six-Pack Wednesday was a crowd favorite, when the club gave six up-and-coming comics twenty minutes each to strut their stuff.

"Heather's next, right?" Skip asked. "She ready?"

"She's ready." My throat felt dry, my palms didn't. Heather's self-doubt bothered me. It was one thing to be a little nervous—many people performed better that way—but she'd gone way beyond a few butterflies. It would destroy her confidence if she flamed out tonight. Maybe there was too much pressure on her. Maybe she *wasn't* ready.

The comedian nailed his final punch line and the audience cheered. A quick bow elicited more applause as Artie strode across the small stage toward the microphone.

"Dave Stebbinski everyone. Let's hear it for Dave!" Artie said. Old-school through and through, he hewed to the traditions whenever he could, even if the entire audience had been weaned on Seinfeld and thought Carlin, Cosby & Klein was the name of the firm handling their parents' wills. To my surprise, Artie held one arm up and pushed his open hand toward the ceiling, like he must have seen a rapper do somewhere. *Raise the roof, suckas!*

Maybe you *could* teach an old-school dog new tricks.

He brought the mic up to his mouth. "How's everyone doing tonight? Having fun?" Another push skyward.

The audience responded, and you could see the pride reflected in Artie's face. "Good, good. We've got a hot comedienne up now, one you'll really enjoy getting to know. I sure did," Artie said, forcing a theatrical chuckle. He waited a beat for the reaction, but only got a few groans. "Hey, I kid because I love," he said, this time to complete silence. There was a reason he'd given up performing to open the club.

He shrugged and cleared his throat into the mic. "Anyway, I'd like to introduce one of the finest young comics to hit this town in a long time. You've seen her as one half of the Dempsey Duo, and now she's taking her solo act out for a spin. Please welcome Miss Heather Dempsey!" Artie swooped his arm out toward the wings to greet Heather as she bounded onto the stage.

No Heather. No bounding.

Artie waited a few seconds, then tried again. "Give a big hello to Heather Dempsey!"

A few murmurs burbled from the audience. "Come on out, Heather. I promise I won't bite. Not this time, anyway." Artie took a few steps toward the side of the stage where the on-deck performers waited, holding the mic away from his mouth. "Hey," he called to someone off-stage. "Where's the girl?" Even without the microphone, most of the crowd could hear the confusion in Artie's nasal voice. He kept walking until he disappeared behind the curtain.

I left my position behind the bar and rushed through the room, weaving my way between the tables. Before I reached the wings, Artie had returned to the stage, microphone in hand. "Sorry about the delay, folks. Miss Dempsey's not feeling well. So let's give it up for Pokey Paulson!" A short, fat guy trudged into the spotlight to polite applause.

I met Artie as he came off stage. "Where is she?" he asked. Concern seemed to crowd out the irritation in his voice.

I shrugged. "I don't know. She was nervous. I'll see if I can find her."

Artie gave me a knowing glance. "Yeah, yeah," he said. He'd been a little leery of putting Heather on stage by herself. A big fan of their sister act, I knew he didn't want Heather to fail, afraid she'd give up her dream if she bombed. Despite his gruff exterior, Artie was the most caring individual I'd ever run into in this business. Or any other, for that matter.

Sometimes a comic would drop out, but usually it happened during an open mic night when nerves would propel a newbie into a puking fit. Didn't happen to the pros very often.

I checked the green room. Artie had transformed an oversized storage closet into a waiting room/dressing room for the talent. A two-person loveseat and a coffee table picked up at a garage sale. A 19-inch TV attached to a VCR. A dorm-sized refrigerator stocked with RC Cola and cream soda. All crammed together in a room he'd painted mint green, in a nod toward *The Tonight Show*. We had a long way to go before we were in Leno's league. Unfortunately, Heather wasn't there.

I got Donna to check the ladies' room; she came up empty. I sent her back in to re-check each of the stalls, but they were still empty. I questioned Skip and the other two servers. No sighting. Turned out I'd been the last one to see her.

I tried her cell, but it rolled into voicemail after four rings, and I closed the phone without leaving a message. She knew it was her turn on stage, knew we were counting on her. Knew about the audience waiting to roll on the floor laughing.

That's exactly why she took off.

I went out behind the club again, bracing for the stench of garbage. I thought maybe she'd still be there, frozen with indecision, nerves a-jangle. I couldn't blame her. The accident had really screwed up my head, and I knew it also had affected her deeply, despite her assurances otherwise. I wouldn't blame her if she *never* summoned up the courage to get back on stage. It was something I hadn't been able to do yet and I had a lot more experience than she did.

I leaned against the cinder block wall trying not to think about that awful night, when I'd lost my fiancée and my entire life had disintegrated. I felt myself going under, succumbing to the feelings of guilt. Why did I have to drink that night? Why couldn't I have been the one driving? I was a better driver; I would have been able to prevent the accident.

Why had I survived instead of Lauren?

I closed my eyes and waited for the bottomless feeling of despair to pass.

It didn't. It never did.

TWO

I WENT BACK INSIDE to catch the last two comics. Each stretched his act ten minutes to make up for Heather's absence, and the audience didn't seem to notice. Or if they did, they didn't seem to care. To them—to most of our customers—comics were interchangeable, replaceable. Like car tires. Got a flat? Just slap on another tire. As long as there's enough tread on it, you're good to go. Sad to think I was the only person truly disappointed Heather hadn't performed.

After the place emptied, Artie and I sat at the bar reviewing the evening—our nightly ritual. It was our way of decompressing, and it gave us a chance to float any suggestions we might have—for improving the acts, the food, the drinks, the service, anything—while they were still fresh in our minds. Tonight, Skip hung around and jawed with us. Made him feel useful, so Artie didn't shoo him away. He always thought it important to make the employees feel like an integral part of the team.

"So? Find Heather?" Artie asked. He chewed an unlit cigar, the same one he'd been gnawing on for a week.

"Nope."

"Don't sweat it. I've seen it a million times. Comics think they're ready, then nerves take over. In this business, courage is as essential as talent. Maybe more so." Artie nodded, as if this was the first time he'd ever said it, although I'd been hearing it for years.

I shook my head. "I don't know, Artie. She seemed off tonight, but I'm not sure it was about performing. I mean, she's been on stage a lot."

He pointed his cigar at me. "Yeah, but always with her sister. Never by herself. Big difference. Big, big difference."

Off to the side, Skip leaned on the bar, bony chin resting on one palm. "I'm with Artie. She rabbitted. Happens all the time." He shrugged in my direction. "Hey, not that I blame her or any-thing."

I glared at him and he busied himself with some glassware down at the other end of the bar. Skip was a frustrated young comic himself, but he suffered from what a lot of people suffered from—stage fright. Except his was so bad it brought on stuttering. Tough to be a comic with that hanging around your neck. To make matters worse—because of the stuttering—someone long ago had saddled him with the nickname Skip. I always thought Skip Gold was a better comic's name than Steven Gold, but I wasn't sure he saw it that way.

I returned my attention to Artie, poring over the figures from the night's take. "I'll talk to Heather. Find out what happened. Maybe we can give her another chance?" I raised my eyebrows in his direction. I didn't want one moment of indecision on Heather's part to ruin everything she'd been working so hard to achieve.

Artie grunted. "Yeah, yeah. We'll see." He jammed the cigar back into his mouth and rustled his papers. After a moment, he picked his head up and fire burned in his eyes. "You know that prick Reed?"

"Sure." Gerry "Greedy" Reed owned the Capitol Comedy Club, known by the comics as the CCC. We liked to think of him as competition, but his club was the D.C. area's eight-hundred-pound comedy gorilla, and ours was a spindly spider monkey. "What about him?"

"He waltzed in here earlier. Said he wanted to talk to us about something big. Something we'd want to listen to." Artie's face had turned red. "I told him I was busy and to come back three years from next Tuesday."

"Did he say what he wanted?" I asked, picturing Reed sauntering through our doors, nose tipped high. He was tall, handsome, and charming, and I didn't like him one bit, not with his I'm-better-than-you-and-every-friend-you-ever-had expression permanently pasted on his puss. Sometimes it still rankled me, knowing Lauren and Heather had gotten some stage time there before I bought into The Last Laff and Reed had become my nemesis. It had been great experience for them, but…

"He didn't say, but I know what he's after." Artie paused and fingered his cigar thoughtfully. "Us. He wants to buy us out."

Since I'd bought into the club three months ago, Artie had been trying to scare me with stories about potential conquerors. According to him, every club owner in the area—and by *area* he meant Maryland, D.C., Virginia, and the rest of the eastern seaboard from Maine to Florida—wanted our tiny hole-in-the-wall to fulfill some monomaniacal domination strategy. Or some such nonsense, I never listened too carefully. "Why would he want us? His place is four times bigger and they *make* money. They attract national headliners people have actually heard of."

Artie's eyes narrowed. "Hey, we're still growing. In a few years, we'll be right there alongside him. He must know it's true if he's so anxious to talk with us." He threw air-quotes around the word *talk*.

"So?" I asked. Down the bar, Skip's clinking had stopped. He wasn't facing us, but I knew he had his ears throttled open.

"So what?" Artie asked back.

"So maybe we should listen to his offer. What do you think?" I knew what Artie's answer was, but I wanted to give him a chance to vent. Not healthy to keep everything bottled up. "You've been doing this a long time. Maybe it's time you packed it in. Retired to Boca." I heard Skip chuckle in the background.

"Fuck Boca. And fuck him. He wants a fight? We'll give him a fight. No one underestimates Artie Worsham. And lives to tell about it, that is." Artie got up, jabbed the cigar in my direction. "Lock things up, will ya? I'll see you tomorrow." He stalked off without another word.

Skip came over and slapped me five. Goofing on Artie was enjoyable, even if it wasn't very challenging. *We kid because we love.*

Twenty minutes later, I'd made it home to my high-rise condo in Dunn Loring. I was about to slide my key into the lock when a few strains of a classical piece drifted through the air. I stepped across the hall and touched my ear to Erin's door. The violins were clearer. I knocked softly.

The music stopped; a moment later the deadbolt *snicked* and the door opened. A single eye and a nose appeared in the crack. When Erin saw me, the door closed for a second and I heard the chain lock being undone. Then the door reopened. "Good evening, Channing. Want to come in?" she asked, face bright.

"If I'm not interrupting anything."

"No, just wrapping things up. Be done in a minute. Have a seat, won't you?"

I followed her in and flopped on her couch, like I'd done many times before. She excused herself and went into the kitchen, where I knew she worked at her laptop.

Erin Poole made her living as a writer, penning what used to be called "pulp novels." Her most popular series featured a hard drinking ex-sheriff who roamed the West looking for black hats to kill—written under the alias Colt Hannigan. In another series, written as Dirk Rogers, a seven-foot-tall, muscle-bound bounty hunter tracked down fugitives. Those stories always ended in death and disaster—especially for the fugitives. Luckily, in real life, she was gentle and caring, more like an Erin than a Colt or a Dirk. I guess most people needed an outlet for their inner feelings. For her it was violence and gore. For me it was comedy.

Erin returned to the living room. "Another week and I'll be done with my latest masterpiece," she said, laughing. "What drivel." She shrugged. "But it's a living, right?"

"Your fans enjoy them."

She laughed again. "You've never read any of my books, have you?"

My face felt warm. "Lauren loved your books," I said, evasiveness transparent. Erin had given us every one of her paperbacks.

Lauren had tried to get me to read some, enticing me with intriguing character descriptions and thrilling plots, but I'd never gotten around to it. Too busy writing my own material to read someone else's.

She patted my arm. "It's okay. I haven't been down to your club either, so I guess we're even." She laughed once more, a melodic sound that couldn't have been more different than Lauren's staccato laugh. Yet it reminded me of the life I'd never have.

Erin lowered her voice. "How are you doing?"

"Okay. I guess."

A half smile from Erin and another pat on the arm. "I miss her too."

All I could manage was a nod. Every day the feeling of emptiness persisted. I'd come to realize it was now a part of me, as much as my lungs or my brain or my spleen.

"She was a good person. A good friend," she said. When Lauren and I had moved into the building eighteen months ago, Erin had been the only one on the floor to show any true hospitality. The three of us had become fast friends, with similar tastes and sensibilities and ways of looking at the world. Erin's preference for working at night even meshed with our nighttime gigs.

I felt tears welling up, but I blinked them away.

"Channing, I've told you before, if there's anything I can do for you, just let me know. You're a good friend, too. And friends watch out for each other, right?"

We sat there, side-by-side on the couch in comfortable silence, while I thought about Lauren and The Last Laff and that elusive thing called comedy and other weighty things. Like why Heather Dempsey had skipped out on her big night in the spotlight.

THREE

THE NEXT MORNING, I woke up around ten, early for me. Downed a bowl of Cocoa Puffs, skimmed the Sports section, then flipped on the Cartoon Network. After a few minutes without finding anything remotely humorous, I turned the set off. Where were Ren and Stimpy when you needed them?

The great thing about working nights was sleeping in and having your days free to watch mindless junk on TV. What better way was there for a thirty-three-year-old to spend his time? Besides thinking about Heather's disappearance, of course.

Two possibilities came to mind. Either she bolted due to a gigantic bout of stage fright, or something else was going on in her life. Something bad enough to freak her out.

If it was just a bad case of nerves, like Artie and Skip thought, then I needed to pump her up. Make sure her psyche hadn't crumbled. Lauren had been stolen in a cruel accident, but I'd be damned if I was going to let the tragedy affect her sister's career— as long as I had something to do with it.

On the other hand, if something bad had happened, I wanted to know about it. To help, if I could.

Bottom line, I needed to talk with her. Now.

I called her cell but didn't get through, so I left a message asking her to call me as soon as she could. I tried the phone at her apartment, too, but it rang until the machine picked up. I left another message for her to call me, and this time I was pretty sure the urgency I felt came through loud and clear, despite the static-filled connection.

Lauren always complained about my lack of patience, but I was never patient enough to sit down and consider changing my ways. After waiting about half an hour for Heather to return my calls, I decided to drive out to her place. Maybe she was hiding in her apartment, ashamed of what happened last night, unable to leave the safety of her bed and unwilling to answer the phone to talk about it.

As I unlocked the door to my vintage 1983 RX-7 in the parking lot, I remembered my first date with Lauren. We'd done the boring—dinner and a movie—but what had stayed with me was her expression when I told her I'd named my car Rex. For a moment, she'd stared at me, trying to determine if I were putting her on. Then her face contorted into a grimace Edvard Munch would envy before she exploded in laughter. Her reaction had surprised me. Didn't all guys name their cars?

Now, though, the joy I got driving Rex had diminished considerably. A car was just a car, after all.

I took I-66 away from town to Route 50, heading west along three or four miles of commercial congestion, passing shopping centers and fast food restaurants and blossoming townhouse developments. Traffic was sluggish, and the roads that had once been bad only during rush hour, now were clogged all day. The trip to Heather's Chantilly apartment, which would have taken about fifteen minutes sans traffic, took about thirty-five.

Her complex was only a few hundred yards off the main drag, yet it felt much farther from civilization. The parking lot was mostly empty, and those cars that remained were old, American, and in need of Earl Scheib's deluxe package.

Heather lived on the second floor of a three-story building, one of four buildings laid out around a central common area. Two toddlers played next to a dilapidated playground set, their mother—or sitter—watching them over a newspaper from a nearby wooden bench, cigarette dangling from her lips. She glanced in my direction as I climbed the stairs, saw I wasn't Ed McMahon toting an oversized multi-million-dollar check, and returned to her Daily Horoscopes.

A three-inch rectangle of paint had peeled off Heather's front door, right below the number 223, revealing a layer of yellow paint beneath the more recent washed-out brown. I rapped on the door a few times, loud enough to wake her if she were still in bed. Lauren and I had tried to talk her out of living here, but Heather yearned for independence, and most of the nicer places, closer in, were too expensive to swing without a roommate.

I waited a minute and knocked again. Waited fifteen more seconds, then rang the bell. I didn't hear it chime inside, so I pressed it again, listening more carefully. And again. Nothing. Busted, right along with everything else around this forsaken place. I glanced down at the play area, and the two kids seemed to be wrestling over a doll, one of them wailing pretty good. The mother kept her head in her paper, no doubt inured to the crying and tantrums. I guess it helped to be inured to a lot of things if you lived in this dump.

After a final rat-a-tat-tat, I left to find the property manager.

Back at ground level, I followed a small sign pointing the way to the rental office, located in a building on the other side of the play area. As I approached the mother on the bench, I nodded and said hello. She glared at me and opened her mouth to respond, but thought better of it, returning to her paper, careful not to engage me in any way. You try to be friendly and all you get is heartache.

The rental office occupied the corner unit on the first floor; a tiny laminated piece of cardboard on the door instructed visitors to RING BELL FOR SERVICE. I poked the doorbell button with my finger but didn't hear anything. After another poke, I gave up and knocked on the door.

I heard someone yell something unintelligible from inside, and the door opened a moment later. A stocky woman with curly red hair—not a shade found in nature, or on most people's heads for that matter—peered at me over a pair of bifocals. Her pinched face scowled at me. "Can't you read the sign? Ring the freakin' bell next time."

"I did. Must be broken."

Her eyes narrowed to slits. "We've got two vacant units. Both one bedroom. Both ground floor. First month, last month, and two-month security deposit." She stepped back a smidge and looked me up and down. Twice. "Assuming you qualify, the rent's—"

I held up my hand. "I'm not interested in an apartment. I'm looking for Heather Dempsey."

She cocked her head at me.

"Unit 223? Pretty blond?"

She gave me a quick nod. "Unit 223's in the first building, across the way." She jerked her thumb over her shoulder and started to close the door.

I slipped my shoe into harm's way. The door bumped against it and I felt the pressure as the landlady continued to try to shove it closed. "Yes. I know. She doesn't answer."

She looked down at my shoe, then at me. Didn't say anything, just glowered. I imagined her anger causing her scarlet hair to ignite.

I shrugged and withdrew my foot. "Sorry. Have you seen her?"

"I've got forty-eight units. You think I keep tabs on everybody's whereabouts? I got a life, you know."

Some life. "Can you let me in? I'm worried something might have happened to her."

"Who are you, David Caruso? I can't just let you in because you're worried. I don't even know who the hell you are." She snorted. "I haven't seen *you* around here before."

I'd dropped Heather off or picked her up a dozen times, sometimes with Lauren, sometimes without. I didn't recall seeing her either. "Well, I—"

"She's probably with one of them other guys."

"What guys?"

She tossed her head, as if everyone on the planet knew about them other guys. "Four or five different ones. All hours. Got a few calls from the neighbors. Walls are a little thin in spots. Know what I mean?"

When I'd first met her, Heather used to go through boyfriends like tissues. But she'd been trying really hard since the accident to get her life together, and I thought she'd been doing a good job of it. Even introduced me to some reasonable-looking guy a few weeks ago named Ryan, who turned out to be a roommate of Skip's buddy. "Look, I'm a friend of hers and I'm concerned. She doesn't answer her phone or her cell. Or the door. She could have had some kind of seizure or something. Or fallen in the shower."

"And she didn't answer when you knocked?"

"Nope. She sure didn't." I gave her my best puppy dog face.

"Well, then. I guess she ain't home. Sorry, buddy. Can't let you in." She drew herself up and stuck her ample chest out. "Now, if you want to rent a place, we can keep talking. Otherwise…I got stuff to do."

I sighed loudly to make sure my displeasure was noted. "Listen, if you see her, could you give me a call?" I reached into my pocket and pulled out a business card. Held it up to her.

She plucked it out of my hand, examined it. "The Last Laff, eh? What are you, a comedian? You don't seem very funny to me."

I got that a lot. "Will you call me?"

Her hand dropped to her side and she squinted at me with one eye. "Why should I?"

"If you do, I'll introduce you to my friend Andrew Jackson."

Something awakened behind her porcine mask. "You got a friend named Grant and we'll talk."

"Sure," I said, but the door had already shut.

FOUR

WHEN PEOPLE DECIDED TO go to The Last Laff for the first time, they often got lost and ended up calling the club for directions. Must be tough to imagine a comedy club located in a nondescript shopping center along a past-its-prime commercial stretch in Vienna, Virginia. Tucked between Lee's Palace—Home of Very Famous Peking Duck—and Sofa Showroom, the club didn't stand out like you'd expect. I wondered how many customers pulled up, took one look at the plain-Jane façade crying out "dull suburbia," and hopped back into their cars to go drinking at some downtown hotspot instead.

But home was where the laughs were, and this was our home. Artie had done quite a tap dance to get a favorable deal on the lease, convincing the property managers he'd still be in business six months down the road. That had been fifteen years ago.

The Last Laff wasn't the most popular comedy club in the D.C. area, but it managed to hold its own despite its aging appearance and hard-to-find location. Truth was, there weren't too many

comedy clubs in Northern Virginia, and we provided good entertainment at a fair price to the not inconsiderable number of people who wanted something fresh and exciting without having to
drive the extra forty minutes into the District. Plus, we had plenty
of free parking.

It was Thursday afternoon, the first day of our headliner's
three-night stand, and when I arrived at the club, comedy superstar Jon Jermaine—J.J. to his fans—was already there yakking
it up with Artie at one of the VIP tables near the stage. J.J. and
I went back a few years, both of us breaking into the business at
around the same time, trying out our material at the same clubs
around town. He'd broken through to the next level—star still rising—while I'd settled in at a spot closer to the middle of the pack.
We had what I would call a friendly rivalry, although I hadn't seen
him in about a year. "Hey, hey, there he is," I said, bumping fists.
"How're you doing?"

"Spectacular. Couldn't be better." J.J. sported a big grin. He'd
done both *Leno* and *Letterman* within the past three weeks, and a
few months before he'd logged serious minutes on a Comedy Central anthology show. "Heard about your accident," he said, glancing at my bad hand. "Rough, man. Real rough."

"Yeah, thanks."

Artie wedged himself into the conversation. "Okay, okay. Let's
not get all weepy here. This is a comedy club." He touched his temple with one finger. "Think laughs."

I frowned at Artie, but he'd been in the hospital with me, hour
upon hour, in the first days after the accident. I knew who the
weepy one was. "Everything okay at the condo?" I asked J.J. Artie's
"comedy condo" was actually a townhouse where he put up the

out-of-town headliners. The comedy condo was an old-school tradition and Artie believed it made the talent more comfortable. Made them feel like a regular "part of the family."

J.J. said, "It's great. Beats staying at a Holiday Inn, sleeping with one eye open so the rats don't sneak up on you." He winked at Artie. "At least your rats *ask* permission before they turn on the TV."

"I hope your stuff tonight is better than that, my friend," Artie said.

"Don't worry. I'll bring my 'A' game. As usual. Who am I working with?" Each show had a special guest opener, a featured middle act, and a headliner.

"We picked a quirky opener from last night's smorgasbord," Artie said. "And Rick Fortunis is in the middle. Know him?"

"Round guy, bushy moustache?" J.J. asked.

"You got it," Artie said. "Not as funny as you, but he's pretty good."

J.J. smiled. "The middle guy's never supposed to be as funny as me, right?"

"You're *all* supposed to be funny," Artie said, then turned serious and pointed his cigar at J.J.'s chest. "Don't forget that."

J.J. nodded, not sure if Artie was yanking his chain. "Sure, man. Don't blow a gasket or something."

"Blow a gasket. Hah, that's a good one," Artie said, rising from his chair. He shook his head. "Try to get all those rotten ad-libs out of your system now, okay? Before your set. Our customers expect *funny*, not *crummy*."

"Uh, sure." J.J.'s expression settled somewhere between confusion and bemusement.

"All right, then. I'll let you two gals catch up. I'm sure I've got something useful to do." Artie shuffled off, chewing on his stogie and mumbling to himself.

J.J. nodded after him. "What a guy, huh? This business needs more old-timers like that. Think one day we'll be like him?"

"I hope not."

J.J. winked at me. "Gotcha. Listen, I really am sorry about your accident. I would have called, but..." He held his hands up. "You know how it is, right? On the road, and everything."

Yeah, I knew. "Sure. I'm fine."

He looked relieved. "Good. But listen, you need anything, you just call, okay?"

"Sure."

"Seriously. Just pick up the phone."

Enough about me. "Hungry?" I asked. Despite a fully stocked kitchen in the condo, not too many comics availed themselves, heeding the old adage: *never eat the mayonnaise at the comedy condo*. Most survived on junk food, cigarettes, and alcohol—not necessarily in that order.

J.J. rose and clapped me on the back. "No thanks. I'm going to meet a buddy of mine for a quick bite. What time you want me back?"

"First show's at 7:30. Sometime around then would be good, although you don't really go on until about 8:30. Second show starts at 10:00." Everything had been spelled out in the contract, but I knew J.J. played so many clubs, in so many towns, that everything blended together. A little reminder never hurt.

J.J. nodded. "Seven-thirty. You got it. Now, how do I get to Hooters?"

As soon as Rick Fortunis took the stage, I left to get some fresh air. I'd seen his act a dozen times before and had subconsciously memorized his punch lines—an occupational hazard of club owners.

Just before I got to the entrance, I stopped at our Wall of Fame, where dozens of autographed publicity glossies hung in cheap frames. About half the comics who performed here signed one for us, and about half of those tried to inscribe their photo with something witty. I found J.J.'s, from about three years ago. *"Artie. Good to see you're still alive and kicking. Try to stay that way, at least until the check clears."* Obviously, some were wittier than others.

I located mine. The shot was taken about two years ago, and the look on my face reflected the happier times. *"The Last Laff— what Heaven must be like, if St. Peter imposed a two-drink minimum."* Not much wittier, but not as caustic either.

I felt a presence at my side. Tyrone Taylor, our greeter, ticket taker, and *bouncer extraordinaire,* had joined me. "What's the word, Ty?"

"Everything's cool. No problems tonight," he said. "Or any other night, either." On Thursday, Friday, and Saturday nights, Artie hired Ty to fulfill his notion that all *real* clubs needed bouncers. Never mind that Vienna wasn't exactly a hotbed of gang activity or that Artie hadn't had a single major problem in his fifteen years running the club. Image was everything in this business, and Artie subscribed to the theory that bouncers were judged like male appendages, the bigger the better. Ty was bigger than most.

"Don't expect any problems. Not with you here." I playfully chucked him in the shoulder and felt no give whatsoever. Ty stood six-six and weighed two-seventy-five, with an androgynously beautiful face perched atop a body carved from a single slab of ebony granite. No seams or cracks anywhere. He looked like he'd started lifting weights when he was seven and hadn't stopped.

"J.J. packs them in, doesn't he?" he asked.

"Yes he does. But I like to think our club's reputation helps."

Ty rolled his eyes. "I guess tomorrow and Saturday will be hopping, too."

"Better be."

The door opened and a trio of attractive young women entered. Ty smiled, and two huge moon craters opened up on his cheeks. Six female eyes dilated. He took their tickets and checked their IDs carefully, as Artie had instructed. We couldn't afford any trouble. If we lost our liquor license, we were dead.

"Welcome to The Last Laff. Have a great time," Ty said.

"Thanks, we sure will. *Now*," one of the women said, and the other two giggled as they headed toward the bar. Artie figured Ty's sex appeal alone accounted for a significant upswing in business from the female persuasion, and Artie was nothing if not a shrewd businessman.

A group of guys came in next, smelling of beer and falling all over themselves. Ty gave them the evil eye and they straightened up without a word. Ty winked at me and checked them through. "Enjoy the show, but be cool." Each one nodded solemnly as he entered the club. Ty grinned after them, head shaking.

"How's school?" I asked.

"Crunch time, man. Semester's winding down." The way Ty said it, you could tell what really mattered. For him, working here was simply a way to make a few bucks to help get through George-town Law.

"Well, I'm sure you'll do fine," I said. A few seconds of silence passed between us. "I don't suppose you've seen my friend Heather around?" I'd called a few people during the afternoon, but no one had seen or heard from her.

Ty eyed me. "Not recently."

"You sure?"

Another smile. "I know you think I space out sometimes, but this isn't a job that requires a lot of brainpower, you know?" He straightened. "Don't worry, I can do my job even if I'm spacing out a little."

I had no doubt about that. Ty didn't have any comedy aspirations—that I knew about—but he could run this place if he wanted to. Maybe after a long and distinguished legal career, he'd open up a chain of comedy clubs as a hobby.

"Why are you asking?"

"She ducked out on her set yesterday."

"Hey, man. It happens. Nerves get the best of them sometimes." Ty shrugged, every muscle in his neck becoming taut.

"Yeah, that's what Artie—"

Ty snapped his fingers. "Hey, did Artie find you? He was in a lather about something."

"When?"

"Few minutes ago. You'd better go see what's up. Sounded like his boxers were on fire."

I found Artie chomping on his cigar in our office. Although he always said we "shared" the office, he got the leather chair and the desk, while I got the folding chair and the wobbly card table. I guess owning seventy percent of the club gets you your choice of furnishings. "What's up?" I asked.

"Just talked with Greedy Reed."

"What?"

"I said, 'Just talked with Greedy Reed.'" Artie enunciated each word and spoke slowly.

I made a face. "I heard you the first time. Where?"

"He's sitting in the front. Brought his own entourage," Artie said. "Prick."

"What did he say?"

"He said he's got an offer for us we'd be foolish to refuse. Worst Brando I've heard in a long time. Prick." Artie plucked the cigar from his mouth and waved it in the air. "I don't care what it is, we ain't selling." He glanced at me. "Right?"

I wasn't in this for the money. Although money *was* nice. "Whatever you say, boss. I'm behind you. You know that. But I still don't get why he would care about our club?"

"Who the fuck knows? Maybe he wants to establish a beach-head in Northern Virginia. Maybe he's looking for a write-off. Maybe he's got a jones for Peking Duck and loves Lee's. Point is, he wants our place."

"So just tell him no. He'll move on to his next target."

Artie sighed loudly. Obviously I didn't understand the situation. "Reed's vindictive and we haven't always seen eye-to-eye in the past. If we don't sell, he'll come after us. Poach our talent, find some reason to bad mouth us in the press. Maybe he'll start another club right down the street. He'll try to ruin us." Artie never backed down from a fight, but he sounded worried now.

"You'd think he had better things to do than harass us."

Artie ran a hand across his face. "He wants us to meet with him next week. At his lawyer's office." He stuffed the cigar back in his mouth and talked around it. "His lawyer's probably a prick, too."

"What did you tell Reed?"

Artie flashed me a tight smile. "I told him to enjoy the show. Just like I tell all my guests."

———

The second show was better than the first, and Artie and I left the club together after the place had cleared out. The take was way above average, and thoughts of having to deal with Reed had receded into the misty background as so many bad dreams do. That is, until we saw J.J. and Reed leaning against a Town Car at the far end of the parking lot, forty yards away under a streetlamp. Artie and I froze by the front door. The sounds of their laughter carried well in the night air, and I saw Reed reach over and grasp J.J. by the shoulder at one point, great companions sharing a joke. Off to the side, a few members of Reed's group huddled, engaged in their own muted conversation.

Next to me, I could almost feel Artie's body tense, and I knew only bad things would happen if I didn't intercede. I gently pulled Artie to the side and spoke in the calm voice I reserved for upset children and wild dogs. "Relax. They're just talking. J.J.'s played his club in the past and they're probably just reliving a few choice moments. I'm sure it's nothing personal. It'd be a big mistake if you go over there and make a scene or something."

Artie bared his teeth and snarled out the words. "He's trying to steal him. Turn him against us. J.J.'s got friends, plenty of them.

If his friends go with him, it'll be tougher for us to get the big names."

"Don't let your imagination get ahead of yourself. They're just gabbing. Go home to Sophie. Get some rest."

"Sophie's at her sister's. In Vegas. For a month." As he spoke, his eyes didn't leave Reed and J.J.

That wasn't good. Sophie was the only person who could tame Artie when he got like this. "Well then, I guess you'll really be able to get some rest," I said, hoping to extract a smile.

Instead of a smile, Artie's jaw clenched, and the muscles in his cheek rippled like waves of grain. "You're still a rookie, kid. I've been around enough. Too much, maybe. And I know Reed's type. Hell, I *was* his type years ago. He's got something up his sleeve, all right." Artie seethed, but he also was smart enough to know I had a point. Without a word of protest, he let me steer him to his Caddy, and I watched with concern as he started it up, jammed it in drive, and roared off.

When Artie was out of sight, I glanced back over my shoulder at Reed, who raised a hand in my direction. Then he turned his back and continued schmoozing our headliner, Jon Jermaine. I didn't see it, but I could just imagine the shit-eating grin on the prick's face.

FIVE

THE NEXT MORNING, I still hadn't heard from Heather, and I was beginning to get worried. Before the accident, Heather had a reputation as being flighty and flaky, dizzy and shaky—not always the most dependable person. But since the accident, I'd noticed she'd made great strides in becoming more respectable, as if she'd sobered up from a long drunken spell. I guess seeing your sister die—and coming face-to-face with Mr. Death himself—changed your way of thinking. I know mine had changed, more than I cared to admit.

I called Skip at home and got the number and address of his friend, the one sharing a place with Heather's latest boyfriend, Ryan. Maybe Heather had gone off to warm her cold feet at his place, a little loving to make everything okay again. I called his number, hoping that even if Ryan were at work, Heather would pick up the phone.

A man's voice answered after the first ring. "Hello?"

"Uh, yeah. May I please speak to a Ryan Skczdlgbrr…" When in doubt, go with the ol' gibberish routine.

"This is Ryan Rizzetti. What can I do for you?"

"Oh. Wrong number." I hung up. Skip had given me a Reston address, about fifteen minutes away. Better to talk to Ryan in person. It would be harder for him to blow me off, although my presence hadn't really swayed Heather's landlady. *David Caruso?* Maybe I needed to step up my tough guy image. Act more like Magnum or Mike Hammer. Or Spenser. Those guys seemed to fare pretty well on the daytime TV reruns I gorged on. Of course, people on cable seemed to live a different—and more exciting—life than mine.

On the way to Ryan's townhouse in Reston, my mind shifted into overdrive. Was Artie right? Had Heather simply chickened out like so many other comics standing on the threshold looking out over their careers? In her act with Lauren, she'd seemed so comfortable on stage, in the spotlight. Had her comfort been solely due to her sister's presence?

Comics weren't exactly the most reliable and predictable people around. They seemed to be wired differently than normal people. Over the years, I'd seen tons of weird stuff. The comic who couldn't perform unless his girlfriend was in the audience, with her eyes closed. A ventriloquist who bombed after his dummy chipped a "tooth." Another guy who couldn't go on stage without his oboe.

I hadn't been back on stage since the accident, but my roadblock was more nebulous than a missing reed instrument. Artie kept telling me to take my time, that I'd know when I was ready again. I trusted him, going so far as to repeat his words as my mantra. Would I get some kind of sign I was ready? Or would I just have to make the leap, hoping for a soft landing?

I turned up the radio as I continued my drive to Ryan's, happy to put my self-analysis aside while I concentrated on my immediate goal: finding Heather.

Thanks to a brisk tailwind, I made it to Ryan's Reston townhouse in twelve minutes. Red and white azaleas bloomed in his small front yard, a green swath of grass blades on the concrete walkway a sign the lawn was freshly mowed. When I pressed the doorbell, a clear chime resonated from within. Somehow, I knew the bell would work here.

"Yes?" The voice from the phone greeted me in person. Tall, with curly black hair, Ryan wore a George Mason T-shirt and green shorts. A ring of sweat darkened his shirt collar and a slight sheen covered his face.

"Remember me? Channing Hayes. Heather introduced us a few weeks ago. At the club."

Ryan tensed. "Sure. I know who you are." The beginnings of a sneer formed. "Heather talks about you non-stop." He made no move to invite me in.

"Sorry if I disturbed your workout."

He waved me off. "Heather's not here," he said. "If you were looking for her." His clipped voice didn't come across friendly. There seemed to be a lot of that going around lately.

"Do you know where she is? She was supposed to do a set at the club the other night, and she, uh, disappeared."

Ryan cocked his head, then shook it. "Haven't seen her in a few days. I had a business thing in Philly. Got back late last night. Was supposed to stay another day, but I wrapped things up early." He swept his arms down at his clothes. "That's why I'm working out instead of just plain working." He grinned at his wordplay, but I gave him the stone face.

"Have you talked to her today?"

The grin morphed into a look of indecision. Then his face softened. "I tried calling her. No answer. Left a message. She'll call back. Eventually." He accentuated *eventually* and nodded at me, as if I knew what that meant. Heather always returned my calls promptly so I wasn't sure what he was getting at.

"Has she disappeared before?"

A small, biting laugh escaped Ryan's mouth. "Heather's right. You are a stitch." He paused, waiting for another reaction from me. I maintained the poker face. "Seriously? Heather? She's queen of the disappearance. High-Tail Heather. Craves her personal space. Always ditching town to 'clear her head.' If her head were any clearer, you could see right through it." Ryan grinned again at his attempt at humor, maybe not fully realizing I was a professional and he was making an ass of himself.

"Any idea where she might have gone this time?" I asked. Ryan was describing the old Heather, and it made my stomach clench. Had she reverted to her unreliable ways?

"*Dude.* You need to chill. She'll come back. She always does," Ryan said, and then a scowl appeared, as if an internal switch had been thrown. "What do you care, anyway? You got a thing going with her? First her sister and now Heather? What next, her mom?"

Ryan seemed to be in pretty good shape, but I figured I could take him, even with only one good hand. If I were lucky, maybe someday he'd start something and we'd get a chance to mix it up. I took a deep breath and focused on my reason for being there.

"Relax, *dude*. I'm worried about her. She's been working hard on her act, and Wednesday night was a big step. Or would have been, if she'd gone on. I know she wanted to prove herself."

His face darkened. "You know, do you? You know all about what she wants, huh? Maybe you should just leave Heather alone. Let her do what *she* wants to do, not what she thinks *you* want her to do." When he'd finished his little speech, the veins in his neck bulged.

Even though he was a jealous twerp, Ryan's words stung. Was he right? Was Heather doing all of this to please me? Trying to make up somehow for Lauren's absence in my life? I needed to find her so I could ask her. Hear it directly from her mouth. I held up my hands in a gesture of peace. "Look. You don't have to believe me. You don't have to like me. All I want is what's best for Heather. If you could help me find her so I can talk to her, I'd really appreciate it." I wiped every bit of animosity from my voice that I could, adding, "Seriously, I'm concerned about Heather and I need to find her."

I didn't know if it was my sincerity or what, but Ryan seemed calmer. Then it hit me. He didn't care a whit about what I felt. He just wanted someone to find Heather, someone who wouldn't catch shit for violating her personal space. Someone who could do the dirty work and deliver his girlfriend back to him.

"What do you want from me?" Ryan asked.

"You know the name of the store where she works?" I knew it was at Seven Oaks Mall, but she'd never told me which place. Heather wasn't always forthcoming with details.

"Brianna's Body Shoppe," Ryan said. "She works there with a friend of hers. Amber or something. Cute chick, but…" Ryan held his finger up to his head and spun it around. *Crazy.*

"Thanks," I said. "Anything else that might help me find her?"

"She'll resurface soon. You're just wasting your time," he said, meeting my eyes directly for the first time in the conversation. When he saw I wasn't going along with him, he swallowed and his eyes flitted around. "Come on, nothing could have happened to Heather, could it?" His pleading eyes met mine again.

I just shrugged.

———

At one minute past one o'clock, I eased onto my therapist's couch. I didn't recline, choosing to sit upright and face things head-on, like the man I sometimes wished I could be.

"How have you been, Channing? Still having trouble sleeping?"

"Yeah. Takes me a while to doze off, then I wake up three or four times every night. It sucks." I looked for some kind of confirmation, but all I got was the steady, thoughtful gaze I'd become accustomed to.

"And the dreams?"

I closed my eyes. "Nothing's changed. It's still me and Lauren, at the store or at the gym, or wherever. She's moving her mouth but not speaking. I talk and she can't hear me." My eyes fluttered open. "Some of the details change, but the gist is the same."

"Have you been thinking about what we discussed last time?"

We'd spent the last session talking about guilt, as well as the time before that. And most of our other sessions usually touched on it, too. Over the past five months, I'd become an expert on the subject. "I can't *not* think about it. It's my fault Lauren's dead, plain and simple."

"Yes, that's what you believe. But that's only your point of view. I think you'd agree someone else, someone who wasn't directly involved in the accident, might come to a different conclusion. Many times we're not in the best position to process our own experiences objectively. Or *accurately*—however you wish to define it."

My pulse quickened. "If I hadn't been drinking that night, I would have been driving. And—you can ask anyone, so I think it's pretty objective—I was a much better driver than Lauren. I wouldn't have run off the road. I wouldn't have landed upside down in a ditch." We'd been through this before. Many times. Why was I forking over $150 per hour? Or, more *accurately*, per fifty minutes?

"You say you don't remember what happened. How do you know things would have been different if *you* had been behind the wheel? You said it wasn't your car, that it was Lauren's. Maybe you wouldn't have driven any better than she did that night."

"I'd driven her car plenty." We'd been driving Lauren's car because the three of us—me, Lauren, and Heather—couldn't fit into Rex's two seats. "I know what I know. I could have avoided the accident."

"Many excellent drivers get into accidents. Sometimes things happen that are even beyond the control of the most careful, most prudent person around. It was an accident, Channing. Perhaps no one's to blame. You or Lauren."

It was true, of course. I blamed myself and I blamed Lauren. How could she have done this to herself? To me? To *us*? Why had I encouraged her to do stand-up in the first place? I didn't speak, letting the thoughts and questions tumble in my head. On stage, silence was deadly. Here, it gave me time to sort things out, quiet the cacophony in my mind. After a long two minutes, I spoke. "The guilt's bad enough, but I could live with that. It's the anger and depression that are really starting to eat at me."

"Go on."

"Not all the time. It alternates. One day, I'll be royally pissed. At everything and everybody. Then the next day, I won't feel like climbing out of bed." I swallowed, knowing where this would lead.

"We've talked about this before. You're struggling to deal with an incredibly tragic situation. Your life has been turned upside down. I think you owe it to yourself to explore all your options. So, despite your mother's, ah, history, I think we might want to consider medication. Medication, like Prozac for instance, could prove to be very beneficial to you."

I didn't respond right away. My mother killed herself at the age of forty-two with a Valium and gin cocktail, heavy on the Valium. The thought of taking drugs scared the shit out of me. "I think I'll pass." I shifted on the couch, stretching my legs and crossing them at the ankles. Time to take this session in another direction, any direction, as long as it led away from my mother. "I'm worried about my act. At first, I figured I was too shaken up to go on. That things would be better in a couple of months. But things *aren't* getting better. I've lost my confidence. And that's a death blow for a comic."

"Let me ask you a question: If you go back on stage, what's the worst that could happen? You don't get a few laughs and you what, bomb?"

"Don't make it sound so trivial. If a comic doesn't get laughs, he has to go find a real job." I rearranged myself on the couch. I'd bought into The Last Laff. Gone into management. Did that mean I'd already thrown in the towel?

"When you were starting out, you must have bombed a few times. Yet you managed to persevere. To succeed. You did it once, you can do it again. And I'm sure now the learning curve wouldn't be so steep. Perhaps it's just a matter of proving to yourself you have the courage to continue with your life. Perhaps it's time to try."

Guilt, anger, despair, destroyed confidence. Just a few of the zillion negative thoughts and emotions haunting me since Lauren's death. "I know I need to get past all this. Get my life back on track. But how?"

"Ah, there's the rub."

SIX

THAT NIGHT, WE HAD to turn customers away from the early show. Donna and Artie tried to persuade the disappointed to come back for the late show by offering discounts and free drink coupons, and although we felt bad for them, it was a nice problem to have. Buzz was good; J.J. had gotten a small blurb in the *Post's Style* section, sending scores of comedy seekers our way. If we were lucky, some of those customers would remember us next weekend, and the weekend after that, and the many weekends after that, too.

Before the show began, Freeman Easter, a friend of mine, found me in the green room trying to put the opening act at ease. With a parting, "Don't worry, you'll do great," I excused myself and walked Freeman back to the office and closed the door. "Hey, man. Thanks for stopping by."

"Planning to come anyway." Freeman gripped my hand and shook firmly. Like he was used to doing it on a daily basis, unlike some of the comics I met who seemed to lack basic social skills.

"How's it going?" he asked, nodding toward the door. "Big crowd tonight. J.J. always brings 'em in, huh?"

"We're not complaining," I said. I'd first met Freeman about ten years ago when I was just starting out. He seemed to do open mics here, there, and everywhere, although he'd never aspired to rise beyond that level. He had some talent but lacked the drive. Loved his regular job too much to give it up. Artie and I had given him a standing pass to the club. Medium height, skinny, and dressed in a conservative dark suit with rimless glasses, he looked more like an accountant than a sharp-witted Fairfax County Narcotics detective.

"You sounded like something was up on the phone," he said.

"Need your help."

"What are buddies for anyhow?" he said. "Need a few good jokes?"

"Always, but that's not why I called. A friend of mine's gone missing," I said. "Heather Dempsey. She was supposed to do a set here Wednesday night. Her big break as a solo act. Then right before her set, she disappeared. Haven't heard from her since and no one I've spoken to has either."

"She's only been missing for two days?" He drew out the word *missing*.

"Yeah, but…"

He raised an eyebrow. "This unusual?"

I swallowed. No denying Heather was a free spirit. Lauren had recounted plenty of stories from Heather's teenage years about her frequent "road trips," a fact pounded home by her boyfriend Ryan. "Well, she's done stuff like this in the past. But…"

"But you don't think that's what happened this time," Freeman finished for me.

I nodded, knowing Freeman probably heard those exact words as often as I heard jokes involving priests, rabbis, and talking giraffes.

"I know you don't want to believe it, but the vast majority of missing persons show up, sooner or later, unharmed. They've decided to go on vacation, or are involved in some kind of relationship hoo-hah, or go on a drinking binge." He stopped and eyed me through his round lenses. "That possible? Drinking or drugs?"

I exhaled again and shook my head. "Listen, I can't discount all of that. I mean, Heather's an adult and she's probably not the most reliable person in the world, so I guess it's *possible*. But I don't think that's what happened here. Really. She's changed since the accident. Matured. And she's always taken her comedy very seriously."

"Two days is nothing."

I stared at him, lips pressed together.

Freeman sighed. "Who'd you talk to?"

"Boyfriend. Landlady. Called her on her phones. Left messages. No one's seen her or heard from her." I snapped my fingers. "Poof, she's gone."

He sighed again as he extracted a pad of paper and a pen from his breast pocket. "Okay, give it to me."

I gave him Heather's description, address, phone numbers—all the information I thought he'd need, including the all-important fact she was Lauren's sister. When I finished, he closed the pad with a practiced flip and eyed me. "Any reason you didn't call the parents yet?"

I nodded and shrugged at the same time, as if it were on my to-do list but I just hadn't gotten around to making the call yet.

"Could be she's there, hiding from the world, just chilling out." When I didn't respond, he let it go. "Okay. I'll check around a bit. Talk to a buddy in Missing Persons. Maybe check out the morgues and hospitals. But nothing official gets done until someone files a report. Usually it's a relative. Considering how you've described her, with her history, I gotta be honest. Nothing much is going to happen from our end. Certainly not without the parents getting involved and raising a ruckus. Even then…" Freeman shook his head. "I can't be the one to call them. Wouldn't want to freak them out, and besides, it's really none of my 'official' business. Sorry, man. I'd like to help more, but…two days? That's nothing." He shook his head as he left the office, closing the door gently behind him.

I pictured Heather's parents puttering around their stately Southern Colonial mini-mansion, William Dempsey fixing a drainspout while Kathleen Dempsey planted impatiens, a perpetual scowl on his creased, middle-aged face, a warm smile on hers. Before the accident, they were going to be my in-laws. My only living "parents." At first, her Republican father resented the hell out of me, a liberal stand-up comic, but we'd achieved a sort of truce—he didn't bother me and I didn't bother him. Lauren's mom, on the other hand, was a real peach.

Despite Lauren's father's overly protective attitude, we'd all gotten along pretty well, and Lauren often joked that she and I would be taking every vacation with them, especially after we blessed their lives with grandkids. Now, the thought of talking to them terrified me.

There was only one reason I hadn't called yet, but it was a beaut. After what happened, William Dempsey hated my guts with the passion of a dozen religious zealots. In his eyes, I was the monster responsible for the death of his daughter.

The late show also sold out, and by the time I helped Skip and the others clean up, it was after two o'clock before I got home and into bed. When my phone rang at four o'clock, I grabbed at it, fearing it was Freeman with bad news: He'd found Heather in a coma at some hospital, or worse, she'd turned up toe-tagged in a chilled drawer at the morgue.

But it wasn't Freeman on the line, it was J.J. "Hey, Channing, my man. I need a big favor." The way he yelled into the phone told me he'd been partying hearty since his show had ended a few hours ago.

"Do you know what time it is?" I spit the words into the phone. I'm sure he knew, but I wasn't too sharp with my retorts on such little sleep.

"Late, man. Real late. Sorry. But I need your help. I did something I prolly shouldn't have. Messed up, super-sized." The words slurred together.

I rubbed my hand across my face and a cold shiver rippled through me when I didn't feel the last three fingers. Their absence still stunned me sometimes. Would that ever stop? I brought the phone back to my ear and heard J.J. chanting my name in a sing-song. "Chan-ning, Chan-ning, Chan-ning."

"Cut the shit, J.J." After one more feeble *Chan-*, his ditty petered out. "Where are you?" I asked.

"At the condo. Lissen up. I need you to come over. But be vewwy, vewwy careful." J.J.'s voice had reduced to a whisper. "And bwing a hacksaw."

SEVEN

At four a.m., I made it to the comedy condo in fifteen minutes. I would have been there sooner, but I doubled back a few times in a Falls Church residential neighborhood to make sure I wasn't being followed. Maybe it was a latent streak of paranoia—Lauren always teased me about locking my car in her parents' driveway—but when J.J. told me to be vewwy, vewwy careful, I took his Elmer Fudd warning to heart. I felt better knowing no one was following me.

After I entered the townhouse development, I hooked down a narrow side street and drove to the end of the row. Parked Rex in front of Artie's end unit. I took it as a good sign there weren't any vehicles with flashing lights or sirens. The townhouse bordered a small patch of woods, and if you sat outside on the cozy back deck—with the conditions just so—you could hear the babble of a little brook cutting through the trees on its way to the drainage culvert out by the main road.

I grabbed my hacksaw and jumped out.

A soft shimmer of moonlight illuminated the parking lot and miniature front lawns. Nothing seemed out of the ordinary. Nothing seemed "messed up super-sized," and I figured J.J. was probably referring to his mental state. A toad bounced into view on the sidewalk in front of me, then stopped. A croak later, it hopped into a row of bushes, eager to bed down with all of its toad friends, no doubt.

On the porch, I removed the townhouse key from my pocket, noticing how odd it looked on the key ring all by itself, without car keys or office keys or locker keys to jingle against. A lone key. Some comics had a way of losing things, while others treated the condo like just another hotel room where nobody cared if you returned your keys. Artie got torqued always having to replace the keys, but hey, the comedy condo was a tradition and sometimes you had to sacrifice to keep the important things going. Or at least that's what he told me through clenched teeth. A couple of months ago, he'd gotten practical and had a dozen keys made. I knew, because he asked me to put each one on its own numbered key ring. Hopefully, that batch would last more than a few months.

I didn't even need key number three; the door was ajar. I peeked in through the gap. All dark. With the end of the hacksaw, I slowly pushed the door open. Nothing jumped out at me, and I realized I'd been holding my breath. I exhaled and stepped in. Flipped the light switch on and checked out the foyer. Looked like it had the last time I'd been there, like it had every other time I'd been to the condo.

"J.J.?" I called out and froze, perking my ears up. Silence. Maybe he'd solved his problem and gone to sleep. Or left the place altogether. I headed for the stairs, glancing into the main living area.

In the semi-darkness, it looked like a tornado had touched down. I turned on the overhead light and the debris came into focus. Two bottles of vodka rested on the coffee table, along with about four or five glasses, a couple tipped over. A few bags of chips laid open, a trail of crumbs marching off the table onto the floor. Pants, a shirt, socks, and underwear draped across the couch and loveseat, as if some neo-wacky decorator had decided to use garments as throw pillows and didn't give a fig about color coordination.

I moved closer, making a conscious effort not to touch anything. Next to one of the bottles were a small mirror and a couple of straws. A single line of coke remained, untouched. To Artie's chagrin, wild parties were not unheard of at the condo. Every once in a while, he'd tell me about some complaint from the homeowner's association. Many comics lived on the edge and reveled in their mania, which was one of the things that made them funny. But it also made them unpredictable, unreliable, and—sometimes—unstable. I thought of Heather. Had Freeman hit on the answer when he'd asked whether she binged on drugs or alcohol? Disappointment washed over me when I realized I wouldn't be surprised if it were true.

I left the living room and searched the kitchen. Aside from a puddle of orange juice on the counter, everything seemed normal. No alcohol, no drugs, no garments. I headed for the stairs to check out the bedrooms. It made sense that J.J. was probably sleeping it off. But then why call me?

"J.J., you here?" I called out louder. This time, I thought I heard something. A gasp, or a grunt.

I climbed the stairs, just another guy creeping around a condo at four in the morning with a hacksaw. The thick carpet on the treads muffled my steps, lending even more of a dreamlike quality to the whole escapade. When I reached the top landing, I stopped. Each of the three bedroom doors was closed and no light shone through the cracks underneath. "J.J., where are you?"

"Hey Channing. That you, buddy?" J.J.'s voice came from the master bedroom, and although it didn't sound peppy, at least he wasn't dead, which was a good thing. Especially for J.J.

"Yeah, coming." I pushed open the door and turned on the light. J.J. lay spread-eagled on the bed, naked except for a pair of frilly pink crotchless panties. Someone else's, I assumed. One arm dangled from high on the headboard where it had been hand-cuffed to a metal rail. On the nightstand were another bottle of booze and an economy box of condoms, a foil strip snaking out of the box and onto the tabletop. Bedsheets mounded in the far corner of the room.

"Hey, man. Thanks for coming. I 'preciate it." A wide grin spread on his face. "Had a spot of bother, I did, I did."

I stood there, staring. Comedians.

"Thank God you brought the hacksaw." He sounded pretty wasted, but he wasn't completely out of it. "After I called and asked you to bring it, I thought that maybe you'd think I was just pull-ing your leg or something. You know, right? But I dropped my cell and it bounced under the bed. And…" He rattled his cuffed hand. "Thank God you came, Channing. Otherwise, I'd be here days from now when the maid came. I owe you, big time."

J.J. obviously didn't know Artie very well if he thought a maid cleaned the condo. "Well, here I am. Mr. Handyman, at your ser-vice." I saluted with the saw, then noticed something on the floor.

J.J.'s wallet. I picked it up and looked inside. Empty. J.J.'s eyes had been tracking me and he let out a groan.

"Shit. Shit, shit, shit. I knew it. I knew it was too good to be true. Bitch set me up. Cleaned me out."

"Who did?"

J.J.'s face lit up as he remembered something else besides the empty wallet. "Smoking hot black chick with a super-super-superlative ass. Did you see her at the show? Front row, on the left." His eyes rolled halfway back into his head. "Awesome."

"Know her name?"

"Yeah, sure. Rolanda. No, no, it was Roweena." His face contorted. "Maybe Rhonda. Or Yolanda or Betty or Jane. Shit, I don't fucking know. I had more than $300 in there!" A loopy smile appeared. "But man, it was awesome. Worth every dollar."

I sawed off the handcuff, cringing from the metal-on-metal squeal. Fortunately, it didn't take very long; the cuff was more toy than a real, honest-to-goodness-police-issue model. But it had done the job, all right. When I finished, J.J. made no move to get up.

"Nice panties, by the way," I said. "You wear those on stage?"

"Maybe I did." He nodded at the dresser. "Get me a pair of shorts, will you?"

I opened his drawer, fished out a pair, and tossed them on the bed. As I did, something caught my eye on top of the dresser. Something that seemed incongruous there in the comedy condo where national headliner Jon Jermaine was staying.

On top of the dresser was a little towel. Dumbo the Flying Elephant stared at me.

Laughed at me.

EIGHT

"WHERE DID THIS COME from?" Saliva escaped my mouth in a fine spray and I'm sure my face turned crimson. I waved the towel in J.J.'s face while he lay on the bed, one arm over his head, half-shielding himself from me, Channing Hayes, Raving Lunatic.

"I don't know. It was here, man." He peeked out from under his arm.

"Bullshit." I backed off a tad, still hot. Was the story about Rolanda just that, a story? Had Heather been the one to party with J.J., then cuff him to the bed and clean him out?

"That towel was here when I moved in. On Wednesday afternoon," J.J. said. His slurred speech had cleared a bit.

"Really? Then how come I saw it at the club on Wednesday night?"

J.J. glanced at the dresser, glanced at the clock. Then he looked my way. "What's the big deal, anyway? It's just a stupid towel. And a little one at that. I need a man-sized towel." He attempted a grin, but my scowl chased it away. "You can have it, if it's so important to you."

"I don't care about the towel. I'm just looking for Heather. Heather Dempsey. It's her towel. Know her?"

J.J.'s face colored. "Should I?"

I waved the towel again, resisting the urge to wad it up and stuff it in his mouth. "Goddamn it. Tell me the truth. Was Heather here tonight? Did she chain you to the bed?"

J.J. laughed and some of the tension drained from his face. "Naw, man. Tonight was the black chick. I swear. And I wouldn't lie about *that*. Even though she ripped me off, I'd do her again in a heartbeat." He paused for a moment, then exhaled. In a quieter voice, he said, "*Two* nights ago was Heather."

"*Two nights ago*? You had Heather here Wednesday night?"

"Yeah. Nice girl." J.J.'s eyes widened. "But, man, I didn't know you were into her. If I did, I never would have—"

"Shut up. It's not like that. She's Lauren's sister. We never had anything going. I was helping her with her act and she disappeared."

"Oh. Okay. Cool." J.J. said. "Then why are you attacking me with her towel?"

"Sorry." I folded it up and squeezed it as I spoke. "Tell me about her."

"What?" J.J. seemed perplexed, as if I wanted smutty details about my friend.

"How did she get here? When did she leave? Where did she go?"

He blew some breath out. "Let's see. She called me on my cell, wanted to—"

"Hold on." I held up my hand. "How did she get your cell number?"

A small, uneasy laugh from J.J. "Yeah, well, she said I gave it to her months ago. After some show I did. But I don't remember, man, I swear." He held up three fingers like in the Boy Scout pledge. Some Boy Scout.

"Okay. So she called you. When was that?"

"I don't know. Ten. Eleven." He shrugged.

"Where were you?"

"Here. Artie invited me to come down to the club if I got in early enough, but I was tired. Wanted to stay in and curl up with a book or something."

My eyebrows arched. It was the "or something" that bothered me.

"Seriously, dude. I don't party every night. Just after my shows. Keeps the buzz going." Of course, being on the road meant he did shows most nights.

"Just like that. She calls wanting to see you."

J.J. tried to suppress his smile but failed miserably. "Yeah. Just like that. Happens sometimes, I've got to admit."

"So she came over? Then what? Liquor and drugs? Orgy? What?"

J.J.'s smile vanished. "No. Nothing like that. We just hung out. Talked. For a while. Then we went to bed." He shook his head. "It wasn't freaky or anything. Just…normal. Nice." An odd look came over him. Something unusual for J.J. Concern, maybe.

"And then?"

"And then we went to sleep. She was gone in the morning when I woke up." He nodded at me, as if stuff like this happened every day of the week. For him, it probably did.

"Did she say where she was going?"

J.J. shook his head.

"What did you guys 'talk' about?"

"See, that's the thing. She was pretty torn up, about a bunch of things. But she kept changing the subject, talking in circles. Hard to understand, really." He clicked his tongue. "You know what I'm talking about, right? Chicks."

I didn't, not really. "Can you give me any specifics? Anything that might help me find her? She skipped out on her set the other night, and I need to talk to her about it. She was pretty pumped about her new act."

"Hmm. Bagging out on your set. That's not good." J.J. pulled on his chin. "Not good at all."

Comics knew the gravity. "Yeah, that's what's got me concerned. She mention her boyfriend?"

J.J.'s eyes flashed. "Shit. She has a boyfriend?"

Asked and answered. "Think, J.J. Did she say anything useful at all?"

"I wish I could help, but she seemed pretty confused by things. If I had to guess, I'd say *she* didn't even know what was bothering her." A shrug. "Sorry. I don't know what else to tell you. She was frazzled. Even after we, uh, did it, she still seemed tense. Nice girl, though."

"Maybe she said something? About where she might be going?"

J.J. rubbed his wrists where the handcuffs had been. "Nope. I figured, you know, she'd just go home, or whatever."

"Well, she didn't." I turned away from J.J. and paced the bedroom floor while I thought. As I moved back and forth, J.J. simply watched, unsure of what I'd do next. Another unpredictable comic on the verge of a meltdown.

Although I'd finally gotten a whiff of Heather's scent, the knot I'd been carrying in my stomach stayed taut. I hadn't really learned anything that changed the situation. Heather still hadn't returned my calls, and Ryan hadn't seen her or talked to her, either. No one seemed to know where she might have gone, or what was bothering her.

And her hopping into bed with a booty skunk like Jon Jermaine didn't do much to allay my concern about her state-of-mind. Something was still very wrong with this picture.

"Channing?" J.J. asked from his prone position on the bed.

"Yeah?"

"I really am sorry. I hope you find her. Let me know if there's anything I can do, okay?"

"There is one thing you can do." I glared at him. "Clean up this fucking mess before Artie comes around."

NINE

I GOT ABOUT FOUR hours of sleep before the tag-team of the sun and my empty stomach forced me from bed. At first, I thought the episode with J.J. had been a dream, but when I saw the hacksaw sitting on the kitchen table, I knew all the wishful thinking I could muster wouldn't change the ugly facts.

After a quick breakfast—two bowls of Froot Loops and a banana—I called Heather. No one answered at her apartment and I left a terse message. How eloquent can you be on your fortieth message, anyway? I repeated my futility on her cell phone, and I considered driving by her place to stake it out but figured it would be a waste of time. Of course, I was beginning to believe my search for her was going to be fruitless, too.

But I needed to find her, if for no other reason than to ease the growing pain in my gut.

Seven Oaks Mall was like every other mall in America, full of trendy clothing and shoe stores, with places like Candy City selling jellybeans by the pound. At one end, or in the grand Centre Court, or tucked away upstairs near a movie multiplex, you'd find an eatery offering the latest greasy permutations on fast food from McDonald's, surrounded by a gaggle of pretenders to the crown. If you were blindfolded and airlifted into the middle of the mall, you wouldn't know if you were in Kansas City, Nome, or Fairfax, Virginia. It wouldn't surprise me if the first outpost on Mars boasted a Mrs. Fields Cookie store. Right next door to the Starbucks.

I consulted the mall's store directory and found Brianna's Body Shoppe, situated down a little sideshoot on the path to Macy's. In the store's display window, shimmering aqua and pink lights greeted shoppers, and those who weren't repulsed entered another world, with a décor that was part Atlantis and part Atlantic City. More garish lights backlit translucent, water-filled walls encapsulating tiny streams of rising air bubbles. Salves and balms lined the walls of the entire store. In the center, futuristic displays showcased more bottles, arranged in odd groupings, no doubt some kind of testimony to Brianna's cosmetological genius. To me, the store simply smelled bad.

It wasn't even ten-thirty, yet the girl behind the sales counter was sneaking bites of a cheeseburger as I walked over. "Hi. Can I help you?" she said, backhanding a few crumbs from her mouth, then smiling.

I smiled back, giving it every watt I had. The last couple people I'd talked to about Heather hadn't warmed to me. Might as well replace the vinegar with some honey. "Hi yourself," I said, forcing a chuckle. "I'm looking for Amber."

She picked a nametag off the counter in front of her and showed it to me: Ambyr. "That's me. I'm Ambyr." She reduced her voice to a whisper. "The nametag looks dorky, so I don't wear it. You're not from the home office, are you?"

I whispered back. "No. You're safe."

With her two-toned hair cut short, purple eye shadow, and green nail polish, somehow it made sense she spelled her name with a y. "Well, Ambyr, it's nice to meet you. I'm a friend of Heather's." I leaned against the counter nonchalantly, hoping she believed in the transitive property of friendship.

"Hi," she said, but I noticed her wary eyes settle on my scar. I turned my head to the left and jammed my left hand deeper into my pocket. No sense shocking her, right from the get-go.

"Not too busy this morning, huh?"

She glanced around. I was the only one in the store. "Nope. Dead, as usual. Things will pick up this afternoon." Her smile faltered. "So…"

"Heather called me the other day and I've been trying to get back in touch with her. She hasn't answered her phone and she hasn't returned my calls. You know where she might be? I really need to talk to her."

Ambyr recoiled, and I realized I came off like a jilted boyfriend, or worse, a crazed stalker, showing up at her place of business with a sketchy line of bullshit. "Wait, that didn't sound—"

She said, "I…I don't really know Heather. I don't think she works here anymore. Sorry." She smiled, two insincere rows of perfect white teeth, as she glanced at the entrance, hoping there would be a real customer so she could get rid of me. Unfortunately for her, no one sauntered in.

"Look, my name's Channing Hayes. I've been working with Heather on her stand-up routine."

Ambyr unwound in front of me, letting out a big breath. "Why didn't you say you were Channing? I thought you were…" She swallowed and a dark cloud passed in front of her face, then dissipated. "She talks about you all the time. I'm sorry, I didn't mean to get weird on you, but…" She shrugged. "Do you mind?" she asked, as she held up her sandwich.

"Go ahead."

She took a healthy-sized bite and masticated it thoroughly. Washed it down with a slurp from a jumbo-sized cup emblazoned with the name of the restaurant in Day-Glo script letters. "Sorry. Didn't get a chance to eat breakfast." She blinked several times, then seemed to get back on track. "Um, Heather's not here."

"Yes, I gathered. Have you seen her?"

"No. I haven't seen her in a few days. She missed her shift last night. Must be sick, although…"

"What?"

Ambyr shrugged. "Heather doesn't get sick much. She wouldn't miss her shift unless she had a good reason. She needs the money."

"When did you see her last?"

She closed one eye, squinting into the past. "I was off Wednesday and Thursday. I saw her on Tuesday, though. Our shifts overlapped."

"And she seemed okay?" I asked. I wondered if her case of nerves started before she came to the club the following night.

Ambyr pursed her lips. "Well, now that you mention it…"

"What?"

"Something was freaking her out." Her head started bobbing, faster and faster. "Some guy was bothering her. She said some guy had called her and was hassling her. Wanted to get together. She seemed pretty upset by the whole thing."

"Did she say who he was?"

"No. I asked, of course, but she acted like she wanted to forget the whole thing. Like not talking about it would make it go away. I asked a couple more times, but Heather got sorta mad so I dropped it. Figure she'd tell me if she wanted, when she was ready." Ambyr slurped some more from her cup. "But I *was* worried."

"Got any guesses who the guy might be?"

Ambyr issued a small laugh. "Heather's a friendly girl. A real friendly girl, if you catch my drift. Guys were always coming in here and it wasn't to buy our products. It was like she gave off some kind of mysterious vibe that attracted guys, like catnip or something. And it was all kinds: preppies, studs, losers. Didn't matter. She always had dudes chasing her. Like always."

"And you didn't know any of them by name?"

"Well, there's Ryan. He's Heather's current obsession. Good looking, but a little…" She made a face.

"A little what?"

Ambyr screwed her face up even more. "He's a control freak. Jealous. Always calling, checking up on her. Always telling her she's got to go where he wants, do what he wants." She shrugged. "Heather puts up with it, so who am I to say anything, right?" She took another enormous bite of cheeseburger.

"Do you think it was Ryan bugging her?"

She swallowed and gazed upward, as if the answer were written on the acoustical tiles. "I don't think so, but you never know, do you? Some guys…" She raised an eyebrow at me.

"Know any of Heather's other, uh, boyfriends?"

"Just Brooks. Brooks Spellman, I think it was. She shoulda stayed with him. He was cute. Funny, too." She pointed at me. "You probably know him. He's a comedian, just like you and Heather. I think that's how they met. At a show or something."

Didn't ring a bell with me. I'd have to ask Artie about him. He knew every comic in America and half the ones in Canada. "Could Brooks have been hassling her?"

"I doubt it. He seemed normal to me, but that was around the time of…" Ambyr stopped talking and her eyes gravitated to my scar again.

I resisted the temptation to touch the hard, ridged patch of skin. "What?"

Ambyr looked away. When she spoke, her voice was barely audible. "The accident really messed her up. Lost her sister. Broke up with Brooks, got depressed. Since then, her life's been screeching downhill. Poor girl." She grabbed her cup and wiggled the straw, pushing it up and down, causing a shrill, squeaky noise as it rubbed against the plastic lid.

Had I been wrong about Heather getting her life together? Had it been wishful thinking? How much did I really know about her private life? Although Heather and I had worked pretty closely on her routine, she never talked much about it, never confided anything intimate to me. I'd always assumed that's just how she was, probably because she'd never revealed many personal details to Lauren over the years. But maybe there was some other reason.

Ambyr slurped from her cup and set it down. "I've tried to help her, but…"

"What?"

"Well…" She twirled her cup on the counter as she seemed to debate something.

I seized the opening. "Listen, I'm trying to help her, too. But I need to find her. You have any idea where she might be?"

"No, but…" She glanced around the store again.

"You can tell me, Ambyr."

"I overheard Heather on the phone the other day. Talking about getting a…" She stopped speaking and pointed a forefinger-and-thumb-gun at a display of shampoo next to the register. Then she cocked the thumb and whispered, "Bang."

"Heather said she was getting a gun?" My stomach lurched.

"Yeah, a gun. I'm pretty sure that's what I heard," Ambyr said, nodding with her lips pressed together.

"Know who she was talking to?" The idea of Heather wielding a weapon—besides her sharp tongue—seemed almost ludicrous. And more than a tiny bit frightening.

"Nope. Sorry. I told you, she was, like, really freaked. At least now she can protect herself, huh?"

TEN

My sense of dread flared up, and I knew better than to ignore it.

On the surface, everyone's argument about Heather's disappearance sounded logical. Flighty, unreliable girl gets nervous, bails out on her set. Nothing more than that. But Heather had been performing with her sister for a while, and she'd never shown even a hint of nerves.

True professional comedians never skipped out on a gig, especially not minutes before they're about to go on stage. Not if they wanted to keep working. Not if they wanted their careers to go somewhere. The stand-up community was too tight-knit for stuff like that to happen without the important club owners and bookers finding out. And in all the time I'd known Heather, she'd always acted with complete professionalism when it came to her career. Never late for a show with Lauren, never went on stage drunk or high. Never flipped off a promoter.

When it came to her stand-up, Heather was very serious.

That's why I was so worried. I didn't expect the others—Ryan, her parents, even Freeman—to fully understand. They'd never had to go on stage with their careers on the line. But I knew how much Heather's act meant to her. Even if she hadn't matured as much as I'd thought, she'd always worked hard to separate the turmoil in her personal life from her career.

Something was wrong. The clincher: why would she want a gun?

I pulled out my cell and called Freeman.

"Hey, buddy. Enjoyed the show last night," he said, genuine in tone. "That Jermaine, he's damn funny. For a white guy, that is."

"Yeah, he's a card," I said, deciding not to bring up J.J.'s adventure. If he wanted to report the robbery, that was his choice, but I had the feeling he'd let the whole thing simply fade away. Another wild tale from the road to impress his buddies with.

"So, did you call for a reason, or do you just like listening to my voice?"

Wiseass. "Did you talk to your buddy about Heather?"

Freeman sighed. "Yeah. Said he hadn't heard anything. Checked a few things out, nothing turned up. Said he'd keep at it, though. I hear something, you'll be my first call."

I wasn't going to let him brush me off so easily. "What things did he check out?"

Another sigh. "Let the man do his job. Give him some time. And relax. What I said last night? About most missing people showing up within a few days?" He paused.

"Yeah?"

"That's so you won't worry. Take my advice. Don't worry. Odds are, she'll show up, bright-eyed and bushy-tailed."

"I don't think so. Something's not right here." I felt it at my core, but how do you tell someone that and have him believe you? "Something's up. I know it."

"Uh-huh. You a seer now?"

I considered telling Freeman about Heather's booty call and about the gun, knowing that if I didn't, I'd catch holy hell for it later. But since he and his buddy in Missing Persons already were looking for her, I didn't want to say anything that might curtail the search or confuse the issue.

She was still AWOL, and I knew something wasn't right, whether he believed me or not. And I wasn't too proud to accept all the help I could beg, borrow, or finagle. I needed to find her before something bad happened. To her, or because of her.

"Channing?" Freeman sounded as if he were about to lecture his daughter about avoiding boys with long hair and skateboards tucked under their arms.

"What?"

"Seems to me the only person who thinks she's really missing is you." He paused, giving his words time to sink into my thick skull. "Talk to you later."

———

The spring morning was warm and inviting, so I took Rex for a drive along the country roads that meandered through parts of Vienna and Great Falls, windows wide open, radio blasting. It never failed to amaze me how rural the area became only a few miles from Fairfax County's high-density population centers. Forty minutes of aimless driving later, I pulled into the gravel parking lot of Meadowspring Gardens.

The gardens were maintained by the county through a combination of entrance fees and tax dollars. But because it cost a few bucks to get in, they were never as crowded as some of the other—free—county parks and gardens, which was nice, especially if you wanted a little peace and quiet in which to commune with nature and contemplate life.

I paid my five dollars and wandered down the main path. Azaleas and rhododendrons bloomed all around, alongside scores of other brightly colored flowers and shrubs, most of which I couldn't identify if I had a field guide and Ranger Rick next to me.

After a few minutes of strolling through the gardens, I arrived at a small pond where a couple of benches had been set up. I took a seat on one with a view of some platter-sized lily pads floating near a thick thatch of cattails. A soft breeze set their slender stalks swaying to some subliminal orchestra.

Would it be too much to ask for Heather to emerge from the pond, like some medieval Lady of the Lake? I envisioned her, dressed in white, holding a trident or a scepter or maybe just a mic stand, as she arose from the depths, garland of tiny white flowers in her long flowing hair. *Why, Channing, so nice of you to meet me here. Just going for a swim to clear my head, don't you know? Working on my act, too. Hey, did you hear the one about the priest, the Rabbi, and the talking giraffe?*

I banished the silly images from my head and considered Freeman's words instead. Was Heather simply off somewhere doing whatever carefree, happy-go-lucky girls do? She didn't strike me as carefree, not with the indecision and lack of confidence she displayed the other night, but maybe it was the fear of going on stage without Lauren by her side that made her bolt. In many respects, I knew exactly how she felt.

Okay, she'd sought solace—or at least a brief moment of physical comfort—with J.J. But why hadn't she answered any of my many messages? Was she ashamed about running out on me? Had I made her solo debut so important in my eyes that she felt bad for me when she couldn't go on?

I hated to think that was true. I was doing this for Heather, wasn't I? This wasn't some kind of vicarious trip I was on to recapture the rush of being on stage. I'd get my act together and get out there soon, wouldn't I? I'd been asking myself these questions a lot lately, and I wasn't too keen on the answers I'd been getting.

On the far side of the pond, a few geese gathered. They strutted awkwardly, deliberately, and I wondered if they mated for life like I'd heard. Mating for life, a nice concept. I couldn't hold myself back any longer. I'd been drawn to the gardens for a reason. I left the pond and the geese behind as I continued along the asphalt walkway. About one-hundred-and-fifty yards down the path, around the second bend of an ess curve, a huge white tent occupied one side of a perfectly coiffed grassy lawn.

The tent was erected in early April and stayed up through September. It provided weather insurance for a multitude of events the gardens hosted—charity benefits, political schmoozefests, community gatherings. Not surprisingly, weddings were far and away the most popular things at the gardens. I knew this because Lauren and I had planned to be married right next to that very tent.

Tomorrow.

Now, the tent stood as empty as my life had become.

Lauren had always dreamed of getting married outside under fluffy white clouds, and she and her mother had checked out a half-dozen possible sites. The instant they saw Meadowspring, their search ended. We'd booked the place over a year ago, and Lauren—again, with her mother's counsel—threw herself into the other aspects of wedding planning. My only goal was to make her happy, so I wisely stayed out of the way and nodded noncommittally when asked my opinion about anything and everything wedding-related.

Heather was going to be Lauren's maid of honor. Had the wedding "ghost" affected her, as it was haunting me? Caused her to run away from the harsh realization that her sister was really gone for good? Had Heather succumbed to survivor's guilt, too?

A young couple rounded the bend on the path across from me. The woman gasped when she saw the tent and rushed ahead, crossing the grass to peer inside. She disappeared through one of the floppy doors while the man ambled over to my side. "Big tent, huh? Looks like they could fit a whole circus inside. Maybe two." He didn't look at me when he spoke, keeping his eyes glued to the tent.

I nodded noncommittally. A floral fragrance wafted by on the wind, and across the field, the grass rippled in waves, an undulating sea of green.

He stuffed his hands in the pockets of his shorts and pointed to the tent with his chin. "We're getting married tomorrow, and the weather report said there was a twenty percent chance of rain. She wanted to check things out one last time," he said. "She'll probably get me up in the middle of the night to come back 'one more last time.'"

His tone exuded excitement. I tried to pump some into mine. "Uh, congratulations."

He turned toward me. "Thanks. Thanks a lot."

From inside the tent, the woman called to him, a disembodied voice full of hope and joy. "Todd. This is wonderful. Come check it out."

Todd shrugged. "The boss calls. Have a good one," he said, and then he skipped off to join his future wife under the big top.

I returned to my car and drove away, still wondering about the geese.

ELEVEN

I DIDN'T DRIVE HOME.

I hadn't been able to locate Heather, but there was one place I hadn't looked yet, two people I hadn't talked to: her parents. I'd been avoiding this moment, hoping Heather would show up so I could skip the unpleasantness. From what I knew of her relationship with them, I doubted she'd be there, but I knew if our positions had been reversed and my daughter had disappeared, I'd want to be told. In person. And I fancied myself as someone who did the right thing, no matter how painful.

I drove to the Dempseys' house in Great Falls, enjoying the rolling countryside. I passed megamillion-dollar mansions with multimillion-dollar guesthouses, interspersed with plenty of horse farms and huge spreads and fancy cars, but for some reason the wealth didn't seem as conspicuous as it did in McLean or Potomac. Maybe the Great Fallsians could just afford to hide it better.

Heather's parents lived in a relatively older section, where five-car garages were the exception, rather than the norm. I pulled up to their house and debated on whether I should park in their circular driveway or on the curb of the wide street. I settled Rex in at the curb.

I'd spent many hours there with Lauren and her family, celebrating holidays and birthdays, gathering for summer cookouts and pool parties. At first, I was just another of the "boys" Lauren felt strongly enough about to parade before her parents. Her father kept his distance, but the bond I had with her mother grew over time. She provided me with something I'd missed in my life—stability from a parent. And she was pretty cool, at least for an impending in-law. Even insisted I call her by her first name, no matter how awkward it made me feel. She made me call her husband by his first name, too, even though I was sure it pissed him off big time. Truth was, I only called him William when he wasn't around to hear me.

I strode up to the porch and conjured my game face. It wouldn't be easy asking them if Heather was there. Actually, the asking wouldn't be so difficult; it was explaining she was missing that would be hard.

The door swung open before I could bang the brass duck-head knocker. Kathleen Dempsey, trim and fit in a cranberry top and white shorts, beamed at me. It was easy to see where Lauren and Heather got their stunning looks. "Channing! How nice of you to come by. Please, come in."

I entered, and she engulfed me in a hug. "Good to see you. How are you doing? We've missed you." The words flowed swiftly, and the undercurrent of emotion almost swept me away. I hadn't been ready for this. I should have been, but I wasn't.

We broke apart and her eyes glistened, and I was certain they weren't tears of joy from seeing me. Her gaze floated to my scar and hovered there. "How are you? Really?"

I opened my mouth to answer, but she didn't let me. "Oh, my manners! Please come in. Have a seat. What can I get you to drink?" The sentences streamed together. "You like iced tea, right?"

"Sure, that would be great."

Her smile widened. "Terrific. Have a seat and I'll be right back." She pointed to the living room and went to get our drinks.

In the living room, every available surface—on tables, on walls—teemed with photographs of the Dempsey clan. Portraits, candid shots, vacation photos. At the beach, at their mountain cabin, at sporting events. The room reminded me of the waiting room at a photography studio. In addition to Heather, Lauren had a brother named Justin. Two years younger, he lived nearby in Reston with his wife and young daughter. There were plenty of pictures of them, too. Guess you couldn't have enough pictures of family members. I took a seat on the couch, girding myself.

Kathleen swept into the room and handed me a tall glass of iced tea, slice of lemon stuck on the rim. She held an identical glass in her hand and sat in a chair across from me, on the diagonal. "So. How have you been, Channing?"

Talking with Kathleen had always been easy, even after the accident. She hadn't blamed me. "Okay, I guess. It's hard at times, but I'm managing." I took a sip of tea. Extra sweet, just how I liked it.

"Good, good." She stared at me as if there were some question she wanted me to ask her.

I aim to please. "How have you been? And William?"

When I said her husband's name, I detected the faintest flicker in her eyes. "It's hard. Hardest thing there is, losing a child."

I sighed. We'd been through the early stages of mourning together. I didn't want to rehash that now and risk tearing open still raw scabs. "Is William here?"

She glanced at her watch. "No. He went to Home Depot. He'll probably be there, wandering the aisles for days." She chuckled, but it was forced and mirthless.

I felt relieved. "How's Heather?" I blurted out. No sense dawdling any more.

Kathleen's eyebrows shot up. "I…I don't know. I thought you were working with her on her act."

"Yes, yes. I am. And she's good. It's just…"

She set her drink down on the side table. "What? It's just what?" She seemed on edge, as if her other baby was about to be ripped from her arms.

"I'm sure it's nothing, but when did you last talk to her?"

"Why? Has something happened?"

I shook my head quickly. "No, nothing like that. I just haven't seen her in a few days. And she hasn't returned my calls."

Kathleen exhaled. "Oh. Thank God. I thought you were going to tell me…" Our eyes met. "Don't worry, Channing. This is nothing unusual. Heather's not like Lauren. I love her dearly, but…" Her head moved slowly from side-to-side.

The sound of a door slamming reverberated from the back of the house. "Kath, where is he?" Dempsey's deep baritone echoed right alongside the door slam. He'd seen my car parked out front. Thoughts of making a quiet getaway dissipated.

Kathleen motioned me to stay put, somehow reading my intentions. She whispered, "Don't worry. He'll calm down."

I rose anyway, measuring the distance to the door.

William Dempsey burst into the living room, holding a beige plastic bag and an eighteen-inch pipe wrench. "Well, here he is." His lupine grin made my knees wobble. "To what do we owe this pleasure?" He gripped the wrench in his hand and the muscles in his forearm bulged.

Kathleen stood. "William. Channing came by to talk. It seems Heather hasn't been forthright in returning his calls."

Dempsey cocked his head to one side, searching for the real reason I was there. Nothing so trivial as a few missed calls would bring me out here, and he knew it—it was no secret I feared him. He'd wanted it that way and he'd gotten his wish, through endless berating and countless threats beginning the day after the accident while I recovered in my hospital bed. "Bullshit," he said after a moment. He lifted the wrench in my direction. "You waited until we'd started to heal—however slightly—and you came out here to torture us again."

"William!" Kathleen said. "That is not true. Channing is genuinely concerned about Heather." Then she leaned toward him and hissed in a lower voice. "Stop it. You're being an ass."

I cleared my throat, deciding I'd have to speak if I was ever going to get out of there. "Mr. Dempsey. I *am* concerned. Heather was supposed to do her act but disappeared. And she hasn't called me back."

"Girl must have finally come to her senses. Given up all that comedy shit." He glared at me, doubly hard, when he mentioned the comedy shit. "You'd think both of my girls could find something more rewarding to do with their lives than try to entertain drunks."

Kathleen took the calming approach and smoothed out her voice. "William, I don't think that's the point. No one seems to know where Heather is."

"And that's new exactly how? Since that girl turned fifteen, we've rarely known where she was. Or with whom." Dempsey set the bag down on the floor with a thump and switched the wrench to the other hand. The muscles on that arm bulged, too.

Kathleen's face flushed and she turned toward me. "When did you say this was?"

"Wednesday night. She was about to—"

"That's all? She's only been gone for three days and you're worried?" Dempsey raised his voice and his face colored, as well. "Try having your daughter go missing for three weeks. See what that does to your insides. See how well you sleep, how well you work, how well you function. Have a loved one disappear and see what it does to you."

"Yes, sir," I managed. Lauren told me about the time Heather hit the road and hitched to Milwaukee with some guy she'd met at the mall. She'd just turned seventeen and it had been three weeks of living hell for the family. Exuding calm while delivering an unpopular message was a tough task, but I tried my best. "It's just that, well, she's worked very hard on her solo act and she wouldn't just skip out on it without a good reason. It was too important to her."

"Three days? Hah." He tapped the wrench against his outer leg as he spoke and it rattled with a metallic ping. "You call her boyfriend, Ryan?"

"I've spoken to him, yes." I shook my head. "Nothing."

Dempsey licked his lips. "Probably some other guy involved. Always is."

Kathleen shot her husband a disgusted look and turned to me. "Did you try the store at the mall?"

"Yeah, they haven't seen her."

"Maybe we should contact the police," Kathleen said. "I read that the odds of finding a missing person go down the longer you wait to start searching." Before I could answer, Dempsey stepped forward, waving the pipe wrench around.

"Not again. Remember what happened last time? The ridicule. The embarrassment. Plus, they didn't do shit. Girl got all the way to Wisconsin and they did nothing." He spat out the words, took a breath, and barreled on. "She's done this to us before, more than once. Hell, she's disappeared more than a half dozen times, doing God knows what. She's twenty-three years old. An adult. She's got to be responsible for her actions. We can't keep trying to rescue her." Dempsey's chest heaved.

"We're her parents," Kathleen said. At my angle, her face looked hard and weathered. I wondered why I hadn't noticed it before. "That's what we do. Rescue our children when they need us."

Dempsey jangled the wrench. "What about Lauren? We protected her all her life, and then…" He shifted his attention to me, eyes narrowed to slits, cheeks flaming. "And then *Channing* here, good ol' reliable *Channing*, goes out and gets her killed. Nice going, my boy. Why weren't you driving anyway? Don't you know a gentleman is supposed to take care of his lady? What was going through that pea brain of yours?"

All the saliva had evaporated from my mouth. I stared straight ahead, wondering how such a great night had turned to disaster in a split-second.

Dempsey moved closer and got louder. "Are you disappointed my other daughter's disappeared? So you won't have a chance to kill her, too?" He flung the wrench onto the coffee table where it smashed into a few framed photographs, sending broken glass flying. Then he stormed off, leaving Kathleen and me gaping at the debris, glass shards glinting in the light.

Kathleen met my eyes and she was beyond tears, in that place of indescribable despair. A place I visited all too often. "Oh, Channing, I'm sorry. So, so sorry." She bent over and rescued a picture from the mess, a beaming Lauren in her graduation gown. Slowly, she traced her finger along Lauren's bright face. "So sorry," she said. "So, so sorry."

I let myself out.

TWELVE

When you're hot, you're hot.

After I left the Dempseys, I decided to talk to Lauren's brother, Justin. Since I was already battered, what was a little more abuse? When Lauren was alive, Justin had been pretty cold to me. Not overtly hostile, but not very welcoming. He had his manicured wife and his newborn daughter and his big house in North Reston, and he pretty much kept to his own, showing up at the obligatory Dempsey family functions, but always arriving late and leaving early. I got the sense the elder Dempseys preferred it that way, at least before their granddaughter came along.

After the accident, I'd had absolutely no contact with Justin, aside from a cool handshake at Lauren's funeral. I guess I preferred it that way, too.

Justin had always been closer to Heather than to Lauren, so maybe he'd know where Heather was. If not, maybe he'd know where she might have gone. I knew one thing for sure; my visit to him couldn't be any worse than my visit to the parents.

Justin lived on a cul-de-sac near the main drag, a couple of miles north of Reston Town Center. The houses were large and the lots small, which made the houses seem even larger. It was a fairly exclusive zip code, although he still had some upscaling to do before he was swimming in the same pool as his parents. I bet that fact burned him, too. And I think something else burned him. The money to buy the house hadn't come from his job as a lab technician; Lauren told me his wife, Bertie, was the niece of a generous chemical company CFO from Delaware and had gotten a fat check as a wedding gift.

A piece of cardboard was taped over the doorbell button so I knocked. A moment later, the door opened and Justin scowled at me, holding a finger to his lips. He ducked his head back inside for a second, then closed the door gently behind him and came out onto the porch. He wore running shorts and a Nike T-shirt; his bare feet and uncombed hair told me he hadn't showered yet today.

"I'd invite you in, but Annie's napping. Sorry." He didn't sound apologetic.

"How are you, Justin?" I asked. "Been a few months."

He tilted his head at me, the same way his father had. "What do you want?"

The five months hadn't thawed him out a bit. I felt I'd owed his parents some respect, but Justin had never earned a speck from me. I dropped any pretense of courtesy. "Heard from Heather lately?"

"No. Why?"

"I thought you were pretty close. When did you talk to her last?"

"Few weeks ago. Why? What's going on?"

I repeated what I'd told his parents. He listened, nodding every so often. When I was done, he simply shrugged. "Yeah, so?"

"So? I think it's odd she bailed on something she's wanted to do so badly for such a long time. This was important to her."

He glanced back at the house, but I hadn't heard any crying. Maybe a father's ears were tuned to a different frequency. "You know Heather. This sound so unusual to you?" he said, tone dripping with condescension. I guess Justin's apple hadn't fallen far from Dempsey Senior's.

"So none of what I've said concerns you?"

"Heather's a big girl." He paused to consider something, something profound by the way he nodded his head. "Why don't you leave her alone? Leave us all alone. Don't you think you've caused enough damage?"

"Just trying to help Heather," I said, tired of people dumping on me. The irony sliced me into little slivers. The night of the accident, I was looking out for Lauren's—and Heather's—safety by not getting behind the wheel after having a few drinks. I paid the ultimate price for that good deed. And would continue to do so for as long as I lived. Why didn't anyone else see that? Were they so torn up themselves to see my pain?

Justin glared at me. "Anything else?"

Nothing subtle about Justin. "No, I guess not."

"Adios," he said, as he turned back to the house without another glance in my direction.

———

I knew when I wasn't welcome. I left, grabbing a couple of burgers on my way to the club. Artie wasn't around and I had the office to myself, so I tilted back in his leather chair and hoisted my size elevens up on the boss's desk. What Artie didn't know wouldn't hurt him. Besides, I needed to be as comfortable as possible as I reviewed the stack of audition tapes before me.

We still called them tapes, even though most of the current ones came on DVD. Despite the fact we were starting to get more and more emailed to us in purely digital form—like what you'd see on YouTube or something—we still preferred something solid you could hold in your hand. Or put in the filing cabinet. Of course, technophobe Artie had another reason he hated those electronic versions—he wasn't on speaking terms with our computer, preferring to let me handle all the club's tech needs. As much as I tried, some tricks you just couldn't teach an old dog.

Balanced on a rickety aluminum stand, a small TV showed a young guy with a microphone in his hand giving it his best shot. The video image jitterbugged and I could barely hear his lines over the static. I hit the stop button on the DVD player's remote. The production values were the first things I noticed on the tapes.

The worst, like this guy's, were little more than shaky camcorder home movies of some nervous comic wannabe sputtering through a wedding toast. Many sounded like they were gargling underwater. At least it made my job easier. I got up, ejected the DVD, and slipped it back into the manila folder Artie insisted we keep on every prospect, no matter how lame. Across the front of the folder, I scribbled the words *NO WAY* in red Sharpie.

I'd planned on spending an hour or so parsing them, but if the rest were as bad as this guy's, I might have to cut things short to preserve what little sanity I had left.

I popped in the next DVD. A catchy intro theme played under a flashy title sequence. The comics with more experience understood the importance of appearance, and it was obvious in their slicker presentations. I let a minute roll by. This tape had clean edits and audio you could actually hear, which made watching it a lot less painful. Audition tapes were supposed to be a montage of the comic's primo stuff, clipped from club appearances or corporate jobs or, in the best cases, TV shows. Unfortunately, this comic's old recycled jokes and stilted delivery told me he wasn't going anywhere. Another *NO THANKS*.

I stopped the DVD and something occurred to me. Ambyr said Heather's old boyfriend was a comedian. If so, it was likely we had his audition package on file. Any aspiring comic worth his weight in laughs knows enough to pepper every possible venue with audition tapes.

I swiveled around to the four-drawer file cabinet next to Artie's desk. We got about a dozen—or more—audition packages from eager comics every week, and Artie had squirreled away every package he ever received during the past fifteen years. Not so much for filling our slots—after all, a comic's act changes so quickly and what's hot one moment is ice-cold the next—but because he wanted some archival evidence in case someone broke through big-time—a kind of "we knew him when" deal. Touting The Last Laff as the launching pad for the next Jerry Seinfeld or Kevin James would be dynamite for business.

I paged through the S – Z drawer. Some of the older files were thick, back when people sent in VHS tapes. We even had cassette tapes, which never made much sense to me. I mean, wasn't it impossible to tell how a comic would perform without actually *seeing* him? But Artie kept everything. I wouldn't be surprised if deep in the bowels of the filing cabinets, I came across a reel-to-reel tape full of jokes about Eisenhower.

It took me all of eight seconds to locate the file: Brooks Spellman, dated six months earlier, before I'd joined Artie. I pulled out his folder, laid it on the desk, and flipped it open, coming face-to-face with Spellman. Instead of a single professional 8 x 10 glossy, he'd sent in a couple 4 x 6 Polaroids. In one pose, he faced the camera with a sly grin. In the other, he wore a fake-nose-and-glasses get-up he'd bought at the dollar store, complete with bushy Groucho facial hair. Some guys were born funny and some guys were named Brooks Spellman.

I slid his DVD into the machine and hit the play button. Low-budget video, crappy sound. I'd never heard Spellman perform, but I'd heard all the jokes before, innumerable times, right down to the hand gestures and the same accentuated syllables in the punch lines. Three minutes in, I stopped my torture and ejected the disk. This was more evidence—in addition to what I'd observed and what Lauren had always told me—Heather's taste in men wasn't very good.

I fished Spellman's resume out of the folder. It listed a few small clubs, mostly around Frederick, Maryland, and up into southern Pennsylvania, neither region known for being a comedy hotbed. There was no description of the types of appearances, only club names, a ploy common among tyros trying to fudge their qualifications. I suspected the majority of Spellman's appearances were bringer gigs—where comics had to bring paying audience members with them—or play-for-food deals, both stretching the definition of "comedy professional" to its breaking point.

One club name hit my radar screen hard: the Capitol Comedy Club. As much as I disliked Reed, I had to give him credit for spotting talent and it wasn't like him to give hacks stage time. Either Reed had suffered a momentary—and monumental—lapse of judgment, or Spellman had decided to list his open mic sessions. Of course, a third possibility existed: Spellman could have been lying through his fake nose and bushy eyebrows. I copied Spellman's contact information on a scrap of paper, folded it, and stuck it in my wallet. If Heather didn't show up soon, I'd be giving him a call.

I started to put the whole package back into the file cabinet when a name on another file folder caught my attention. I jammed Spellman's package into the drawer and pulled out one in front of it labeled Skip Skitters.

Inside, a picture of our very own Skip Gold stared at me, same gap-toothed smile, same mousy hair. The folder was dated eighteen months earlier, well before he started bartending at The Last Laff. I scanned his resume. Even less impressive than Spellman's, but one similarity unnerved me. Skip Gold also had been on stage at Reed's club. At least Skip had the decency to label his appearance as an open mic. Skip and Lauren had been friends but she'd never told me he'd hung out at the CCC. Curiouser and curiouser.

The door swung open and Artie entered.

I slammed the file drawer shut and sprang from his chair. "Don't worry, I wasn't just sitting at your desk with my shoes up watching audition tapes. Really."

Artie scowled and waved me away from his desk. "Find any gems?"

"Nope. As usual." I squeezed by him and took a seat in my folding chair while he reclined in his leather throne. Most of the guys we "discovered" arrived via referral. Not all, though, which was why we kept reviewing the tapes, hoping for that one diamond in the rough. "But I did find a couple I had questions about."

Artie said, "Okay. Shoot."

"Skip Skitters."

Artie stared at me. Not even a grin. "Don't mention that. In this business, we've all done things we wished we hadn't. We've all made mistakes, every single one of us. Me. You. Everybody. Just part of becoming a professional. Skip wasn't ready when he made that. Don't bust his balls over it."

I remembered the first tape I'd made. Artie had a point. "Okay, if you insist. Fact is, I didn't look at it yet."

"Well, do us all a favor and don't. Besides, he's been working hard over the past year to improve. He's just got that…that thing. Weird." He shook his head.

No one could say "stuttering" out loud. Some kind of superstition. "Yeah. I feel bad for him. He's got some funny stuff, but…"

"Give him time. And space. He's a good kid, just a little sensitive about it." Artie pointed at me and glared. "Promise me, Channing. He's the best bartender we've had in awhile, so don't make me choose between him and you."

I bugged my eyes out in mock horror for a second. "Don't worry. I know where I stand around here. Next question. Guy named Brooks Spellman. Ring a bell?"

Artie started to shake his head, then cut it short. "Wait a minute. Asshole with the fake nose thingamabob in his headshot? All bluster and no luster?"

"That's the one."

"Annoying jerk. He came in one day wanting an audition on the spot. I was busy so I told him to send in a package. Got all huffy, like his time was more important then mine." Artie scratched his nose. "Raised his voice and got in my face. Just so happens, Ty was here picking up his check." He stopped talking, eyes sparkling.

"You didn't?"

"I didn't," Artie said. "But Ty most certainly did."

"No broken bones, I hope."

Artie seemed offended. "Please! I just had Ty talk to him. Mano a mano."

I shook my head. Knowing Ty, he probably bought Spellman a beer and let him down easy. *It's not you, kid, it's us.*

"The funny thing was, Spellman sent in his package the following week. As if nothing had ever happened here," he said.

"I watched a couple minutes of it."

"Ouch," Artie said. "Take a Motrin, that'll help. I've got Pepto-Bismol, too."

Everyone's a comedian. "You know he says he played at Reed's? That true?"

"Inferior clubs get inferior talent," Artie said, shrugging. "How did his name come up anyway?"

"Old boyfriend of Heather's."

He pursed his lips. "You talk to her yet? Find out what happened?" Leaning forward, he softened his tone. "She okay?"

"Working on it. She's been hard to catch up with." I didn't mention Heather's interest in firearms. Maybe Ambyr had gotten it wrong. A guy could hope, anyway.

"Well, she's got some serious talent, but without someone like you working with her, she'll never get it focused. I hope you're successful." He paused and locked eyes with me. "And I hope you're ready to get back on *your* horse soon. Let me know what I can do for you. You're a funny man and a good shit, Channing Hayes. Don't let your talent go to waste."

"Uh, thanks, I think." High praise, coming from the legendary Artie Worsham. High praise, indeed.

THIRTEEN

SATURDAY NIGHT WAS THE club's biggest night, where we made the week's nut or lost it. That's why we booked the best talent, ran the most promos, and scheduled the best employees for Saturday nights. Made sure Ty had on his smoothest threads. Thanks to the blurb in the *Post*, we were hoping tonight's take would be the biggest we'd had all year.

The employees also knew how big Saturday night was, and even though they got paid an hourly wage, they all realized how important the club's success was to their paychecks. A string of bad Saturday nights could send the club plummeting into the depths of bankruptcy, their jobs along with it.

I left the office to stretch my legs and found Skip behind the bar. "Hey, what's up?"

"Nothing much, boss," he said. "You talk to Heather yet?"

I watched Skip arrange his work area. "Nah. Not yet. Hopefully, she'll turn up soon." From my lips to God's—or George Burns's—ears.

Skip nodded toward the back. "Artie's in a mood today, boy. Chewed me out for breaking a glass. Hell, I break two or three a night, he don't say a word. You know what's eating him?"

I had a few guesses, but I just shrugged. Mapping out Artie's moods could be a full-time job. "How's your act coming?" Everyone in the club knew he was working on something, but no one had any particulars. Evidently, they didn't know about his audition tape tucked away in the office.

Skip eyed me suspiciously. "Fine. Why? You haven't asked in a while."

True. I'd asked him about it a month ago and he'd responded like he didn't want to talk about it. After a few more tries without getting anywhere, I'd left him alone. "Curious. Tell me about it."

"Nothing much to tell. I get nervous on stage. Stutter." He looked down at a row of bottles, all lined up, labels facing out. "That's why they call me Skip. Funny, huh?"

"I've heard funnier. You used to go on over at Reed's place? Open mics and stuff?"

Skip bent over and pulled a poly bag of lemons and limes out of a small refrigerator. He set them on the counter in front of him and began washing the fruit, carefully removing the tiny stickers with his fingernails. "A year or two ago. Tried some other clubs, too. Why?"

"What's he like, Reed?"

Skip sorted all the limes into one pile, lemons into another. "Okay guy, really. Hard-nosed, but he never treated me bad or anything. Most people either loved him or hated him." He picked up a knife and pointed it at me. "Me? I was lukewarm on the guy."

"How come you put your act on the shelf?" I kept my voice quiet, in case someone—like Artie—walked by. I didn't want my interest to be misinterpreted as needling.

Skip shrugged. "Wasn't ready yet." He quartered a lemon and put the pieces in a small white bowl. "I'll get back to it someday. In fact, I'm thinking about seeing a hypnotist. For my problem."

I didn't know what to say, so I watched him slice a few more lemons in silence. He filled up two bowls, then started on the limes with quick, sure cuts.

"Know a guy named Brooks Spellman?" I asked.

Skip's knife kept slicing. "Struggling comic. Met him at the CCC. Always scrapping for stage time. A few of us—me, him, my man Nathan—were working on our stuff around the same time. Hung out together some, you know how it is, waiting around for your chance. Haven't seen him in a long time. Went out west or something, I think. Seemed okay to me."

Everybody seemed okay to Skip. Guess that was a good way to go through life. "Did you know he was dating Heather a while back?"

Skip dissected the last lime and swept it off the cutting board into the lime bowl. "Heard something about that, sure. Don't really know how it ended." He covered the bowls with Saran wrap and stuck them back into the refrigerator.

Donna waltzed up. "Hey, boys. Watcha talking about?" She lived for gossip, but she'd be the first person to tell someone else to mind his own business.

"Nothing. Guy stuff. You wouldn't understand," Skip said.

"I've forgotten more guy stuff than you'd ever understand," she said. "Now how about letting me talk to Channing alone?" She nodded to the back. "I think there's some citrus needs your attention in the kitchen. You're the expert with the knife, I hear."

Skip stuck his tongue out at her as he left.

"What's on your mind?" I asked Donna. She stared at me, and the unblinking attention made me uncomfortable, like when my high school chemistry teacher would lock me in his sights for a long moment before nailing me with detention.

"How are you holding up?"

"Okay."

She nodded, as if I'd just confessed something. "Tomorrow would have been the big day. If it hasn't hit you yet, it will, and I think you should be prepared for it."

"I'm okay." I didn't tell her about my trip out to Meadowspring Gardens earlier. Didn't want her to get a big head about being right.

"Honey, it's okay to be sad. Good, really. Means you can start to move on." She patted my hand.

"I'm fine. Really. I've already been through all the stages of grief. Hit some of them more than once." I smiled as I pulled my hand away.

She nodded, not believing me for a second. "Well, if you need to talk about it, I'm here for you."

"Thanks." I looked up and Artie stood at the end of the bar, glowering at us. He crooked a finger at me, then turned around and headed back to the office.

I shrugged at Donna. "Sorry. Gotta go."

In the office, Artie said, "Don't get comfortable. J.J.'s coming in and I'm buying dinner next door at Lee's. You're invited."

The last time Artie sprang for dinner was never. "What's the occasion?"

He leaned back and clasped his hands behind his neck. *Portrait of a Schemer as an Old Man.* "We need to find out what Reed's trying to do with J.J. The past couple of years, J.J.'s alternated clubs when he comes to D.C. I'm afraid Reed's trying to lock him up exclusive."

"Don't you think you're letting your imagination run wild? Even if we 'lost' J.J., there are plenty of other funny fish in the sea."

Artie shook his head. "I told you before. J.J. fills up this place. And if he goes with Reed, then a bunch of his buddies might do the same—and he's got a lot of followers who take their cues from him. Pretty soon, they'll be no big names left for us. And that prick Reed will have beaten me."

"I'm not saying your scenario is plausible, but—if it is—what are you going to say to J.J. to persuade him to keep coming here?"

He pointed at me. "You'll think of something, champ."

FOURTEEN

LEE'S PALACE WASN'T CROWDED at the early hour, and the owner, Thomas Lee, waited on us himself. He and Artie had formed a fast friendship when The Last Laff first moved into the strip center, and Lee kept the relationship stoked with free eggrolls and Moo Shu Pork. One night nine years ago, Artie, along with a good deal of Tsingtao, convinced Lee to channel his natural playfulness and perform at an open mic. Since then, Lee had returned—often—to subject the crowd to his comedy stylings. In nine years, the material hadn't changed a bit, if anything his timing had gotten worse.

"Jon Jermaine, I have seen you many times and each time you are funnier than last," Lee said, menus tucked under his arm. "It is great honor to serve you." Lee spoke to J.J. in a thick Chinese accent, and I rolled my eyes at Artie. Normally, Lee spoke as if he were born on Long Island. Which he was. He only used his accent on stage and—evidently—when ribbing headlining comics.

J.J. soaked up the phony adulation. "Thanks. Glad you enjoyed the show. I do my best, you know."

Lee bowed. "I will be back with your food, wonderful funny man." He winked at Artie before he headed back to the kitchen.

"Hey, we didn't order yet," J.J. said.

"He'll bring us out something special, don't worry," Artie said. "Lee knows how to treat people right."

I made eyes at Artie. *Easy, go easy.*

He gave me a little nod and said, "So, J.J., enjoying your stay at the luxurious comedy condo?"

J.J. glanced at me, and an unspoken acknowledgment of secrecy passed between us. "Sure. Just what I need between shows. A quiet place where I can recharge my batteries."

I stifled my snort and took a sip of ice water, avoiding eye contact with J.J.

"Glad you like it," Artie said. "Some guys say it's too quiet. I guess everybody's different." He dry-swallowed. "Saw you talking with Gerry Reed the other night."

"Yeah. Good guy. He gets me." J.J. scanned the restaurant. "And he's got a nice club. Gets a lot of big names there. Always packs them in."

"Yeah, just like us," Artie said, and I couldn't tell if he was trying to be serious or facetious. I wondered what J.J. thought.

Next to me, Artie played with his fork and squirmed around. Then he cleared his throat a couple times.

I leaned back in my chair, enjoying my role as a spectator. Even though Artie had joked I'd be the one to hash it out with J.J., I knew Artie didn't trust anyone but Artie to handle the situation. And really, that was fine with me.

"So what did you guys discuss?" Artie asked.

"Huh?" J.J. asked.

"What did you and Reed talk about?"

J.J. waved his hand. "The usual."

"The usual?" Artie asked. "What's that?"

"Look, we didn't talk about anything specific. He just wants to book me more often."

Artie chuckled. "Hey, who doesn't?" He stopped laughing. "What did you tell him?"

Before J.J. answered, Thomas Lee arrived with the food. He set out several platters heaped with a variety of dishes, some old standbys, some I'd never seen before. Enough food for a gastronomic orgy. Artie was right, Lee knew how to treat people well. "Enjoy, folks. Let me know if you want anything else. Okay?" Lee said, sans accent.

J.J. gave him a quick double take, then reached for the closest platter. Lee departed after a curt bow, returning to his post at the front door where he waited to greet his guests like a true host.

We dug in, and J.J. never answered Artie's question. Across the table, I knew Artie was trying to figure out a way to get the conversation turned back to where he wanted it without seeming desperate or conniving.

"Channing, what's up with your act? When will you be getting back out there?" J.J. asked, mouth half-full of Moo Goo Gai Pan. Artie's head bobbed up from his meal and he turned toward me too, eyebrows raised.

The skin on my face felt hot, and I didn't think it was from the Szechuan String Beans. "Working on it. Trying to get my timing back. The accident, and all." I lamely held up my left hand and concentrated on my food, hoping to deflect any more questions. I'd get "back out there" when I was damn well ready, thank you.

The table fell silent and Artie seized the opening. "What did you tell Reed?"

J.J. glanced from me to Artie. "About what?"

"About working his place more often?"

J.J.'s face hardened. "Told him he should talk to my agent." He pointed his fork at Artie. "Why? What should I have told him?"

"You should have told him there's another club in the area that treats you right. Gives you a nice paycheck. Promotes your appearances. Puts you up at the condo. Buys you a seven-course dinner." Artie smiled, sweeping his hand over the table. "Seriously, though. What would it take for us to become your exclusive D.C. area venue? You name it and it's yours."

My mouth fell open. Artie *never* groveled. His feud with Reed must be nastier than I thought.

J.J. shook his head. "Man, you guys are something else. I've been doing both of your clubs for years. Years! And now each one of you is trying to get a grip on me like I'm some kind of wishbone." His fork clattered as he dropped it on his plate. "I'll tell you what I told Gerry. If you've got some kind of proposal you want me to consider, call my agent. He's the one who does the business. Me? I'm just the clown who makes people laugh."

———

J.J. did indeed make people laugh: loud, hearty, and often. Both shows were terrific and the snapshot I had in my head of Artie's ebullient face after he tallied the take stayed with me during the drive home. In the hallway of my condo, I peeked through Erin's peephole and although I couldn't see anything concrete, I saw a glimmer of light. I knocked softly.

Dressed in a flowing red and silver caftan, with her sultry complexion and dark flowing hair, Erin reminded me of some exotic Persian princess. She invited me in, only to break the fairy tale illusion when she blew a pink bubble-gum bubble and popped it on her lips. "How are you, Channing?" She led me into her kitchen and took a sip of water from a glass on the table. Her laptop was open and a small conical desk lamp illuminated a jumble of papers scattered beside it. The lamp's cord stretched taut through the air to the wall socket three feet away.

"I'm good. Had a great night at the club."

"Can I get you something?" she asked. Her smile lit up the dark kitchen.

"No thanks." Clearly, she was working and I felt bad for interrupting. I just wanted to share the buzz I still had going from the banner night. It was times like these I missed Lauren most. I wondered if Erin remembered tomorrow—make that today—was to be my wedding day. "You're busy. Just wanted to say hi." I didn't move. "So, hi."

Erin set her glass down and came closer. Reached out and gathered both of my hands in hers. Except for nurses at the hospital, it was the first time a woman had actually held my mangled hand. I resisted the urge to yank it away and hide it in my pocket. In a soft and comforting voice she said, "It's okay. This is a tough time for you. Rightly so. Don't worry about disturbing me."

I nodded, tears welling. I'd felt so good at the club during the late show, not two hours ago. The crowd had been raucous and Artie and I had been pumped up right along with them. Now coming home to an empty condo terrified me.

"I'm here for you," she said.

"Thanks." She hugged me and patted my back, rocking me back and forth, the embrace motherly solace. Erin held me in her kitchen while I leaked tears onto her shoulders and ached, picturing Lauren so beautiful in white on our wedding day.

FIFTEEN

THE PHONE RANG. THE clock read 10:35 a.m. The caller ID displayed W. Dempsey.

I rolled onto my side and covered my head with my pillow, wishing today would be over and I could just move on to Monday, *Do Not Pass Go, Do Not Collect $200.* After a few rings, the phone shushed. I exhaled and curled up, preparing to finish my slumber, when the phone rang again. I considered jerking the cord from the wall and hurling the phone across the room, but that would require effort. I glanced at the caller ID again: W. Dempsey. Persistence, to go along with his hatred of me. A bad combination. I picked up the phone, hoping he was calling to tell me Heather had shown up.

"Hello? Channing?" Kathleen Dempsey's voice greeted me.

"Good morning, Kathleen." I flopped onto my back, keeping my eyes closed.

"I hope I didn't wake you." She paused, but I was too tired to answer. "Well, I'm sorry if I did. It's just that I'm worried about Heather. Did you find her yet?"

"No. Not yet." I took a deep breath. "I thought you and William said Heather does this all the time. He didn't seemed worried about her in the least."

"William took Lauren's death hard. We all did. But he turned his sorrow into anger." She lowered her voice. "He doesn't really blame you for Lauren's death, you know."

Why not? I did. "He's a pretty convincing actor then."

"He needs to blame someone, needs to believe it wasn't just some senseless accident. So you're convenient. It's not fair, I know. Please don't take it personally."

Hard not to take it personally when a father practically accuses you of murdering his daughter. I shook my head, scattering the unpleasant memories. Back to the now. "About Heather? Any ideas where she might have gone? Maybe she went to visit a friend out of town?"

"Channing, you may know Heather has to fight a lot of distractions. And she bounces around from thing to thing. But she was quite devoted to her comedy. So it seems unlikely to me she would just run away from it. That's why I'm worried. If it was something else, I might agree more with William, that she's just taken off, as usual. But not now. Not like this." She paused and her voice hardened. "I'm worried something bad has happened. That we're finally going to get that call we've been dreading so much. And despite waiting for it all these years, I'm still not ready."

"I'm doing my best, Kathleen. I've looked everywhere I can think of." On the other end of the line, I thought I heard sobbing but it was subdued. Genteel, even in despair. "But I'll keep searching. She's bound to turn up somewhere soon, right?"

"Yes, yes. I'm sorry," she said, pulling it together. "And Channing?"

"Yes?"

"I wanted you to know I'm thinking of you today. And praying for both you and Lauren." Then she burst out crying.

"Ditto, Kathleen. Ditto," I whispered to myself.

———

I puttered around the condo all morning, trying to stay above water. Finally, after lunch, I decided to go on a long walk. I grabbed a bottle of blue Gatorade, and for the first time since the accident, I took a blank notebook along with me, just in case I got any sudden comedic insights I needed to get down on paper before they escaped, never to be heard from again.

I walked along the main road to a nearby school, then cut around back, across the playground, to a dirt trail. A hundred yards later the trail joined up with a popular paved path. I paced myself, alert for "on your left" calls from cyclists sneaking up on me from behind, and tried not to think of Lauren, our wedding, or Heather. I wasn't entirely successful, but I didn't get mired in pity, either. After about an hour, I stopped and hoisted myself up onto a stone wall that bordered the path, thirty yards behind a 7-Eleven catering to thirsty bikers.

I pulled out my notebook and flipped it to the first page. Grabbed a ballpoint pen from my front pocket. Clicked it open. Put pen to paper and waited for the muse to appear. After a couple minutes staring at the blank page, I clicked the ballpoint shut.

Most comics carried something to write on—a notebook, a little pad, or even a folded-up piece of paper—because you never knew when the perfect joke would strike you. You'd be waiting for coffee at Starbucks, the gag would pop into your mind, and you'd want to make damn sure you captured it. So you jotted down the exact wording, including every nuanced expression necessary to make the joke dynamite. On those occasions when you didn't write it down and couldn't recreate the magic later, you'd kick yourself for hours about the one that got away.

They weren't always gems, however. Far from it. Out of the dozens of ideas I'd get in the middle of the night and scribble on a scrap of paper I kept on my nightstand, only one or two would ever pan out. Writing material was a numbers game. You had to generate an awful lot of "possibles" before you got an idea that worked.

I stared at the blank page. At home, I dedicated one entire shelf of an old bookcase for my "inspiration notebooks." Every so often, I'd haul them out and mine them for undiscovered ore. I always thought it fascinating how I could tell what kind of mood I was in or what things were going on in my life simply by thumbing through the notes and commentaries. Some books I'd written in blue periods, while others were striking in their optimism. Turned out a lot of my best material came from some of the darkest times in my life. I wondered if that was a common theme among the great comics. I hoped so; it was a small consolation to know your depressed periods weren't a complete waste.

I stared at the blank page. A successful writer I once knew said if you waited for inspiration to hit or for the muse to arrive before you started writing, you'd end up in another line of work, but quick. Writing comedy was hard, and often—too often—there was nothing funny about it. Just another job in the entertainment industry. I wasn't sure I agreed with that. I couldn't think of anything more enjoyable, more fulfilling, than getting up on stage and making people laugh. Sure, there was a ton of unseen hard work required—and plenty of luck—to get to that point, but it was worth every single excruciating second.

At least it *had* been worth it. I hadn't been on stage in five months. What was I waiting for? The ghost of Richard Pryor to whisper in my ear? I had enough material ready and polished to do shows five nights a week without repeating myself. Then what was the problem? Was I afraid? Afraid of how the audience would react when they saw my scarred face and mangled hand? Or was I afraid of what would happen if I bombed and there was no one around to console me, besides Artie whose idea of comfort was a bottle of scotch?

I stared at the blank page. I'd made my bed and I'd have to lie in it the rest of my life. Dempsey was right about one thing. Lauren was dead because of my actions. Premeditated no, but dead is dead. And now his other daughter was missing, and I wouldn't be surprised if that was my fault, too. For pushing her too hard. For taking up her cause and driving her to succeed as some sort of twisted effort to garner Lauren's forgiveness. Part of me wished I would run into William Dempsey in a dark alley and he'd have had the foresight to bring along his pipe wrench.

I closed the notebook. Took a sip of Gatorade. I'd have plenty of stuff to talk about with my therapist this week and I didn't think I needed to take notes to remember any of it. I hopped off the stone wall and headed down the path. A minute later, my cell phone chirped.

"Hello?"

"Come over to the condo right away," Artie said, gulping air as if he'd just completed an Ironman competition. "I need your help. J.J.'s laid out on the floor. And he ain't breathing, my friend. He ain't breathing."

SIXTEEN

Artie had stationed himself in a chair by the front window so he could peer out onto the parking lot. I got a glimpse of his face as I bounded up the front walk, then the curtains fluttered closed. A moment later, the front door opened a crack and Artie made sure I was alone before letting me in. "You didn't tell anybody, did you?" he asked, out of breath. For a split second, I thought he might frisk me for a wire.

I stared at him. "Did you call 911?"

Artie held up his phone and wiggled it in the air. "Just about to."

Why he'd waited until I got there was beyond me. "Call them. Now," I said, as I pushed past him into the living room. Everything looked like it had the other night when I'd come over. Drugs, booze, clothing. Except this time, J.J.'s body sprawled on the floor by the couch. A small vial of white powder stood open on the table and a dusting covered J.J.'s upper lip, like a faint milk moustache. *Got Coke?*

My breath quickened. A picture of my mother, lying dead in her bed, a vial of pills overturned on the pillow next to her, floated before my shimmering eyes. I'd been the one to find her.

Artie trailed behind me. "That's how I found him."

The mirage vaporized. J.J. stared at us, rictus frozen in place, skin unnaturally pale, almost bluish. "You positive he's dead?" I asked, making sure to cover all the bases, but I knew the answer.

"I know dead, Channing. And he is most definitely," Artie said. He still held the phone in his hand. "No pulse, no breath. No nothing."

"Did you call?"

"Not yet." He made no move to dial 911, kept staring at the tableau of death. "Maybe we should clean up a bit first. Come up with a story? Make him look better? I'd hate for his family and friends to have to deal with this."

I glanced around, then eyed Artie, whose face had blanched to a hue approaching J.J.'s. "Look. They're going to do an autopsy. They'll find the drugs. No sense trying to clean anything up. It'll just make us look guilty of something." I paused. "The drugs? They're not yours, are they?"

Artie must not have heard me because he didn't react, just kept staring.

I snapped my fingers in front of his face. "Artie? Call 911. Tell them we found J.J. dead. I'll call Freeman."

He scuttled off to the kitchen and I heard him talking to the emergency dispatcher, imploring him to *hurry up, hurry up, there's a dead guy here, hurry up*. J.J. wasn't going anywhere, but I understood Artie's urgency. No one liked having a body in the living room of his condo.

I returned to the foyer and navigated through the contact list in my phone. Dialed Freeman's number. He didn't answer, so I left a message, a sort of generic I-could-use-some-serious-help type message, careful to omit any mention of bodies or drugs—you never knew who might be listening in when the message got retrieved. Of course, in his line of work, I'm sure he got plenty of gory, graphic messages. Maybe he'd appreciate my change of pace. I stuffed the phone in my pocket and drifted over to J.J.'s body.

From the extra forty pounds he carried and the rolls of doughy flesh, I'd guess the most exercise J.J. got was moving the microphone stand out of the way. But he clocked in at about my age, give or take, and most thirty-three-year-olds didn't have heart attacks, no matter how poorly they ate or how much couch time they logged watching poker on ESPN.

The smart money was on a drug overdose. J.J. lived hard; it was fitting he died hard. He'd brought it upon himself, and if only a small fraction of the legendary tales about J.J. had been true, it had just been a matter of time. Dead from his own excess.

In my mind's eye, the white tent door flaps billowed in the breeze. Lauren, who exercised religiously, avoided red meat, and didn't drink anything harder than root beer, had also died. But she was dead because of *my* drinking a little too much. I wasn't in the same class as J.J., was I? Maybe I was worse—at least *he* died from his own actions; Lauren died from *mine*.

Artie joined me in the living room, and although a sheen of sweat glistened on his face, he seemed calmer. "They're on the way." He nodded vaguely in J.J.'s direction. "I came by to clean up. He told me yesterday he was planning on getting an early start to Pittsburgh." He shrugged. "Musta happened last night."

"Yeah, looks that way."

"You know what I always say. Fifty percent of comics are depressed, fifty percent are neurotic, and the other half are just plain nuts." Artie said.

I had no response. Funny what a corpse will do to a conversation. We stood there side-by-side for a moment. I hadn't told Artie about freeing J.J. from handcuffs the other night. He'd find out, of course, probably from the police report after I told them, but I didn't see any reason to tell him now. He didn't need the added aggravation at the moment. Neither did I.

I jerked my head toward the front door. "I think I'll wait on the porch."

———

Police interviews and waiting around and watching the police technician photograph the scene and waiting around and waiting around some more killed the rest of the day. Artie and I must have repeated our story thirty times for various EMTs, detectives, and neighbors. Artie kept asking when he'd be able to use the condo again, and the cops kept shaking their heads and telling him to cool his jets. Artie responded by scowling and grumbling and chewing on his unlit cigar.

When I told the detective about the handcuff incident, Artie simply glared at me.

———

Sunday nights were slow at the club, and Artie usually showed old comedy movies on a big projection screen that descended from the ceiling. Tonight, neither of us felt like working—or even being around other people—so we called in and told Skip and Donna they were in charge, without telling them the reason. They'd find out soon enough and I didn't feel like rehashing the story one more time. They were happy with their temporary rise to power, and Artie and I needed the time to recover. We went our respective ways with hardly more than a parting nod.

Finding Heather was still my number one concern. But I didn't know where to look or who to ask, so I went home and left a message with my therapist requesting the first available cancellation. Then I nuked some fish sticks, scarfed them down with a boatload of ketchup, and went to sleep.

The next day, I arrived at the club a few minutes after four and found Skip waiting for me by the door, like the family dog minus the drool. "Oh, man. J.J. od'd. There'd always been plenty of stories about him, and I figured there had to be some truth to them, but… man. Right in Artie's condo. Bet he was plenty pissed." Skip's inquisitive eyes searched my face for some emotion, some sign this was big news. If he'd seen death up close and personal, he wouldn't be so enthralled.

"Well, hello to you too, Skip," I said.

"Saw it on the news last night. And it made the *Metro* section this morning," he said. "Page three. Above the fold. Not bad."

People reacted differently to a person's death. Some cried. Some withdrew into silence. Others prattled on as if they'd just come back from the circus. "Skip. Take it easy. It's not like on some TV show. J.J. was lying there, dead. Right on the floor. It was pretty unnerving." I tried to say it calmly, without reproach.

Skip's face sagged. "Sorry. You're right." He closed his mouth, then it popped open. "But man, right in the condo. What's Artie going to do? Sell it and buy a new one? Who's going to want to stay there now?"

"Give it a rest."

Skip shrugged, and after waiting for me to say something else, wandered off to work when I kept my lips pressed together. I headed back toward the office, but stopped when I heard my name being called. Justin Dempsey came slinking my way. "Hey Channing, got a minute?" His tie was too tight and his blue suit too old. I didn't look down, afraid I'd see a pair of scuffed brown wingtips.

His defiant manner from the other day had eroded. Now he seemed almost apologetic. Something must be up. Maybe he'd gotten a line on Heather. "Yeah. Sure. This way." I led him to the office, offered him my chair while I sat in Artie's.

"So. To what do I owe this unexpected treat?"

His face shaded. "I'm here about Heather."

"What about her?"

Justin glanced around the office, eyes flitting about, not settling on anything. Then he fixed on me and blew out a big breath. "She's been at my place. Hanging out."

"Heather's staying with you?" Skepticism coated my words.

"Yeah. Since last Thursday."

I leaned across the desk. "You're telling me that Heather's been at your house since last week. Since she 'disappeared'? When I came over to talk with you, Heather was there?" I felt like reaching out and grabbing Justin's neck and squeezing until his eyeballs popped.

He looked down into his lap. "Yeah. She was there."

"And she's okay?"

"Yeah. She's okay." Slowly, he brought his head up and faced me. "At least she was. Now…"

"Now what?" My heart beat faster.

"Now she's gone."

SEVENTEEN

"What do you mean *she's gone?*"

Justin gave me a hangdog expression. "She took off. I gave her a key and everything. Free run of the house. She'd leave in the morning and come back in the evening. But Saturday night, she never came back. So I checked the guest room and her stuff—not that she had much stuff—was gone." He held his hands out. Empty.

"Today's Monday. Why did you wait to tell me?"

"Thought maybe she'd come back. I called her. No answer. She hasn't returned my messages. So I figure she's gone into hiding again. Someplace else. Thought it was time to tell you, seeing as how you're looking for her, too."

I thought a moment. "Why was she staying with you anyway? Something wrong with her apartment?"

Justin shook his head. "She wanted to, uh, keep a low profile. Said there were some people mad at her, and she wanted to let things cool down."

"She say who?"

"My parents for starters. They were constantly on her case. About guys, about jobs, about her, uh, bad habits. About that *comedy shit*. That's how my father refers to it." He chuckled.

That wasn't new. Heather had never gotten along with them. "Who else?"

He stared at me and licked his lips. "Your name came up."

My neck snapped back as if I'd been punched. "I'm not mad at her."

Justin's left eyebrow scooted up a millimeter.

"Well, I am now. Because she took off and I've been busting my balls to try to find her. But I wasn't before." Was I? I blinked a couple of times, trying to remember my interactions with her. Had I been taking out my anger over the events of my life on Heather? Had the pressure been too much? Was *I* the reason she'd run off?

"Don't take it personal. I don't think it was you or my parents she was really hiding from. Some guy's been hounding her. Threatening her. Heather didn't say it, but I wouldn't be surprised if he even slapped her around a bit. She was really freaked out, and for Heather, that's saying something. You know how she can be. I thought she felt safe at my place, but…" He trailed off and cocked his head to the side. "She even parked her car a couple of blocks away in the church lot. Didn't want to be found, all right. And Heather's a clever one when it comes to sneaking around." He smiled, the sneering kind you reserve for someone you're about to insult. "She got lots of practice as a teenager."

This all sounded pretty thin. I'd never thought of Justin as a straight shooter, and Lauren had corroborated those feelings, albeit not directly—it wasn't her style to call her brother a flat-out liar. "Did she mention the guy's name?"

"Nope. I asked, too. More than once. But she played it cagey."

"She should have gone to the cops if this guy was really bothering her."

"Yeah. I brought that up. But…" Justin stopped, sighed. "Cops and Heather don't mix. Plus, despite what she said about this guy, I got the impression she still had the hots for him. Didn't want to see him get into any trouble." He shook his head. "Heather was like that. Going for the bad boys. They'd treat her like crap and she'd just go back for more. But hey, there's only so much we can do." A stupid grin appeared on his face. "I mean, I'm not my sister's keeper, right?"

I willed my hands to stay on the desk, palms down, but inside my anger threatened to boil over. Justin must have read my mind, because his gaze settled on my mangled hand. When he broke off and looked at me, his pupils jumped as he realized I'd busted him staring.

I needed more information and escalating things with Justin would only be counterproductive. I took a deep breath and concentrated on fluffy clouds and cuddly kittens. Modulated my tone. "Tell me Justin, why do you think she decided to leave on Saturday? As opposed to Friday or yesterday?"

Justin frowned. "With her, who knows? After you came sniffing around, maybe she thought you'd find her soon. Wanted to run to a different hiding place."

"Uh-huh." A picture of J.J. at the comedy condo flashed in my mind. Could Heather have gone there? She'd been there on Wednesday night. Could she have gone back to open arms on Saturday night? Then fled when J.J. od'd? It sounded preposterous, simply a wild explanation of two unrelated events. At least I hoped that's all it was.

Justin rose. "Just thought you might want to know. And I wasn't sure you'd talk to me on the phone."

I got up but made no attempt to shake his hand or thank him. If he'd told me the truth when I'd gone to his house, I could have talked to Heather and discovered what was bothering her. Helped her. "You sure you don't know the name of the guy stalking her?"

"Sorry, man. It's ironic, isn't it? In the past, I never paid much attention when she started jabbering about guys. Now, when I wanted to know, she wouldn't tell me."

I nodded. It would have been nice to get some confirmation, but I didn't really need it. I think I knew the creep's name.

———

Tracking Heather from place to place, a step behind, was getting old. If Justin was correct about Heather always going back to her bad boys, then I ought to go pay Ryan Rizzetti a visit. And if Justin was wrong and she didn't want to go back to the bad boy, then I ought to pay him a visit anyway, if only to give him a little re-education on how to treat people. My only decision was whether or not to take Ty along for support, but I didn't feel like bothering him with my problem, and besides, I thought I could do a pretty good job by myself.

At The Last Laff, Mondays meant open mic nights, which Artie liked to host, so he didn't mind when I told him I had an errand to run. He was still shook up from J.J.'s death, although he told me he'd spent the day cleaning up the condo with about five gallons of industrial-strength chemicals. Life goes on, I guess.

I drove over to Ryan's townhouse in Reston without calling. No need to give him a chance to slip away. If he wasn't there, I'd camp out in his parking lot until he returned. I'd brought a book, a bottle of water, and a box of Balance Bars to tide me over.

He was home.

And this time, he recognized me right away. "What do you want? She's not here," he said. Snappy conversationalist. He didn't open the door one inch wider than he needed to.

"Have you heard from her?"

"Nope."

"Can we talk about it?"

A grudging nod. "Sure." He opened the door and waved me in. Today he wore black shorts with his George Mason T-shirt.

"Have you tried calling her?" I asked.

"Of course. No answer," he said. "Look, we've been through this. She takes off sometimes. Drives me crazy too, but…" He shrugged. "We're just having fun, me and Heather. She's not the love of my life or anything."

"Uh-huh." Why were all the people in Heather's life jerks? I didn't lump myself into that category, but if you asked Justin or Ryan they might have a different take on it. "You ever hit her?"

Ryan's eyes widened. "Fuck no. I don't hit women." He straightened. "Who told you that?"

"I've got my sources."

"Well, your sources are full of shit. I like Heather. Why would I hurt her?" He cocked his head at me and his eyes narrowed.

I cocked my head back at him and stared. He seemed pissed in that way people sometimes got when they were being falsely accused. I didn't know for sure, but his outrage seemed genuine.

114

Ryan blew out a short blast of breath and was about to say something when a scrawny guy came down the stairs behind us.

"Oh. Hey. Didn't know you had company." Wispy hair swirled on the skinny guy's head like a soft-serve ice cream cone, and the pupils of his eyes seemed to move independently of each other. Woody Allen had nothing on this guy in the nebbish department.

Ryan produced a tight smile. "This is my roommate Nathan. Nathan Borghat." He nodded at me. "Channing Hayes."

Nathan's face lit up. "Sure. Skip's told me all about you. We met once before, too. After one of your shows," he said, looking to me for an acknowledgement. I didn't remember him, but I half-nodded anyway. He cleared his throat. "So, when will you be performing again?"

"Not sure," I said, instinctively moving my left hand behind my hip.

A switch flipped and his face darkened. "Anybody talk to Heather?"

Ryan spoke first. "Nope. She'll come back when she's ready."

Nathan bared some teeth, but it came out closer to a sneer than a smile. "Yeah, maybe. I hope she's okay."

I noticed something pass between the two roomies. And it made Nathan nervous, because he glanced from me to Ryan then to me again. "Well, nice meeting you. I…I gotta run," he said, voice wavering. He slipped between us and hustled out the front door, keys jingling in the pocket of his baggy jeans.

Ryan's flat brown eyes focused on mine. "Anything else?" he said, no inflection in his tone. I knew a dismissal when I heard one.

"No. Thanks. If you hear from Heather, you'll call, right?"

"You'll be the first," he said, still straight-faced.

Snappy comeback. Snappy dresser, snappy repartee, Ryan Rizzetti was just plain snappy, any way you cut it. I took off, contemplating what I'd just seen. Something was up. Ryan knew what. Nathan knew what. I didn't know squat.

What else was new?

———

On my way home, Freeman called.

"Just got a heads-up about J.J.'s tox screen. The coke wasn't pure. In fact, it only resembled cocaine in form and color. A good portion of it was cyanide."

My money had been on overdose. I guess I should have known that something more sinister was a possibility the way the cops handled things at the condo. But what did I know about police procedure? On TV, the cops always treated every death like a crime scene. "You're saying someone murdered J.J.?"

I could hear Freeman's sigh over the phone. "I'm saying there was cyanide in the coke J.J. snorted. That's all I'm saying."

"But what are you *thinking*? Someone intentionally poisoned J.J.?"

"Well, someone intentionally put cyanide in the coke. And I don't think it was J.J. himself. Whether or not someone wanted to kill J.J. *specifically* is unknown, so it could be just an unfortunate case of getting some tainted coke. We'll know more about that if anyone else shows up dead from cyanide. That's not something you see every day, you know."

I hadn't thought about it. "Yeah, I guess."

"Channing?" Freeman's tone turned softer.

"Yeah?"

"You got any theories? Supposing someone targeted J.J. specifically?"

I thought a moment. "Probably some irate husband or boyfriend. J.J. had a loose zipper."

"Oh, you're a bundle of information. Talk to you later." Freeman clicked off, leaving me with a big question on my mind.

Had someone intentionally murdered Jon Jermaine? And the follow-up: Who?

EIGHTEEN

I PLUCKED A PIECE of lint from my shirtsleeve and rolled it between my thumb and forefinger. It was 11:25 a.m. on Tuesday morning, according to the calendar/clock combo hanging on my therapist's office wall. We'd spent the first part of the session discussing my reaction to J.J.'s death. The death itself, seeing the body, talking to the cops. My responses and feelings all seemed within normal bounds, considering the body belonged to a guy I knew.

"Channing. I'd like to back up a moment. You said you had just closed your 'idea notebook' when you got the call from Artie. If I remember correctly, you hadn't been carrying the book around with you. Was this the first time in a while that you've done so?"

I thought a moment. "Yeah. I guess it was."

"Did any particular event inspire you to bring it?"

"Not that I can recall. Just thought it might come in handy." Something loosened in the back of my brain.

"Don't you find it, ah, interesting that you decided to bring it along on the day you were supposed to be married?"

I hadn't thought about it. But as I was discovering during my sessions the past months, a lot of important stuff happened when I didn't consciously think about it. "Maybe I was hoping to write down some of my feelings. On some level, I figured I'd be pretty emotional and would want to capture it on paper."

"And did you?"

I saw the blank sheet of paper, my pen poised above it, fingers frozen in place. "No."

"Why didn't you? Was it because you didn't have any feelings, or was it something else?"

I exhaled. Always with the hard questions. "At the time, I wasn't thinking anything either way. But reflecting back on it, maybe I didn't want to write anything down because I didn't want to make it 'final.' I didn't want to write down something about Lauren or about our wedding day that I would later rip out of the notebook and throw away." My voice got very small. "Like I threw away our life together."

Silence pressed against me.

"Channing. I know you blame yourself. But blame won't do you any good. It's an anchor weighing you down. You must find a way to get past it." A pause. "Let's shift gears. Look at this from a different angle. Suppose you didn't bring along the notepad to write down your feelings about Lauren. Suppose you wanted it in case you thought of some material. Isn't that the primary purpose of the notebook?"

"You mean sometimes a cigar is just a cigar?"

"Well?"

Again, I tried to remember exactly why I had taken the note-book. Maybe it *had* been to jot down ideas. "Okay, so what? What difference does it make why I took it? I still didn't write anything down." The frustration erupted, loud and clear. Frustration, anger, sadness, guilt. I was a giant ball of negative emotions. And they always seemed to flare up during these sessions.

"I think we should concentrate on your intention. The first step. I think it's a big first step you've taken, not something that should be discounted or glossed over. It tells me you're ready to get on with your life. Ready to get on with your career. The fact you didn't write anything down is minor. It will come. You have to believe, Channing. With time, it will come."

———

Artie and I sat in the office, shooting the shit and watching audition tapes with the sound off, which didn't make them any more difficult to judge. Body language was enough to get a good indication; unfortunately, most amateur comics didn't speak "body" very well.

By some sort of unspoken agreement, we'd avoided talking about J.J. and about tomorrow morning's meeting with Reed at his lawyer's swanky K Street office. It was hard having any kind of interesting discussion when the two most pressing issues were off the table. And it was surprising how boring watching comedy routines can be knowing there was stuff inside we wanted to talk about, but were afraid to.

After a while, we ran out of bullshit to bat around. "So?" Artie said, unlit cigar in place.

"So?" I eyed him.

He stared at me for another few seconds before cracking. "Hell of a thing about J.J. "

"Yeah. Hell of a thing."

Artie frowned, then relaxed, the creases on his face softening. "Okay, okay. Tell me what you really think. Accident or murder?"

I smiled, winner again. "Tough to call. J.J. could be abrasive. And obnoxious. And a host of other unpleasant things. But murder? You had to piss somebody off pretty damn bad."

"Did you know he had drugs in the condo?" he asked.

Was he putting me on? Probably eighty percent of the comics who performed for us used some kind of mood-enhancer. "Comedians. What are you going to do?"

"What did the cops ask you?" Artie asked, pulling the cigar out of his mouth and reseating it.

"Same things they asked you, I'm sure." I grinned. "Why? What did you tell them?" After our initial statement, they'd interviewed us separately to make sure our stories matched. I'm sure they did, unless Artie had decided to spin some wild tale to make J.J. look better. I doubted it, but…

Artie scratched his cheek. "Did the cops ask you about it? The drugs, I mean."

"Yeah, sure. Told them everything I knew. Which wasn't much." Actually, I didn't tell them everything I knew. I didn't mention Heather's visit, not wanting my paranoia to turn an innocent coincidence into a nightmare for her. Despite my bad feelings, I still had no proof Heather was involved in anything illegal. She could have just buckled under the pressure of performing without her sister and taken off, like people had been telling me. I needed to talk to her first, just to put the niggling thoughts to bed. Of course, if it turned out she were involved, I'd call Freeman as fast as my seven fingers could dial.

Artie frowned again, then dropped the subject and moved on to something he could relate to better. "I guess Reed's pretty pissed now that his golden boy won't be making any more curtain calls," he said, a cold glint in his eye. "By the way, there's no need to get dressed up for tomorrow's meeting. I'm not. Fact is, I might not even shower."

"Tell me again why we're going? Since you've made it abundantly clear you have no intention of selling."

Artie's eyes narrowed. "This is war, my friend. And in war, you need every scrap of intelligence you can get your hands on."

Since when did intelligence have anything to do with running a comedy club? "Uh-huh. And what, you think he's going to spill his state secrets to you?"

"You never know. War is hell, don't ever forget it. If he gets the opportunity to ruin us, he'll take it. Mark my words. Gerry 'Greedy' Reed cannot be trusted." Artie pointed his cigar and scowled, and if you squinted just right and imagined a few pounds worth of jowls hanging on his face, it—almost—seemed like he was channeling Winston Churchill.

I rolled my eyes, and in case Artie missed it, rolled them again. "Maybe we should just tell him we're not interested. 'Thanks, but no thanks.' Then we can all move on. Otherwise you risk pissing him off. And I don't think we want that, not from what I've heard. Not from what you've been telling me."

Artie didn't flinch. "This is what we're going to do. Tomorrow, we're going to go and listen politely and ask a billion questions. We're not going to let on that we wouldn't sell our club to him if he were the last prick on earth. No, we're going to act very interested. Get his guard down. Then," Artie wound up his fist and drove it through the air. "POW!"

I laughed to myself, thinking about the headline in the *Post*: *Explosion on K Street, One Arrogant Prick Maimed. People Rejoice.*

Artie leaned forward. "I've got an assignment for you."

My ears perked up. I'd been counting on being merely an observer. An amused observer, sure, but still a non-participant. "What?"

"I want you to go over to the CCC tonight and scope it out. Gather some additional intelligence. No telling what information might come in handy."

"I don't know, Artie. I think we should duck and cover on this one. Let it all blow over."

Artie glared at me like an English bulldog. "Remember: 'Without victory, there is no survival.' Really, Channing, we have no choice."

I shrugged. I hadn't been over to Reed's place since he renovated two years ago. Besides, what could a little intelligence hurt?

NINETEEN

The Capitol Comedy Club was modern, happening, glitzy, and cavernous. In other words, it was everything The Last Laff wasn't. And popular, too. I wore a silk Nationals warm-up jacket and matching cap along with a pair of dark glasses, nighttime be damned. I might not be fooling anyone with my disguise, but at least I *felt* like an A-lister. As I entered the club alongside a knot of six or eight others, I was a bit disappointed. There was no one to sneak past. Reed wasn't glad-handing customers by the door as I'd imagined.

I snagged a table for two in the back and dragged the extra chair to a nearby table so no strays could join me. Settled in and ordered a burger and Sprite from the server, who was better looking and far friendlier than any of ours. She repeated it without writing it down, beaming at me the whole time. Let's just see if she got the order right.

The customers flowed in and the place filled quickly, efficiently. Three levels of seating fronted the stage in a semi-circle, affording every seat a clear view. The well-padded chairs were from this century with nary a rip in the fabric, certainly none big enough to stick your fist through like those at The Last Laff. I'd been after Artie to replace our chairs for months now—at least the ones with so many stains they looked as if they'd been upholstered with the hides of Holstein cows.

The food arrived and the server had nailed the order. Big burger with lots of trimmings next to an Everest of curly fries. A half-pickle. Sure it looked good, but how did it taste? I took a bite of the burger. Hot, juicy, delicious. Maybe we should send our servers and cooks here for training. Hell, maybe we *should* sell out to Reed—from what I'd seen so far, he had a good thing going.

Tonight was an open mic night, just as it was at The Last Laff, and it probably ran like the open mic nights at most clubs. Sometime earlier—a half hour, two hours, yesterday—aspiring comics signed up for a five- or seven-minute slot. At some places it was first come, first served; other places put your name in a hat and assigned positions randomly. Depending on how strictly the emcee enforced the times and the club's popularity, you could go through eight or ten comics an hour—mostly amateurs—all trying to make the most of their valuable stage time.

Once in a while, you'd get a more experienced comic trying out some new material, doing a little favor for the club owner, or simply slumming. When that happened, it made you realize just how far some of the amateurs had to go before they were polished enough to compete in the big leagues.

The lights dimmed and the emcee was some guy I'd never heard of. Hit a few good jokes before introducing the first comic of the evening, a big fat guy with a shaved head. Fat guys were funny and shaved heads were funny, too, so I was optimistic. I slipped into evaluator mode, paying special attention to how the comic moved, how he spoke. The rhythms and the cadences of his delivery were every bit as important as his material—if not more so. You could always improve the material. Changing your natural rhythms and speech patterns was much, much tougher.

How a comic related to the crowd was a fairly reliable indicator. Those who could engage the audience fully and transport them into their own worlds stood the best chance of making people laugh—the ultimate goal. Too many comics lost sight of that. Some hacks tried all sorts of creative gimmicks that, while unique, didn't pay off with the funny. Other guys adopted a "mutha-fucka this, mutha-fucka that" persona, counting on shock value. Those guys didn't last long, either. People came to comedy clubs to laugh.

After the fat guy's seven minutes were up, I filled out a mental report card. All in all, he did an okay job. Half of his material was pretty fresh and there were a couple of good setups, so I'd give him a C-plus on his stuff. On the other hand, his delivery was a bit stiff—nerves—and he stepped on a few punch lines. The nervous guys almost always are in a big hurry to spit their lines out so they can rush out of the spotlights. C-minus for stage presence.

About what you'd expect on open mic night. To have a shot at getting hired for a longer set on a Wednesday night, say, you'd have to get two As. Maybe if you had that special *je ne sais quoi*, we'd hire you with an A for delivery and a B-plus for material. Like I said, you can always punch up the material.

The emcee trotted back out and encouraged the audience to buy more food and order more drinks. *And don't forget to tip the bartender*. Then he introduced the next comic. "Put your hands together for Brooks Spellman."

Spellman walked out with exaggerated stiff legs and arms extended in front of him, à la Frankenstein's Monster. When he didn't get any laughs, he cut it short. He flopped a small notebook down on a wooden stool next to the mic stand and removed the mic. For a split second he looked like a deer caught in some mighty big headlights. "How you all doing tonight?" he said, just like he'd seen every comedian do for the last twenty years.

A few murmurs greeted him back. "I tell you, it was hot today, yes it was. It was so hot, I had to take a sauna to cool down."

Silence. Spellman glanced around. Tapped the mic. "Hey, is this thing on?" With his free hand, he played with the mic stand, another tic of the amateur.

Groans, but no laughter. He shielded his eyes from the spotlight and looked out over the crowd, like the captain of a sinking ship gazing at the horizon one last time. "Anybody out there? Hellooooo."

A guy from the crowd yelled out, "Yeah, we're here. Say something funny, dipshit."

Indignation crossed Spellman's face. Or was it panic? "Is that how you treated your fellow inmates when you were in Lorton? Show a little respect, will you? Or I'll have Vito come talk to you after the show. And Vito don't really do much talking, capisce?" He laughed at his own attempt to put down the heckler. "Now, where was I?" He glanced down at his notes on the stool, lips moving silently. Then he cleared his throat and smeared a smile on his face.

"Oh yeah, I went to the bank today, you know, the one where they're always advertising their friendly service? We'll do anything for you, because we value you as a customer? The Friendliest Bank in the State? Anyway, the guy ahead of me in line pulls out a gun and robs the place." Spellman drew a breath and surveyed the audience, nodding, trying to sell it as best he could. "Yeah, so he's robbing the place and the teller's like, 'Yes, sir, coming right up. Your business is very important to us. How would you like it? Twenties and fifties okay? We can have someone cart it out to your getaway car, if that's convenient.'"

He drew a few feeble laughs from the crowd, but it was as if they were rewarding Spellman for not sucking too badly, rather than for saying something humorous.

Spellman plowed ahead. "So the guy says, 'No thanks, I can manage,' and he starts to leave the bank, a couple of sacks of dough over his shoulder when the bank manager comes over. The thief waves his gun in the manager's face, but the manager doesn't even blink. Just smiles real big and offers the guy a toaster—and free checking—for being the first dude to rob the place that week." Spellman waited for a laugh, got a small one. A very small one.

"And on his way out, the security guard holds the door open for the guy, and says real friendly-like, 'Have a nice day and thanks for banking with us.'" Spellman paused a beat before springing the capper. "I can hear the police dispatcher now. 'Be on the lookout. Be on the lookout. White male, early twenties. Carrying two large sacks of cash. And a toaster.'" He held his arms out, then saluted the crowd. "Thanks. Thanks a lot. Brooks Spellman. Thanks." With a final salute, Spellman trotted off.

Sometimes an act was so bad, so pitifully horrendous, it was funny. Spellman would have to improve his act significantly to attain that level. I'd give him a D, D-minus. And judging by the utter silence of the crowd, I was an easy grader.

It was nice to know the open mic nights weren't any better at the CCC.

I left my table and followed Spellman backstage, catching up to him right before he reached the men's room. "Brooks Spellman?"

He whirled around. "Yes, that's right." He stepped back a bit and eyed me. "And you are?"

I offered my hand. "Channing Hayes."

Spellman shook my hand and his head bobbed. "Ah, so you're Hayes. Well, I guess it's nice to meet you. Heather told me a lot about you. Funny we never met before." He licked his lips and I detected the faint aroma of hope. "How'd you like my set?"

"Uh, you know. Funny premise." I nodded noncommittally, something I'd gotten pretty good at during open mic nights. All comics wanted to know how they'd done and normally I didn't have the heart to tell them the dismal truth. Did that make me a bad person? Or a good one? "Have you spoken to Heather recently?"

"Naw. Not since we broke up. How's she doing after the accident? Pretty rough on her, losing her sister and all." His eyes went wide. "Oh, right. She was your girlfriend. Sorry, man. Rough on you, too. What happened that night, exactly?"

I shrugged. "Don't remember a thing." Even if I'd remembered the details, I was pretty sure I wouldn't want to talk about it. I kept my left hand in its usual place, my pocket. "I need to talk with her. Any idea where she might be?"

Spellman ran his tongue across his lips. Being on stage sometimes dried you up. "No. Not really. After we broke up, I went to

129

L.A. and San Diego for a while. Worked some clubs out there. Pretty good scene, you know?"

I'd witnessed his performance. He might have been able to wait tables in a comedy club, but that was about it. "Uh-huh. So, no idea how to reach Heather?"

He shook his head. "She was unpredictable, that's for sure. Is something wrong?"

I was sure he knew about J.J.'s death. Everyone in the comedy world knew. But no one knew about the possible connection between Heather and J.J., and I wanted to keep it that way. If it got out, who knew what the media—or the cops—might do with that information. Or what inaccurate conclusions they may draw. Heather was too fragile to be exposed to something like that, she was as skittish as a day-old colt. "No. I just need to talk to her. She was supposed to go on at our place and she skipped out."

A frown had settled on Spellman's face. "Hmm. That doesn't sound good. Bagging out on your set. I hope something didn't happen to her."

"No, I think she's okay. I found out she'd gone to her brother's for a couple days. But she left there and I really do need to find her."

"Well, if I run into her, I'll tell her you're looking for her." He nodded to the men's room door. "I gotta see a man about a horse." He licked his lips. "Uh, by the way, have you or Artie had a chance to look at my package? I sent it in a while back and I haven't heard anything." Spellman stared at me, the smell of hope more pungent now.

"Uh, not yet," I said, shrugging. "Not yet."

TWENTY

I'D THROWN ON A sport coat and tie even though Artie said not
to dress up. Walking down K Street, I was glad I did, not wanting
to stick out like some country rube gone to gawk at the cityfolk.
Everywhere you turned, a man or a woman in a suit rushed by, cell
phone to the ear, spewing various dialects of lingospeak. Lawyers,
all. Washington was an important town, full of important people.
And if you didn't believe it, just ask any one of them.

I met Artie in the lobby of the mid-rise office building, which
was similar to every other one on the block. Lots of steel and mir-
rored glass windows. He'd taken his own sartorial advice, selecting
an old checked sport shirt to go with his dingy gray workpants.
Country-rube-couture. The only thing missing was the CAT cap.

"Ready?" I asked him.

"You bet," he said as he thumped his briefcase, a well-worn
leather model, the kind every executive used—forty years ago.
Most of the silverplate finish had flaked from the clasps. "Ready
for anything." Small beads of perspiration formed on his forehead,

although the air-conditioning in the lobby would make a penguin shiver.

I nodded at his briefcase. "What's in there?"

He patted it again. "Newspaper, bagel, a sandwich for lunch. Some dental floss I picked up at the CVS around the corner." He winked. "It's just for show. Can't let the lawyers think they can run all over us."

"You know, we don't have to do this," I said. "We can just tell Reed we've reconsidered and we don't even want to hear his proposal. Tell him we're not interested." I leaned closer to Artie and whispered. "Because we're not, right?"

Artie set down his briefcase and glanced around the lobby although we were alone, save for the security guard at a desk with his head buried in the *Sports* section. All the lawyers who worked there had been in their offices for hours, writing briefs, taking depositions, and bilking law-abiding senior citizens out of their life savings. After another glance, he put his hand on my shoulder and spoke in an even tone. "Here's the game plan. We remain totally calm. We don't raise our voices one iota, no matter how outlandish things get. We simply listen to their proposal and nod our heads a bunch and say stuff like, 'sounds interesting,' and 'we'll have to think that over,' and 'very compelling.' Nothing controversial. We want them to drop their guard and say something revealing. Just follow my lead." He grabbed my forearm. "You cool with that?"

"Like an iceberg."

He picked up his briefcase. "Okay, then. Off to battle."

We rode the elevator to the fourth floor suite in silence and checked in at the receptionist's station. With a smile plastered on her face and a restrained K Street sashay, she led us to a large conference room featuring an expansive walnut table. We were the first to arrive for the meeting. "The others will be here shortly. Please, make yourself at home," she said, gesturing to the center of the table with two sleek manicured fingers.

A sterling silver tray laden with muffins and scones sat next to three silver carafes. One was labeled coffee, one decaf, and the third had no label, but judging from the condensation on the outside, looked to be ice water. China coffee cups and crystal water glasses were arranged next to the tray in two pyramids. Fancy.

Artie lowered himself into a chair and hoisted his briefcase onto the table. I took a seat next to him. Neither of us poured a drink, took a muffin, or talked. I knew Artie hadn't spoken since we'd left the lobby because he was afraid the place had been bugged by Reed trying to discover our strategy. I wondered if he didn't take any food because he thought it was laced with some CIA-developed truth serum.

The glass conference room door creaked open and Reed entered, followed by an older guy, tall and patrician, sporting a comb-over that wouldn't fool a blind man and a pencil-thin moustache over a puckered mouth. His blue custom-tailored suit must have cost more than my entire wardrobe. Hell, his tie was worth more than ten of my shirts.

Artie and I rose and everyone shook and exchanged pleasantries and cleared their throats. The attorney introduced himself as Robert Billings Hamilton, and if someone had asked me to picture an attorney named Robert Billings Hamilton, this guy would have come pretty close. I noticed Artie only spoke directly to Hamilton, not to Reed himself. I was sure everyone else noticed, too.

Reed and Hamilton settled in across from us, and Hamilton placed a thin portfolio pad in front of him, carefully squaring it with the edge of the table. The way Artie's suitcase-sized briefcase sat in front of him, it looked like *we* were the ones giving the proposal.

It was their party, so we yielded the floor. Hamilton grabbed the reins forthwith. "Gerry and I would like to thank you for coming." He nodded at Reed as he spoke. "Gerry wanted to approach you himself and give you his offer, man to man." Hamilton glanced at me and amended his statement. "Er, man to men. But I told him this was business and we should conduct it properly. So all of this," he paused, and waved a liver-spotted hand around in the air, "is my idea. Don't hold the formality against Gerry." He smiled and I was reminded of the star of the movie *Jaws*. And I didn't mean Roy Scheider.

Reed also smiled, a placid smile, neither too wide nor too tight. A smile that said he was going to let his lawyer do all the talking. Probably to rankle Artie more than for any strategic reason.

"Before we get started. Mr. Worsham, are you sure you don't want a lawyer?"

"No. I don't need anyone else to advise me. I've been in this business long enough to handle my own affairs. And please, call me Artie." He punctuated his statement with a bright, can't-we-all-just-get-along smile.

"Well, okay then, Artie." Hamilton tapped the pad before him with an expensive pen. "Why don't we get right to it? No sense dragging this out, eh?" He glanced at Artie, then at me, then opened his portfolio and pulled out a document while pushing a pair of glasses higher up on his aquiline nose. "Mr. Reed would like to purchase The Last Laff from you." He licked his lips and clasped his hands together on the table. Again, his eyes bounced from Artie to me, then back to Artie. We'd pretty much known this had been coming, so I was able to keep any surprise from my face. Out of the corner of my eyes, I noticed Artie's features tighten ever so slightly, but only because I knew him. To the unknowing observer, Artie was following his script and playing it cool.

Across the table, Reed's expression hadn't changed. He might have been waiting for his car to be serviced at Jiffy-Lube. Hamilton, on the other hand, seemed a little unnerved by our lack of reaction. "So, how does that sound?" he said, words rushing in to fill the vacuum. The lawyers I knew never liked silence during a negotiation. Most never liked silence any time.

Artie exuded calm. "Sounds interesting. What are the terms?"

Hamilton smiled. "They're spelled out right here," he said, turning around the document so Artie could see it and pointing out a couple of paragraphs. "Please, take your time." Hamilton glanced at Reed, then looked at me and realized I was staring at him. "Oh. I'm sorry. I should have made another copy." He pulled out his cell and punched in a few numbers.

I interrupted him before he completed his call. "Don't worry about it. I'll take a look in a minute. Your offer does sound very compelling, though." I smiled broadly and leaned back in my chair. Mr. Iceberg. Next to me, Artie's breathing revved up.

Artie set the document down in front of him and lifted his head. I reached out to take a look at the proposal, but he slapped my hand away. "Am I to assume that the figure you've spelled out is not a down payment? But it's actually the total price you're willing to pay for my club?" The muscles in Artie's jaw tensed.

"Uh, yes, that's right," Hamilton said, sneaking a quick glance to his right at Reed, who maintained his poker face.

Artie slid the document across the table at Hamilton. "The Last Laff is the preeminent comedy club in Northern Virginia. It's worth three or four times that much."

Hamilton tried to chuckle, but it didn't come out right. "This is just a starting point, of course. But, yes, we feel this price is commensurate with the value, considering the work Mr. Reed here will have to undergo to raise it to the level of the Capitol Comedy Club's standards."

Artie blew quick breaths through his nose, sounding like a cartoon bull about to charge at Bugs Bunny. "What exactly, does *Mr. Reed* plan on doing to The Last Laff to bring it up to his exalted standards?" His voice spiked in volume and intensity.

Hamilton licked his lips. "Well, extensive renovation to the club. New kitchen. Expansion. New signage. He'll also have to sink considerable promotional dollars into what we believe has been an underserved region, vis à vis comedy entertainment."

New signage?

"And, of course, we'll need you to sign a non-compete agreement," Hamilton said.

Artie's eyes bugged out and he bit his lip.

Reed broke his silence. "You enjoy the show last night, Hayes?"

My face got warm. "I…uh. It was about what I'd expected."

"Trying to pick up a few tips on how to run a successful club?" Reed's smirk was all I could focus on. "No need to sneak around. You could have just asked. Always happy to help those who need it."

Next to me, I could practically feel Artie boiling over. "Thanks. Maybe next time."

"So what do *you* think of the proposal, Hayes?" Reed asked, smirk going strong.

I glanced at Artie, saw red fury. "I, uh. I haven't read it," I said, shrugging. "We'll have to think it over."

Reed clicked his tongue twice and smiled. "Has Artie ever told you about the time we worked together?"

"No. No, he hasn't." I looked at Artie, but he wouldn't meet my gaze.

"Well, we worked up an act, a regular comedy duo. Got some pretty good gigs. Had a little success. Then Artie got greedy, thought he knew more by himself than we knew together. Crowned himself act 'manager.' He tried changing some of the bookings and demanding certain terms from these club owners— terms unheard of for two relatively unknown guys. All of it behind my back. I was counting on those jobs." Reed paused, sat up a bit straighter. "When I found out, I begged Artie to call these guys and get our gigs back, but it was too late. Needless to say, our act dissolved."

Hamilton started to say something, but Artie slowly rose and pointed at Reed. "Bullshit. You were a drunk and a liar. Still are a liar, probably still a drunk too. The only reason I made all the bookings was because you wouldn't lift a finger for the act. Too busy drinking and screwing around. You would have done the shows for free booze and free pussy. I just wanted to get paid what we deserved. Comedy is a business."

"Ironic, isn't it? *You* telling *me* that comedy is a business. I know you're in some financial trouble, Artie. Have been for a while. Let me help you out. Sell me your club. Then step back and watch a real businessman make it shine."

Artie looked as if he'd been in the sauna for an hour. I reached across the table to pour him some ice water, but he pushed my arms aside. "A real businessman? Does a real businessman steal another person's product?"

"What are you talking about?" Reed asked.

"J.J. I'm talking about J.J. You tried to steal him from me. Have him to yourself. Then when he said no, you…" Artie froze, limbs extended and rigid. He'd come close to calling Reed a murderer. To his credit, Reed didn't respond. He simply stared, slack-jawed at the crazed man before him.

Hamilton stood up. "Okay, gentlemen. Settle down. Negotiations can be sensitive at times. Why don't we all take some time to think about the proposal? Sleep on it. Review it with clear heads. What do you say?"

"Here's what I say," Artie said, coming back to life. He ignored Hamilton and addressed Reed. "You can take your deal and shove it up your lawyer's ass. And don't even try opening up a club within ten miles of The Last Laff. We'll crush you." Spittle flew from his lips and his voice got hoarse. He grabbed his briefcase and nodded to me. "Come on, Channing. This place is making me ill."

I'd hate to see Artie when he wasn't keeping cool.

TWENTY-ONE

"Artie wouldn't tell me what happened at the meeting today, but it didn't sound good. He just kept swearing under his breath and waving his cigar around. Something about a prick bastard. Or bastard prick. Hard to tell exactly what he was saying," Skip said. "Sounded sorta like Homeless Harry used to sound after a cold winter night."

Skip and I were in the storage room where I was helping him unpack the latest delivery of supplies. With only one good hand, though, I was doing more watching than helping.

"To say it went badly would be an understatement. Things started on the tense side and deteriorated quickly." I shook my head. "Artie's a piece of work, all right. But he doesn't back down. Not from anyone."

With a hook-bladed knife, Skip slit the shrink-wrap on a mini-pallet of beverages and peeled back the plastic. He began stacking the smaller packs on shelves sorted by type, imported beer on one side, domestic on the other. "Yeah. That's what makes him so fun.

Speaking of fun, a detective came by this morning. Wanted all our fingerprints so they can sort out who's been to the comedy condo. Trying to figure out what—or who—killed J.J., I guess."

Artie and I had been fingerprinted already. "Just an accident. I mean, who'd want to kill him?" Even though Artie had Reed number one on his suspect list, I didn't buy it. Why kill the golden goose, even if you had to share it?

Skip set a six-pack of Samuel Adams on the shelf next to a few others. "Probably a couple dozen jealous boyfriends, husbands, and lovers who wouldn't mind seeing J.J. dead. I understand he was quite the swinging dick." A wistful look came over him.

"Jealous?"

"Nah." He paused, seemed to reconsider, then shook his head. "Nah. But someone else might have been."

"Maybe. But giving someone poisoned coke seems risky. Why not shoot him? Or stab him? Seems like that would be more fitting for someone who was really angry. Messing with the drugs seems cold. Cowardly."

Skip shrugged. "Dead is dead, right?" He finished stowing the beverages and moved on to a huge box of paper goods. Napkins, paper towels, toilet paper. It never ceased to amaze me how much disposable crap we went through in a week. Finding space for it all in our cramped storeroom was a perpetual challenge. "Give me a hand, will you?"

I clapped softly.

"Et tu, Channing?"

"Sorry."

He climbed on a stepstool and I handed packages up to him so he could cram them on the top shelf, snug against the ceiling. "What's the deal with Heather? She ever coming back?"

"Wish I knew. She's around. Someplace. I just haven't talked to her. I think she feels bad she ditched and doesn't want to face up to me." In my mind, I'd been vacillating between two extreme explanations for her disappearance: merely a bad case of stage fright and murder. In my sanest moments, I truly believed her disappearance had nothing to do with J.J.'s death, although it sure would be nice to hear it directly from her mouth.

"Makes sense," he said, as he used his fist to pummel a multi-pack of paper towels between two other packages. We'd need a crowbar to get them down again.

"You haven't spoken to her, have you?"

Skip hesitated. "No, I haven't. I'd tell you if I did. But I haven't." I handed up another package, napkins this time, and he squeezed the air from the package before cramming them into an opening I couldn't even see.

"You sure?" I asked. Skip was always a little twitchy, so it was hard to tell when he was shooting straight or just being Skip.

"Yeah, of course. Haven't talked to her."

"Okay then. Next topic. I've got some free time coming up. You want some help with your material?"

Skip took a break from his cramming and jamming, punching and squeezing. "You serious?"

I nodded, keeping my smile at bay. "Yeah."

He beamed. "Sure. I'd love some help." The smile faded. "But only if you want to. I mean, I know you're busy and all, with—"

"I do. Why don't you get some stuff together? Make some notes and we'll find some time this weekend, okay?"

"Sure, boss. Sure," he said. "And thanks."

———

For this week's Six-Pack Wednesday, all six comics showed up. The first two were good, the second two were excellent, and the final two were outstanding. Artie booked the last two for a couple of weeks out on a Thursday night, and we stayed after the show for an hour or so, entertaining all six of them at the bar. Just the club owners and the talent, talking shop, swapping stories about comedy in the trenches. We wanted to make sure they knew how we felt about their performances so they'd tell all their comic friends about how great it was to play The Last Laff. Drumming up a good reputation was key in this business, and we had some work ahead of us to counterbalance the hit we took by having a headliner overdose in our comedy condo.

With a final salute my way, Artie walked out alongside the comics, leaving me to lock up. Skip, Donna, and the others had cleared out a long time ago, and anything else that needed cleaning could wait until the crew got there tomorrow.

I stood alone in the club, hearing the echoes of laughter in my head, from tonight, from past nights. I inhaled deeply, trying to catch a whiff of the French fries or the burgers or the spilt beer on the floor. The electricity from the audience had faded along with the houselights, but the memories lingered and always would. Late night was the comics' time, the time we rode the buzz, basking in our success.

The relationship with the audience was symbiotic. We made them laugh, and they displayed their gratitude with applause and cheers and hearty belly laughs. But I often thought we needed them more—they made us whole, gave us a reason for being. Without an audience, we were simply aimless guys performing in front of the bathroom mirror.

The empty stage beckoned. A blank canvas exhorting me to walk on it, to talk on it, to perform upon it. The idea of getting back on stage didn't fill me with dread anymore, at least not to the same degree it had in those first couple months after the accident. The fingers were gone forever and the scar on my face remained, but the fears about returning were waning. At least I hoped they were, that this feeling wasn't temporary, induced by the evening's success, vicarious though it had been. I needed the fear to ebb because I wanted to be whole again, and starting by getting my career back on track was the easy part. I knew I couldn't get on with the rest of my life just yet. I missed Lauren too much for that. People kept telling me time heals all wounds, but I didn't believe them. My wounds were too deep.

I checked the creaky back door into the alley, making sure it was locked, double-checking the cheap deadbolt Artie had installed himself. Then I pulled the office door closed and turned out the lights behind the bar. Left the club and crossed the deserted parking lot toward Rex. As I reached for the door handle, I heard my name. I spun around as a figure stepped forward from the murky shadows. Mired in my melancholy mood, I hadn't heard him approach.

"Channing," he said again, in a deep resonant voice. In William Dempsey's voice.

"What are you doing here? Is Heather okay?" My heart had taken off like a racehorse's.

"That's exactly what I want to know. Is Heather okay?" His hands were jammed into the pockets of an old trench coat, even though the temperature must still have been in the seventies. It sounded like he'd been drinking.

I glanced around but didn't spot his black Mercedes. Which was good—he wasn't in any condition to drive. "Mr. Dempsey. Maybe we could talk about this later. In the morning would be better. Can I call you a cab?"

"Don't need a cab." He stepped closer. The streetlamp above cast spooky shadows on his face, grotesque and elongated. "You hiding something?"

"No, sir. I haven't seen or spoken to Heather in a week. I wish I could tell you otherwise, but…" I held my palms up.

"The other day, at the house…" He paused.

"No need to apologize. I understand how you felt."

Dempsey issued a harsh laugh and edged closer. "Apologize? No, I didn't come to apologize. You truly are a comedian. No, no apology." He coughed once, twice. Cleared his throat. "Kathleen and I spoke. She seems to think this behavior is unlike Heather. She says Heather's been better lately, more responsible, and I… well, let's just say I've come to see her point. I guess you could say I've changed my thinking here."

Hundred-proof exhalations hit me. "Why don't we continue this discussion in the morning? I think we'll both be able to concentrate then." I wondered if you could fit a pipe wrench in a trenchcoat pocket.

"No. I think we'll continue our discussion right here. Right now. That okay with you, *Channing*?" He spit out my name like a rancid piece of meat.

I nodded.

"So, Kathleen and I think that maybe Heather didn't run off on her own, by her own choice. We think maybe someone coerced her, or influenced her, or tempted her to go with them. Not a cult, but maybe a boy, or a boy's promise of something exquisite. Heather liked to grab at shiny things." Dempsey sounded like my college roommate sounded after a few too many. With him, I'd just nod and agree with everything, knowing it would all be forgotten in the morning.

"Okay. Mr. Dempsey. Say you're right. Say Heather was lured away by some bad element. Why don't you go to the police?"

"Hah. The police. I told you they're worthless." He cocked his head. "No. I'm coming to you." He pulled one hand from his pocket and jabbed me in the chest with it. "Kathleen and I are coming to you. We figure you're responsible for her disappearance. After all, you turned your back and she was gone. She trusted you to help her and you fucked up. Lost her. You're lucky we don't call the police on *you*." Another jab in the chest. My back pressed against the side of my car. Nowhere to go. Nowhere to hide.

"I've been looking for Heather. So far, I haven't had—"

"Shut up. Shut the fuck up." Dempsey grabbed my shirt collar and twisted the fabric until it pressed against my Adam's apple. Brought his face so close to mine I could almost feel his beard stubble scratch my cheeks and taste the booze on his lips. "Listen to me, *Channing*. You killed one daughter of mine. You better not let anything happen to the other one. You better find her, *Channing*,

145

and she better be okay, or I'm coming after you, *Channing Hayes.* And you'll wish you'd never met Lauren or Heather or even been born, if that happens." He twisted my shirt another time for good measure, then let go. "You understand me? You better find Heather and find her fast."

I nodded, not wanting to speak, sure my voice would crack.

"And don't think I'm going to forget this in the morning. *Channing.*"

With my good hand, I smoothed out my shirt collar as William Dempsey receded into the shadows.

TWENTY-TWO

THE TIMPANI BOOM-BOOM-BOOMED IN my head. My eyes sprang open, and I glanced at the nightstand clock for orientation: 7:45. But was it a.m. or p.m.? The fog lifted but the timpani kept pounding. I threw the covers off and padded toward the door of my condo, cursing the noisemaker. Who had the nerve to bang on my door so damn early?

"Hold your freaking horses. I'm coming." I didn't bother with the peephole; anyone wanting to rob me would never call attention to himself by making such a racket. I flung the door open and squinted against the light from the hallway. Before me stood a grinning Freeman Easter, dapper in a brown suit, brown shirt, and brown tie, a Styrofoam cup of coffee in each hand. I was afraid to ask what he was banging on the door with.

"What?" I managed through a mouth so dry and gritty it would give sandpaper a run for its money.

"Good morning to you, too." He pushed past me and strode to the eating alcove. Flipped the light on and set one cup in front of an empty chair, then sat across from it in another, cradling his coffee with both hands.

I shuffled over, one hand holding up my old running shorts, elastic shot years ago, the other hand shielding my eyes from the light. Slumped down into the chair and willed my eyes to stay open, just a crack.

"Too early," I said, not sure if my lips were moving.

"Man, you look like shit." He jutted his chin at me. "By the way, does your face hurt?"

I touched the scar, then let my hand drop. "No, not really."

"Well, it's killing me!" A broad smile lit up his face. When he noticed I wasn't smiling along, he tempered it. "Sorry. Julian tries that on me daily." He shrugged. "What do you expect from an eight-year-old who wants to follow in his daddy's comedy footsteps? Better the lame jokes than him yelling, 'freeze dirtbag or I'll blow your brains out.'"

"Why are you here, Freeman? There's no open mic in my condo, you know."

"Touché." He sipped from his coffee. "Seriously, how's the hand?"

I held it up and wiggled the finger and thumb. "Incomplete. But I guess I'll get used to it. What choice do I have?"

"You might not ever get used to it," he said. "But you'll learn to deal with it."

"I know you didn't come here to ask about my health."

"Nope, don't really care too much about that. Just being polite," he said. I expected a wink or something, but he forged ahead straight-faced. "Perlstein, the new homicide guy, brought me in on J.J.'s case to handle the drug angle. I told him I knew the scene pretty well, so he's given me a little headroom. It's a new world

148

in our department. Fewer turf wars, more cooperation. I like it. Probably go down in flames soon, but at least we'll have a good ride. Anyway, I told him I'd talk to you. See if I can shake something loose from your subconscious that might help us."

"And you had to start now? I just went to sleep."

"Oh? Rough night partying?"

"No. Just couldn't sleep." After Dempsey had accosted me in the parking lot, I'd tossed and turned, but too much adrenaline combined with too much worry kept me awake. So I popped *Caddyshack* into the DVD player, which led to *Animal House*, which led to some Adam Sandler comedy I'd already forgotten. "Don't you know all comics are night crawlers?"

"Maybe that's why I haven't hit the big time. I can't stay up past midnight." He set his coffee down and pulled out a handy pad. "Ready?"

I grunted.

"Okay, then. Tell me again about Friday night at the condo. I love a good S & M story."

I'd already told Perlstein about J.J.'s call and the handcuffs and the girl who ripped him off. And I'd told Freeman, too. But we went through it again to be sure I hadn't missed anything during the first two recitations. Freeman nodded the whole time, not bothering to write anything down. When I finished, he asked me if I was sure I didn't know who this mysterious "black chick" was.

"Nope. J.J. didn't remember her name. And I don't recall seeing anyone that night who matched her description."

"Not even the 'superlative ass' part?"

"His words, not mine. Anyway, I haven't noticed anyone like that in the club since, either."

Freeman's brow furrowed. "And you've been looking."

"Sure. I always like to get to know my customers."

"Uh-huh." He waved his hand. "About the drugs. You know ahead of time J.J. was a user?"

I exhaled. "You know as well as I do what the deal is. J.J.? No specific knowledge. Does it surprise me? Not in the least. I don't partake, but many, many comics do. Need it to 'be funny.' Stuff just messes me up." Coke no, caffeine yes. I'd finally woken up enough to give the coffee a try. I pried off one edge of the lid and took a sip. Felt good going down.

"Okay, man. Now that you've had a few days to think about it, come up with anyone you think might want to see J.J. dead?"

I set the cup down. Thought a moment. "Nope. Can't say I knew the guy real well. Hadn't seen him in almost a year. But…"

"What?" Freeman asked.

"Like I told you before, J.J. was a hound. Chased a lot and scored a lot. My take on this: either he got into it with his dealer, or some guy offed him for screwing his wife."

"Know anyone he was screwing?"

Thought a minute more, then slowly shook my head. "Just the girl he met at the club. And I didn't know her." I felt guilty for not mentioning Heather, but there was no way I was going to give her up to the wolves, at least not without talking to her first. Getting her side of the story. For all I knew, J.J. had embellished the whole sexual conquest story to maintain his reputation. Besides, J.J. had been very much alive when Heather had left the condo.

Freeman closed his pad. "Did you go back to the condo after that night?"

"Nope."

"But you have a key?"

"Yeah, sure. Why?"

"No sign of forced entry. Meant J.J. either knew the perpetrator or someone had a key."

I didn't like where this was headed. "Maybe he just brought in the tainted drugs on his own. From his supplier."

Freeman nodded. "Maybe. But why? Why kill a customer? Besides, most coke is cut with something innocuous—baby powder or something. Not cyanide."

"I cannot believe—"

"Did you have anything against J.J.?" Freeman asked, before I could finish my sentence. His voice was calm. Too calm. "Envious of his success, maybe?"

"You're crazy if you think I had anything to do with this."

He shook his head. "Just getting you prepared. Perlstein's thorough. If we don't find the guilty party soon, he'll be asking you those questions. On the record. And plenty more. Don't want you to get rattled. Sometimes innocent people are the ones who act the most guilty."

"So this conversation is off the record?"

Freeman laughed softly, mostly to himself. "No such thing as 'off the record.' Just some things are more on the record than others." He leaned back in his chair. "How about Artie? He have something against J.J.?"

My good fist clenched. "Artie had nothing to do with this and you know it."

Freeman held up both hands, as if he were stopping traffic at a dangerous intersection. "Yeah, I do. Like I said, just getting you prepared for when Perlstein comes a-knocking. Tell Artie not to take anything personally. We're just doing our jobs."

"Artie? Take something personally?" I rolled my eyes.

"Uh-huh. That's exactly why I'm telling you. Clue him in, will you? For his sake."

"Sure," I said, glad this line of questioning had ended.

Freeman drained the last of his coffee. "Topic B. Ever find your friend?"

"Not yet."

His eyes narrowed. "Talk to her parents?"

"Yeah. They hadn't seen her. Father says her disappearance fits the pattern. Wasn't overly concerned." I didn't bring up last night's encounter with Dempsey, nor his change of heart. Nor the ten-pound pipe wrench he'd flung across the room.

"Uh-huh." Freeman scratched his chin. "So, you think J.J.'s death and Heather's disappearance could be connected somehow?"

My breath caught. Had Freeman discovered something incriminating? Or had he detected something in my tone or manner? "Connected? How so?" Playing dumb had often worked for me in the past.

"I was hoping you could tell me."

I didn't answer, worked hard to control my breathing as I ignored Freeman's stare. I felt like an absolute shit for deceiving my friend, but an overwhelming need to protect Heather kept me from opening my mouth.

"Channing. It wouldn't be prudent of you to withhold information in an investigation, you know." The stare intensified.

I nodded, shrugged. Pasted an innocent expression on my face. "Just a coincidence."

"Uh-huh," Freeman said as he rose to leave. "I'm a cop. I don't believe in coincidences."

———

Freeman took off, and I crawled back to bed and slept the rest of the morning, waking up in time to eat lunch—a bowl of soup, half a turkey sandwich, a mealy plum, and a bag of Doritos. As I ate, I watched a stand-up comedy showcase on Comedy Central with the sound off. I muted the volume for two reasons: so I could concentrate on the performers' mannerisms, and so I wouldn't subconsciously hack any of their material.

These guys were good, even in silence.

I watched the comics perform for a while, but my thoughts drifted back to Freeman's comments. He wasn't simply being polite, asking about my health. He genuinely cared about my hand, my face. He knew how much appearances mattered in stand-up, and how much they factored into a comic's confidence. Audiences made a split-second decision about whether they liked you or not—just like people you'd meet on the street. Only difference was you weren't trying to entertain the people on the street for an hour. It was infinitely easier to entertain people when you didn't repulse them—old show-biz tenet.

I went to the bathroom and examined my scar in the mirror. Hard and ridged, discolored. I could feel people's hot stares on it as I did my errands. Pointing behind my back. Whispering to each other: *Check out the freak. Look, it's the Phantom of the Opera, here in the housewares department of Wal-Mart.* Sometimes I thought I should open up my own circus sideshow, charge a buck, and let people gawk at me freely, above board.

The scarred patch was foreign to me, yet I couldn't seem to remember my face without it. Like my time with Lauren, my unblemished face had taken on a dreamlike quality. I touched the mirror with my left hand, watched my two digits turn into four. Still incomplete. Forever incomplete. My hand had become a metaphor for my life and the pain deep within me seared my heart.

But I was letting the pain ruin me. This was the only life I got, and Freeman was right. I needed to learn how to deal with it. The face in the mirror wasn't the Channing Hayes I knew, scar or no scar. The Channing Hayes I saw was a passive coward, afraid to face reality, no matter how fucked up it was. I used to make fun of people like that.

There had been moments during the past couple weeks when my funk had abated and I could see through the murky present into a brighter future. When I felt the old stirrings, the yen to be back in the game. Now, at least for a few moments, hope had booked a return engagement. I wasn't quite sure why, but who in their right mind argues with good feelings? Ever since I'd been a kid, my moods had changed with surprising speed, often without a tangible stimulus. I'd learned not to fight it.

Maybe it had been offering to help Skip with his act, or realizing you only had so many days left on the planet, or seeing how much of a prick Reed was, I didn't know. All I knew was that I had an urge to roll up my proverbial sleeves and start working up some new material. I needed to seize the moment while I was still in the mood.

The question was how.

Since the accident, every time I'd thought about reviving my act, I figured I'd dust off the old routines. Empty the memory banks to dredge up the tried and true. After all, I'd spent hundreds—thousands—of hours honing my act. Tweaking this and fiddling with that until I'd gotten it how I wanted. To where I knew I would kill with it. But every time I even thought about getting back on the horse, I'd end up obsessing about Lauren. Call it a focus problem or a psychological roadblock or a fear of bad karma, but I couldn't do it. Every time I tried the old jokes, even in the safety of my living room, I froze. Too many debilitating memories. I'd proven to myself that doing the old material would be impossible in my current state of mind.

So I had two choices: change my state of mind or come up with new material. Although working up new material was difficult and time-consuming and painful, it seemed like a walk in the park compared with escaping my depression. My therapist would probably agree.

I left my half-finished lunch on the table and unearthed the box of office supplies I kept in the closet. I pulled out a four-pack of lined notepads, peeled off the cellophane wrapper, and extracted a single blank notepad. Got a cheap Bic pen and a voice recorder from my desk and took everything to the couch in the living area. Kicked off my shoes. Got ready to do some work.

Something was missing.

I bounced off the couch and crossed the room in three steps. On the top shelf of the bookcase, I kept a gigantic brandy snifter full of racquetballs. I'd never played the sport, but it had always been my habit to squeeze a racquetball while I worked on my material. I reached up and snatched one from the glass snifter, giving it a squeeze with my right hand. The blue rubbery sphere felt good, familiar. I took a whiff of the characteristic smell. Reassuring.

A blue Penn racquetball. Some might call it a superstition, a crutch, a security blanket. I didn't care, I called it essential. At some point in my career—I'd forgotten the specifics—I'd discovered the jokes flowed like gangbusters when I squeezed a racquetball while I wrote. I tried a tennis ball, a baseball, and even a pair of Chinese worry balls, but none seemed to work as well as the racquetball. Other comics had their lucky charms: stuffed animals, baseball caps, towels. I had blue Penn racquetballs.

The last time I'd squeezed one had been before the accident. When I had all five fingers on my left hand. I hadn't touched one since, out of fear, plain and simple. Would I be able to squeeze it just the right way? Would the loss of three fingers mean the end of my comedy career as I knew it? Would I be reminded of the accident with every squeeze? Sure, it sounded silly, but to me the power of the racquetball was as real as anything else in my life— and more tangible than many things. I had proof of its effectiveness in these notebooks. Where was the "proof" of my loyalty? My compassion? My love?

I encircled my thumb and forefinger around the ball and squeezed gently. Luckily, the fit was perfect. An omen, perhaps?

I flipped the notepad open to the first page and closed my eyes. Tried to clear my mind and remember how I used to write. My old routine. I thought back to the mundane things I'd accomplished earlier in the week, hoping to flex my comedy muscles. Working, errands, hanging around. Nothing popped out. I took a deep breath and tried again, priming my mind with a few racquetball squeezes. Thought about my trip to the grocery store yesterday. Remembered seeing an old lady trying to change her flat tire on the side of the road. Where was the funny when you needed it?

I retrieved a Sprite from the fridge. Took a few sips. Rummaged around in the cabinets for a cookie and discovered a sleeve of old Fig Newtons behind some cans of tuna. Quickly downed a few. Gulped some more soda, hoping a sugar rush might kick-start things. I returned to the couch, closed my eyes, and let my mind run free, watching the snippets from recent events roll by. Dempsey in his trench coat. Artie pointing his finger at Reed, face about to burst like an over-ripe tomato. The empty stage at The Last Laff. J.J. cuffed to the bed. Heather's Dumbo towel. A sobbing Kathleen Dempsey clutching Lauren's photo to her chest. J.J.'s body on the floor, staring at me. Calling to me. *Help me, Channing. Help me. I'm bombing.* My eyes flew open. Nothing too funny going on in my life.

I closed the pad and tossed it onto the coffee table. Finished my Sprite just as another idea hit me. Maybe I was forcing the issue. I didn't seem to be able to use my old routines, but I might be able to cull some usable stuff from my old notebooks, before every observation had to pass through the veil of depression that had settled upon me after the accident. I fetched two handfuls of old notebooks and stuffed them into a duffel bag. I'd take them into the club and work on them in the office, just like I was going to a regular 9-5 job. Didn't know if it would work, but anything was worth a try at this point.

I showered and changed, energized by the new plan for getting my career back on track. Before heading to the club, I made sure to toss a couple racquetballs into my bag. I needed all the help I could get.

TWENTY-THREE

WHEN I GOT TO the club, eight employees sat in a large circle around a table: Donna, Skip, Ty, a couple of cooks, two servers, and a busboy. All eyes were on Artie, who stood with his back to me, talking and gesturing madly. It was another one of his famous pep talks, usually reserved for times when big name headliners were on the bill or when something of monumental import happened, like the time our beer supplier's truck got stuck in the snow with our shipment aboard.

Everyone but Artie had seen me enter—I could tell by how each head followed me as I tried to tiptoe past on my way to the office. I'd almost made it when I heard Donna's too-friendly voice rise above Artie's. "Oh, yoo-hoo. Hello there, Channing. Come join the meeting, won't you?"

Artie turned and spotted me, then waved me over while the others snickered in the background. They'd all try to sneak past, too, if they had the chance. Donna, especially. I trudged over to the group, duffel bag in hand. I made no move to sit.

"Hey. Just inspiring the troops," Artie said. He stepped closer and whispered in my ear. "Getting them pumped up for our fight with Reed."

I had better things to do than help foment the masses. "Yeah, well, I've got some stuff to go over. Skip can fill me in later." I winked at Skip and he smiled, but most of the others looked bored stiff. Their glances shot daggers at me as I tried to extricate myself. Jealous, all.

Artie stroked his chin. "No, I think you should sit in. You might have something significant to add. This is a team effort and you are a big part of this team." He held his hand up to the rest. "Right, team?"

Everyone chimed in affirmatively, sealing my fate. I guess if they had to sit through it, they were taking me down with them. Pulling up a chair, I noted the smug satisfaction in their faces. For the next fifteen minutes, Artie rambled on about how important it was to treat every customer like a king or queen, how vital it was to get every itsy-bitsy detail right, and how *absolutely critical* it was to make sure every single person—audience, talent, other employees—had a positive experience at The Last Laff. That's the business we were in. Creating joy. And only by doing the best damn job we could would we be able to fend off the dark menace named Greedy Reed.

It was a moving pep talk and every one of us had heard it before. *Ad infinitum.*

I half expected Artie to end with a hip-hip-hooray cheer, but he sort of petered out, telling us to keep a smile on our faces and do our best. He adjourned the meeting, leaving everyone to drift off to his or her duties in preparation for the evening. I followed him back to the office.

He took his seat behind the desk and put his feet up. A pinhole in the sole of one shoe captured my attention. "What are you looking at?" he said around his unlit cigar.

"Nothing."

He frowned and nodded at the duffel bag I'd set on my card table. "What's in the bag?"

"The bag?"

"Yeah, that blue nylon thing on your *desk*." Every time Artie called my little table a desk, the snicker in his voice squeaked through.

"Just some stuff. Nothing."

"You've never brought that bag in here before. In fact, you've never brought any bag in here before that didn't have hamburger grease soaking through."

I shrugged. "So? Now I have. What's it to you?"

"Nothing. It's just a bag." He crossed his legs on his desk, kept staring at me. "Awful testy, aren't you?"

"Don't you have something to do right now? Maybe sharpen some spears in case Reed shows up."

"Reed shows up, I won't need spears." Artie held up his hands and strangled an imaginary neck.

"You *need* to forget about him. We leave him alone, he'll find someone else to bother." I picked the duffel bag off the table and set it on the floor at my feet. I was itching to get started but didn't want Artie's "help." Didn't need his halitosis breath blowing in over my shoulder like the San Francisco fog.

"I've known Reed a long time. He's a phony. Cares only about money and success. Success and money. Doesn't care about people." Artie waved his stogie. "I got a bad feeling about this. A bad feeling." He put his feet down and stood. "You're right. I got stuff to do. You think this place runs by itself? Think I'll start by yelling at Skip. That's always entertaining."

Artie left and I waited a few minutes to make sure he wasn't coming back before I picked up the phone. I dialed the number from memory and waited. My heart picked up speed and I felt like I had during the first six months of my career, back when every little opportunity, every contact with the established comedy world, sent my pulse racing with anticipation.

My agent, Sammi Long, picked up after three rings.

"Sammi? This is Channing Hayes."

A long silence. "Well, hello, Channing," she said, Southern magnolia accent in full bloom. A cross between a snapping turtle and a debutante, Sammi was the only person on the planet I'd back in a fight against Ty Taylor, even though she didn't crack five feet standing atop the 212 phone directory on her tiptoes. "How are you?"

"Doing better."

"Glad to hear it." Another pause. "I'm so glad you called. Every time the phone rings, I hope that it's you."

Pure Dixie sugar. After the accident, I'd told her I was on the shelf for a while. *Don't call me, I'll call you.* Sammi represented a stable of top names, so I knew she wasn't taking a significant financial hit during my absence, but she never treated me as anything smaller than a big name headliner. "Well, it's me now. I've been thinking…"

"Yes?"

"I think I'm ready to get back into it. Get back on stage."

I heard her exhale over the phone and it sounded as if she'd been holding her breath for five months. Or maybe that had been me? "Oh, that's sensational, Channing. Simply wonderful. Shall I start booking you? How about a trip to New York to get things rolling?"

"Hmm. Not sure I'm ready for that. How about a few local things, let me straighten some of the kinks out?" I didn't tell her I wanted to write a completely new act. Didn't want to give her vapors or something. "And I've got a few things to work through yet. Still a bit rusty, I think. So…" I mentally counted out a few months. "How about something in July? Or August? Definitely by October."

I imagined some of the energy draining from Sammi, like a water balloon that had sprung a small leak. "Oh. Okay. I'll get on it. Of course, I assume you'll be ironing the wrinkles out on your own floor. So it'll be spic-and-span by the time you hit the road."

Always the agent. "Yes, ma'am. Spic-and-Span Hayes, that's me."

A giggle, Southern-style. "Stop it, Channing. That's just how I talk and you know it." More giggles. "Don't be such a Yankee. There are a lot of people who find my mannerisms charming."

"Ah'll try to contain mahself, Miss Sammi. Ma'am."

"Oh, pish tosh." Sammi's voice turned serious. "I'm glad you're back. Not so much for me, but for you. You deserve something good to happen, you surely do. Take care now." She clicked off and I pictured her on her veranda, down in Atlanta, sipping iced tea as she got ready to ream out a promoter somewhere for shortchanging one of her clients.

I hung up, letting my conversation with Sammi slowly fade away. When it had dissipated, I returned to reality and sat staring at my old notebooks, wondering if there were any hidden comedy gems that would get me rolling again. October would be here before I knew it.

———

That night, our special guest was a young local guy who'd brought along a pack of his buddies. They whooped and hollered at everything the comic said—lame, funny, or in-between—which was nice. The guy did have a lot of good stuff, but like so many young guns, he needed the kind of polish you only get through years of stage work. After the show, Artie and I would make a point of offering him our assistance whenever he wanted it. It never hurt to encourage the up-and-comers. They were our future featured guys and headliners, and if we got to them early, they'd remember us. Loyalty was important in this business.

Our featured middle act was a ventriloquist who called himself "Trafalgar Squared." Trafalgar the person packed about 250 pounds onto his smallish frame, and Trafalgar the dummy looked like a miniature wooden version of Mr. Trafalgar. To me, they both looked a little like Margaret Thatcher after a hard day's night. The comic adopted a poor British accent and the dummy spoke with a Brooklyn attitude. The Limey-Yankee thing wasn't a bad hook; he—they?—had about ten good minutes. Unfortunately it was a twenty-minute act. I wondered if the audience was confused because tonight's theme was "local rising comedy stars," and with that nutty accent, I'm sure they didn't realize Trafalgar—the person—hailed from Arlington. I didn't know where the dummy was from.

Artie proclaimed ventriloquism a dying art, so we didn't get many ventriloquists, but we wouldn't care if we did. Funny was funny, and we'd put on an actuary reciting the almanac in Armenian if he'd get laughs. Humor was subjective and we always figured the "proof was in the applause." If our customers liked the act, then we liked it too. Trafalgar Squared garnered enough applause for him to remain on our "possible future act" list.

We were very excited about our headliner, Tom Otapi. Another guy with local ties, but he'd cracked the big time with appearances on the late night shows. He'd been at it for a few years, working the clubs in Los Angeles and some of the smaller rooms in Vegas. He modeled some of his act on the late Sam Kinison, right down to the style of dress and the shouting. I thought of J.J. as I remembered one of Kinison's bits: *There's no happy ending to cocaine. You either die, you go to jail, or else you run out.* There certainly had been no happy ending for J.J.

Otapi wore a beret à la Kinison and he flat-out destroyed, leaving the audience begging for more. You always want to leave them hungry, that's why they came back. After the show, Artie dragged Otapi into the office and talked business with him for a few minutes, then left to drive him to his hotel, the Tysons Sheraton. Artie wasn't ready yet to re-open the comedy condo for business; I couldn't say I blamed him. And for Artie to put him up for three nights out of his pocket meant Artie *really* wasn't ready.

The rest of us did the usual—cleaned up the place so we could come back tomorrow and do it all over again. At about two-twenty, I told Skip to go home. He protested—for all of three seconds—before exploding through the front door. I needed a couple of minutes to myself.

First, I turned on the spotlights so their beams hit the "X" we'd taped to the front center of the stage, right next to the mic stand. Then I turned down the houselights and took my position just off stage right. Took a deep breath. Put a smile on my face and got ready for my intro. *Now, let's all give a big hand to Channing Hayes!*

I bounded onto the stage, making sure to hit my mark squarely. Grabbed the mic off the stand and set the stand behind me. I saluted the audience, and in my head a thousand past audiences cheered, their applause making my heart pound, my blood flow. Dozens of opening lines reverberated in my mind. The applause continued as the spots beat down on me. I kept saluting, eager to sustain the ovation.

If only they were really clapping for me, in the here and now. I'd seen too many comics living in the past and had derided them all at every opportunity. Silently scolded them for resting on their laurels, for stagnating, for embracing complacency instead of working to forge a new, brighter future. Move forward or die. How I didn't want to be one of those dying comics. How I wanted to move on.

The applause dwindled. The empty chairs mocked me with their stiff backs and cold eyes. *Say something funny, dipshit!* Put up or shut up. I stood, slack-jawed while the room cooled around me. I had nothing funny to say, so I slinked off stage, doused the spots, and left The Last Laff.

I drove home along deserted Maple Avenue, through the heart of Vienna's business district. The Outback Steakhouse, the Safeway, the dry cleaners, a 7-Eleven. Familiar landmarks, everyday establishments, serving people living normal lives. When had my life become so abnormal I'd even notice these things?

I was about to turn off Maple when I remembered my duffel bag sitting in the office. I wasn't in the mood to work tonight, but I knew Artie would dig through the bag if he had the chance, and I didn't want him to find the notebooks. He'd start hassling me about my act, and I wanted to come back on my own terms, at my own pace. I pulled a U-turn across three lanes and headed to the club.

With the roads deserted, it only took a few minutes to get there. I parked at the curb and hopped out. Opened the door and immediately the acrid smell of smoke set off my body's adrenaline pump. I flipped the lights on, searching for the source. Had someone left the stove on?

I rushed to the kitchen but didn't find anything burning. As I raced down the hall, I noticed a few wisps of smoke coming from the storage room. I dashed back and found something burning in a small metal trashcan in the corner. Looked like paper or rags. I hustled to the kitchen and grabbed the fire extinguisher. Two mega-blasts later the fire was doused.

I leaned against the wall and let my racing pulse slow. The fire hadn't been hot enough to activate the sprinkler system, which was a good thing—the water damage would have been worse than any harm a minor fire would have caused. And this fire could only aspire to be minor. Once the paper or rags had been consumed, it probably would have gone out on its own, contained as it was in the trashcan.

After checking the cash register and finding nothing missing, I discovered the back door had been pried open. Not too difficult a trick considering the weak wooden doorframe and cheap deadbolt. Maybe now Artie would be more willing to open his wallet to fix things right.

Who set this fire? Why?

It seemed like an odd thing for vandals to do. What harm would a trashcan fire cause? Not splashy enough, certainly not compared to throwing a brick through the plate glass front windows. Was it simply an inept arsonist? Torching for fun? Then why go to the bother of breaking in? A much bigger fire could have been started in countless more flammable places.

This fire wasn't meant to cause damage. This fire was a message.

But what was the message? And who sent it?

TWENTY-FOUR

As I batted theories around in my head, my cell phone rang and I flipped it open. "Hello?"

"Goddamn that motherfucking prick. Goddamn him," Artie shouted into the phone.

"What's wrong?" I'd heard Artie mad before, plenty mad, but never like this.

"Fucker fucked us up. Goddamn arsonist prick. I'm going to kill him."

How did Artie know about the fire? "What are you talking about? *Who* are you talking about?"

"Fucking goddamn Reed, that's who. Set the fire. I'm going to annihilate him."

"Calm down. Calm down. How did you know about the fire?"

A pause. "I'm standing right here, damnit." His voice had decreased maybe one decibel.

I glanced around and didn't see him. Surely I would have heard him shouting if he were in the club. "*Where* are you?"

"I'm at the condo. Fucking fucker Reed. That fucking prick burned down my comedy condo!"

I sped over there and parked Rex as close as I could get to the scene, across the access road leading into the townhouse development. Loped across a few lawns to get to the end of the row where a slew of emergency vehicles idled, light bars flashing. Displaced residents gathered in knots, pointing and talking, while the cyclical shadows played across their concerned faces. I scanned the area for Artie and found him alone on the far curb, staring at his charred townhouse, hands on hips.

Hoses snaked through the front door and the urgent calls of firefighters filled the air. I touched his shoulder gently and his head swiveled toward me, in slow motion. The expression on his face was pure hatred. "Artie, I'm sorry. It's…" I took a deep breath. "How bad is it?"

He answered in a monotone. "Gutted. Fire damage, smoke damage, water damage. Totaled."

I nodded. The firefighters seemed to be concentrating on the next townhouse over, trying to limit the extent of the damage. I didn't see any flames, but the portable lights that had been set up on the lawn illuminated a thin trail of smoke rising skyward.

Artie mumbled something.

"What?"

"He's a dead man," Artie said, louder, but still barely audible.

No sense talking a man like Artie down, not while he was in the throes of his fury. I'd get plenty of opportunity to calm him down later. Tomorrow. And during the weeks beyond. To our right, a group of firefighters parted and a dark sedan cruised up, blue light flashing from a dashboard cherry. It screeched to a halt and

Freeman emerged. He spotted us and waved, but he jogged over to a guy standing near the Fire Chief's car. Freeman spoke to him while Artie and I watched all the action unfold before our eyes, as if we were digesting the latest disaster movie sequel down at the multiplex. *Conflagration III.*

After a few minutes, Freeman strode over to us. "I'm sorry, Artie. You too, Channing. This can't be easy."

Artie nodded but didn't say anything. I nodded, too. "They know what started it?" I asked.

"Not exactly. They'll investigate and these guys are good. They'll nail it." Freeman jerked his head at the townhouse. "Anybody staying there?"

Artie stayed mum, so I answered for him. "No. We put Otapi up in a hotel. Artie wasn't ready to open it for guests." A sigh escaped my mouth. It may never be ready for guests again.

"Lucky," Freeman said. "Damn lucky."

"Can they tell if it was accidental?" I asked. I wanted answers and I didn't want to wait for any investigators. I wanted answers now.

Freeman shook his head. "Like I said, they'll investigate. Why, what do you think?"

Artie spoke up. "This was no accident. This was arson."

"Really? You got someone in mind?"

Artie bit his lip. "I'll leave that for the investigators."

"Uh-huh," Freeman said. "You have any ideas, you'll let us know, right?"

"Sure," Artie said, but he didn't meet Freeman's eyes, just kept staring at his condo, at all the hoses and firefighters, and at the water streaming down the front walk.

Freeman turned to me. "How about you? Got any theories?"

"Someone set a small fire at the club tonight, too. In a trashcan. No damage. I think that was just a message. This…I don't know." I shrugged and eyed Artie before saying what I knew he was thinking. "Gerry Reed wanted to buy The Last Laff. We told him no."

Freeman snorted. "And you think he's a poor loser? That he'd burn down your place because he couldn't buy your little club?" He cocked his head. "Or are you just trying to soil your competitor's good name? I know you're overcome and everything, but I expected more from you guys."

I licked my lips. "You're right. Forget we said anything."

Freeman laughed, but it sounded hollow. "We find J.J. on the floor a few days ago and now the condo burns down. Either you've got the worst luck in the world, or something mighty suspicious is going on, and you have the nerve to give me some bullshit story about Reed being involved. If you know anything—*anything*—now would be a good time to tell. How about one eensy-weensy clue to make my job easier? Help me catch this asshole?"

"Come on, you don't think—" I said, but was interrupted by the guy who'd been talking to Freeman earlier.

"Detective, we got something here," he said.

Freeman seemed irritated, more so than usual. "What?"

"One of my guys found a body. We'd have liked to leave it in place for your people, but we can't risk it. Too unstable inside. We're dragging it out now."

Freeman glared at me, but I had no response. *A body?*

The discovery of the body brought more emergency vehicles, cops mostly, and I couldn't help but wonder what they thought, coming back to the scene of a possible homicide less than a week later. This wasn't Southeast or Anacostia, or even downtrodden

Prince Georges County where murders didn't make the front page. This was Falls Church, a homey little place where people walked their dogs at night.

Freeman had gone to examine the body, telling us to stay put. As if we were planning to go somewhere. "Who could it be?" I asked, more to myself than to Artie.

He shook his head and we continued to watch in silence. Anger seemed to radiate from him like the rays of sun in a preschooler's drawing. I got the feeling this wasn't just about the loss of the comedy condo. Even though he had absolutely nothing to do with it, I knew Artie felt guilty about the person who had died. His condo, his responsibility. Reed just happened to be a handy—and reviled—scapegoat.

Twenty minutes later, Freeman returned. "Female. African-American. Probably under forty years of age. That's all we can tell right now. Body's pretty damaged." He glared at us. "You still think your buddy Reed's involved?" He didn't wait for an answer, simply headed back to the body, which now lay on the grass in a dark vinyl body bag.

Was it J.J.'s smoking-hot black chick with the superlative ass? Seemed possible. Why she returned to the scene of the crime beat me, but I didn't believe in coincidences any more than Freeman did. I agreed with him about something else, too. Something fishy was going on here and it didn't sound like Reed's style.

Something clicked in my brain. J.J. was dead. The girl J.J. had sex with the previous night was dead. Could J.J. have a psycho girlfriend on the loose? One who killed him in a jealous rage, then went after the women he'd slept with? Was Heather on her list? I closed my eyes and tried to get a grip on reality, but things were very, very slippery. I needed some sleep. And some answers.

I offered to drive Artie home but he refused, claiming he was fine. I knew otherwise, but arguing with him had never proven to be effective. Not for the first time, I wished Sophie had been around to steady the ship. I managed to squeeze a promise out of Artie that he'd go straight home and go to sleep and call me when he woke up. I waited until I saw his car pull away before I got in mine and drove home.

I wanted to go to sleep, too, and stay asleep for a week—by which time I hoped everything would be over. Heather would be back. The mystery of J.J.'s death solved. Arsonist/murderer apprehended. But I knew life didn't work that way, no matter how much we wanted it to.

I had a tough time falling asleep, worrying about everything. Most of all, I worried about Artie.

———

Artie called around eleven in the morning, sounding a tiny bit calmer. Pissed, but not hysterical. I offered to go with him to sift through the remains of the condo, but he said to forget it, there wasn't anything worth salvaging. He hadn't kept anything of a personal nature there, just basic furnishings, semi-disposable stuff from Sears and IKEA.

We agreed to meet at Lee's at noon for our first meal of the day, which Artie always called breakfast, no matter what time it was. Working nights as comics gave you license to see things in a different way and meals were no exceptions.

I arrived at the restaurant first and Lee showed me to a booth in the back, sliding in across from me. "I've invited myself to join you both. Hope you don't mind." A huge grin dissuaded me from arguing.

"No, that's great," I said. Lee never failed to lighten my spirits. He was one of those guys who would do anything for you and not expect a thing in return beyond a simple thank you.

"What happened to J.J. was terrible."

I hadn't seen Lee all week. Usually I came by every couple days for spring rolls and conversation. "Yeah. And that's not all. Last night, someone torched the comedy condo."

Lee's eyes grew. "You're kidding," he said, but he knew I wasn't. "Holy shit. Was anyone hurt?"

"They found a body in the fire. Don't know who it is yet."

Lee's head dipped as he shook it. "Terrible. How's Artie taking it?"

"You can ask him yourself." I pointed with my chin toward the front as Artie walked up. He nodded hello and plopped down next to Lee.

"Ladies. Thanks for waiting." Artie unwrapped the napkin around his silverware and placed it in his lap. He carefully arranged his utensils on the table.

Lee turned sideways to face Artie. "Channing just told me about your place. I'm sorry."

Artie swallowed. "Thanks. Don't sweat it too much. It's insured."

Lee glanced at me with a puzzled look, then caught the eye of a server. She glided over. "We're ready now, doll. Thanks," he said, giving her a warm smile that somehow seemed to make it okay he called her doll. Not an ounce of condescension in him. He turned back to Artie. "You okay?"

"Sure. Why wouldn't I be? A comic staying at my condo was murdered. That prick Reed wants to wipe me off the face of the earth. My condo burned down." He ticked each event off on steady fingers. "And, oh yeah, they found a body, practically burned past the point of recognition, in the debris. Sure, I'm just swell." The words were chilling, but the matter-of-fact monotone Artie used to deliver them was far more frightening.

Lee reached over and grasped Artie's forearm. "Man, you need a vacation. How about my sister's place? It's right on the beach. I'll call her, hook you up."

Leave it to Lee to offer up someone else's retreat. Gotta love the guy.

Artie's left eyebrow arched. "An invitation to Hyannis Port South? I'm honored." Lee's two nephews were up-and-comers on the local political scene, and his sister's family had a getaway "compound" down on the Outer Banks. Artie often referred to their charismatic clan as the Asian Kennedys, which amused Lee, although he didn't like to admit it.

"Think about it. A whole week with no worries. What do you say?" Lee said, almost pleading.

Artie didn't answer. Worse, his eyebrow had returned to its normal position.

I put as much enthusiasm into my voice as I could muster and jumped in to help Lee's case. "Sounds great. Why don't you take him up on it, Artie? See if Sophie can come join you. When was the last time you two had a real vacation anyway? I'll handle things here. You go and take your mind off things."

"Thanks for the offer, but I'm fine. Really. Thanks for being so concerned. You are true friends," Artie said.

Thanks for being concerned? True friends? Lee and I exchanged glances. With Artie, it was sometimes hard to tell where the sincerity ended and the sarcasm began. He'd been honing his deadpan delivery for forty years. But what we were getting now reminded me of a man who'd finally decided to commit suicide and had accepted his fate.

The server brought our food—five dishes of assorted delicacies—and we helped ourselves. I didn't have much of an appetite, but Artie and Lee wolfed theirs down as if this were their last meals. At one point, Artie smiled my way and sent a shiver rippling through me. Could this *be* his last meal?

Before the fortune cookies arrived, I excused myself to go to the men's room. I entered a stall and locked it. Pulled out my phone and called Skip. It wasn't quite one in the afternoon—still early for him—but he'd just have to get over it. "Hello," his sleepy voice answered. "This is Skip."

"This is Channing." I told him about the fire at the club—I'd cleaned it up before anyone else found out about it—and I told him about the devastation of the comedy condo. Both news items shocked him, but when I mentioned the body they found in the townhouse, he went into full stutter mode. "Oh, sh-sh-shit. I can't be-be-believe it. Oh sh-sh-shit."

"Yeah. It's bad. And the worst part is Artie believes Reed is the one who burned down his place. I'm afraid he's going to go after him."

"What makes you think th-th-that?"

"I know Artie. And he didn't mention Reed's name to Freeman. Like he wanted a crack at Reed first, before the cops got him. I had to mention Reed, even though I don't think he had a thing to do with it." I paused. "Plus, I've never seen Artie this mad. And that's saying something."

I heard Skip whistle on his end. "Where's Artie now?"

"We're just finishing lunch at Lee's and then we'll be at the club. But…" I let it trail off, not wanting to attach concrete words to my nebulous fears, lest they come true.

"But what? What do you think Artie's going to do?" Skip sounded worried. That made two of us, three if you counted Lee, who I'm sure was as concerned as I was.

"I don't know. That's where you come in. I want you to get your ass over here and follow Artie around. Don't let him know you're tailing him, but make sure he doesn't do something crazy. Something he'll regret for the rest of his life."

Skip drew in a breath. "Sure thing, boss. Sure th-th-thing."

TWENTY-FIVE

Today the couch seemed lumpier than normal. I sat erect with my back flush against the cushions, hands in my lap, feet on the floor, knees together, as if I were at church hunkering down for a long sermon. My therapist and I had spent the first twenty minutes talking about the fires, my *feelings* about the fires, and my *feelings* about Artie's *feelings* about the fires. Most of what I expressed must have come across as confusion, except when I spoke about the body. That was pure sorrow. Then my therapist hit me between the eyes with a fastball.

"Why don't you tell me more about your mother? We haven't really spoken in much depth about her."

I'd put it off for so long that some small part of me believed I'd never have to plow those grounds. So much for wishful thinking. I composed myself and blew out a cleansing breath. "When I was about ten and first told my mother I wanted to be a stand-up comedian, she roared with laughter. I figured I was off to a pretty good start." I glanced up to see if I was connecting with my audience. A faint smile—perhaps. "She was a good mother, considering."

"Considering what?"

"She was a dancer and actress, in Broadway shows mostly. That's how I got my name. Sort of a Carol Channing-Helen Hayes amalgam." I paused, not wanting to turn this into a monologue. But I guess that was the nature of the beast, so I pressed on. "It was tough, trying to make ends meet. We were always moving from one apartment to another, sharing the rent with all sorts of Mom's show biz 'friends.' Sometimes I even think she, uh, entertained men for money. But it never seemed seedy or shady to me. Living in New York was odd. It was crowded, smelly, dirty, and kind of scary, but I loved it." I shrugged. "Maybe I just wasn't old enough to see the truth. About the city or about my mother's lifestyle. All I saw was how popular she was. All those friends…" Men's faces paraded before me. Always happy and smiling. I guess they weren't around long enough for me to grow to dislike them.

"Must have been rough. So much upheaval for a young boy. Your mother never married?"

I suppressed a laugh. "No. And I never knew my father. When I got older, I got the feeling she wasn't sure who my father was either, although she'd never answer my questions about him directly. She never answered a lot of my questions directly."

"What questions were those, Channing?"

I pondered that a moment, remembering all those discussions we had, just the two of us, best friends for life sharing everything. A sham, I knew now. There was a lot she hadn't shared. "I don't know. Just questions."

"Try to remember some. They might be enlightening."

I swallowed, trying to loosen my throat. The questions were never far from the surface, but usually I kept them submerged. Now they were ready to breach. "Why did I always have to switch schools? Why did the other kids always tease me and call me names? Why did they call *her* names? Why was she always crying, always sad? Why, why, why?" I stared ahead, oddly unemotional. "Questions like those. She never answered them. Never answered me. Just cried a lot."

"And you never knew why she was sad?"

"Oh, she'd make up stuff but I never believed her. I mean, who would cry because they broke a fingernail?" I said, forcing a chuckle.

"I didn't ask if she *told* you why she was sad. I asked if you *knew* why she was. You're a perceptive guy. I'm sure you had some idea about what was upsetting her, especially as you got older."

I knew, all right. I knew. But I'd been keeping it bottled up inside me for so long, I was afraid I'd feel different if I let it go, let it free. And I wasn't sure I'd feel better. Good or bad, my feelings about my mother were what kept her close to me. I didn't want to risk losing my tether to her. My thirty-three-year-old umbilical cord. If I cut it, would she go floating off into space and out of my memory?

"Channing?"

I blinked, emerging from my trance.

"Did you know what made your mother so sad?"

I leaned forward. "So sad that she'd kill herself, you mean? Yeah, I know. Me. She resented me. Taking care of me, watching over me, providing for me. She could have been living it up with her friends. Traveling around the world. Anything. But she had me. *I* was what made her so sad. *I'm* why she killed herself."

———

Considering how many messages I'd left on Heather's voice mail, I wasn't surprised when the electronic voice told me her mailbox was full. I figured it was time to compare notes again with Ryan, although I guessed he'd contributed his share of unanswered messages to Heather's overstuffed mailbox, too. With the same amount of success I had.

Ryan's roommate, Nathan, met me at the door and his face brightened with recognition. "Oh, hey. How are you doing?" he said, looking over my shoulder to see if I was alone.

"Okay. Ryan here?"

He shook his head. "Nope. Work."

"I thought he worked from home."

"He does, usually. He had to visit a client's site today. Some kind of IT emergency." He smiled. "Want to come in? Help me enjoy my afternoon off?"

"Sure." Maybe he'd overheard something that would help me find Heather. Or maybe I could find out what little secret he and Ryan shared. I followed him through the entry hall, through the living room, and out onto the small back deck. A few cans of Pabst sat on a table next to a thin paperback. *God Save the Child*. Old Robert B. Parker. At least he had good taste in books, if not in beer.

"Want a brewski?" he asked.

"No, thanks." We both sat. "Nice back here." The deck overlooked a small pond bordering a wooded area. Serene.

"Thanks," Nathan said as he picked up his beer. "I guess you're here about Heather. Ryan hasn't heard from her." He squinted at me in the sunlight. "At least he hasn't said anything about it."

"I haven't heard from her, either. And it isn't like her not to call me back."

He nodded. "Yeah. Ryan said the same thing."

"He did? Ryan told me it was normal for Heather not to return calls."

Nathan turned the can around in his hand. "Well, sometimes Ryan says different things to different people. He's not the most consistent guy in the world."

"Gotcha. Is he worried?"

Nathan took a sip of beer. "He says he isn't really worried. But he likes to appear macho about stuff. I know I'd be worried if Heather was my girlfriend."

I nodded, gazed at the pond. The breeze sent a few ripples across its glassy surface.

"We went out once, you know," Nathan said.

"You and Heather?" Instinctively, I gave Nathan the once-over. Yet another example of Heather's poor taste in men.

"Yeah. Maybe six or seven months ago. Didn't really click, so Ryan asked me if he could ask her out. Hey, it's a free country, right? We can all get along." He took a long swig of beer.

"Where did you meet her?"

He made a chucking sound in his cheek. "Let's see. I think we met her—Skip and I—at some party for comics at Capitol Comedy. After some kind of competition or something. I remembered I didn't do well with my act, but I scored Heather's phone number." He snapped his fingers and a cloud descended on his face.

"Her sister was there, too. So sad what happened. I'm sorry." Skip must have filled him in on my relationship with Lauren. It felt weird getting pity from a guy I barely knew.

"Yeah, thanks." I waited the appropriate few seconds before continuing. "So after you went out with Heather, Ryan started dating her?"

"Oh, no. Not right away. She hooked up with someone else after we went out, Brooks Spellman, another comic who spent a lot of time at Reed's. After *they* broke it off, Ryan stepped in. A girl like Heather must have guys queued up." Nathan lowered his voice. "I really don't know how serious it is with Ryan. Seems kind of like it's on-again, off-again. But, whatever. Not my business." He stared off into the trees, sipped some beer. "Sometimes I think all Ryan wants from her is some advice about breaking into the comedy scene."

"What? Ryan's a comic?"

Nathan chuckled. "Not even close. He thinks he's funny, but trust me, he isn't. He likes the idea of being a funnyman, but he doesn't want to put in the time. Which would be wasted, in my opinion. Some people just don't have 'it.' I tried giving him a few pointers, but he was always looking for an easier way." Nathan looked at me sideways. "You know what I'm talking about, right?"

Yeah, sure. "How'd you two become roommates?"

"I answered an ad. I guess the other candidates smelled worse," Nathan said. "Actually, when I told him I did some comedy, that probably sealed the deal. Anyway, I pay my share of the rent, and we coexist in peace. It works, I guess."

I put some caring in my voice. "Him dating Heather bother you?"

He took a sip of beer and looked out over the pond. "Naw. Like I said, Heather and I didn't click. Tell you what, though. If Heather was my girlfriend, I wouldn't give her the chance to date someone else, know what I mean? I'd treat her like a queen. I guess I'm too much of a romantic for my own good."

The more Nathan talked, the more I understood why he hadn't clicked with Heather.

"Sure you don't want one?" he asked, reaching for another beer.

I shook my head.

He popped the top and took a sip. "When are you coming back? You were good. Real good. I wish my act was half as good as yours."

"Thanks." I didn't elaborate about my plans to return. Hard to elaborate on wisps of smoke.

Nathan tipped his can of beer at me. "You know, I've been working on it. My act. With Skip. He and I are 'comedy buddies.'"

"Oh yeah?" Even though it was a common way to develop material, Skip hadn't mentioned anything to me about working with a partner. I'd thought he was on his own when I offered to help him. Maybe he was embarrassed joining up with Nathan.

"My stuff's better now. Maybe I should send you guys another package." He took a sip, but didn't take his eyes off me.

"*Another* one?"

"Yeah. I sent a package to Artie a year ago. Didn't hear back, so I called him. Said I wasn't ready yet." Nathan shrugged like it was no big deal, but he couldn't completely mask his disappointment, especially from me. Over the years, I'd become an expert in disappointment. Most comics did.

"I haven't seen it. But I guess it wouldn't hurt to send in another one."

"You'll look at it?"

"Sure. We look at all the stuff we get."

Nathan's face sagged. He was hoping for some kind of fast-track to the top of the pile. I guess Ryan wasn't the only one looking for an easier way. "Okay. I'll send one in. I'll address it to you, personally, so you'll be sure to see it."

"Okay. Great. I'll look for it." We both knew the words were empty, but it was part of the dance.

Nathan drained the last of his beer and set the empty can on the table with a clink. Picked up another one, turned it around in his hand, then set it back down, thinking better of it. "You get along with Artie?" he asked.

"He's a piece of work all right, but we get along." I glanced at him sideways. "Why?"

"No reason. Just curious. Seemed a bit gruff when I talked to him, is all."

I laughed. "Don't take it personally. He's like that with everyone. In fact, the gruffer he is, the more he likes you."

Nathan gave me a tight grin. "Then he must really love me."

TWENTY-SIX

On most Saturday mornings, I slept until noon. But today, I rolled out of bed at nine, feeling alive and alert and altogether brimming with hope. Despite the events of the past week, the curtain of depression had parted again, and I vowed to make the best of whatever time I had in the light. Last night's show went great—Otapi was even better than he was on Thursday—and Artie's mood seemed to have stabilized, although I still had Skip tailing him just to be sure.

I inhaled four toaster waffles and a Granny Smith apple for breakfast before gathering my notebooks. I was heading down to the park again to write some new material, hoping my creativity would be enhanced by fresh air and sunshine, two substances usually avoided by comics. I made sure I had a trusty Penn with me, too.

Before I made it out the door, Freeman called. So much for my good mood. "Got an ID on the body from the fire," he said, skipping the pleasantries. "LaTasha James. Working name: Honey Pot.

Was a call girl with a pretty high-priced outfit working the downtown hotels. Her prints were among those we found at the scene of J.J.'s death. You got any idea why she'd go back after cleaning him out?"

"How would I know?" I said. "Maybe she didn't know J.J. died." I explained what J.J. said about wanting to see her again, regardless of the theft. "Maybe she was after an encore performance."

Freeman grunted. "Uh-huh. Thanks for your input. We've processed most of the prints we took from the townhouse. In addition to James's, we found J.J.'s , of course. And yours, Artie's, and everyone else's from the club."

"No surprise there. Artie held staff meetings at the condo from time to time. Thought it fostered bonding. I think it was an excuse for him to feel like a gracious host."

"Uh-huh. He gracious enough to invite Gerry Reed to those staff meetings? We found his prints there, too."

My breath caught. "I don't know what Reed was doing there. I'm pretty sure he and Artie weren't reminiscing."

Freeman said, "What I figured. So I talked to Reed."

"How did he explain his prints?"

"Simple. Said J.J. asked him to come over for a drink, and he did."

J.J. invited him over to talk turkey, in Artie's own townhouse? J.J. had balls, all right. "When was that?" I asked.

"Wednesday. Couple nights before your handcuff rescue. He's got an alibi for the night of J.J.'s death. Was working late at his club, got a few witnesses. You can pass that along to Artie when you see him, maybe that'll help convince him Reed's not involved in some nefarious scheme," Freeman said.

"I'll tell him." It would take more than that to get Artie off his Reed jag, but I'd pass it along anyway. "What about the night of the fire?"

"Things are less locked-down that night. Said he was working late, alone. Then drove home. Wife was asleep when he got home. So…"

"So he could have set the fire," I said.

"I try not to speculate. I prefer to rely on facts." Freeman cleared his throat. "And here's a fact you might find interesting. We've identified one other set of prints from the condo that might be important. Heather Dempsey's." He paused, waiting for some comment from me. When I didn't respond, he asked, "You got anything you want to tell me?"

As much as I hated keeping something like this from Freeman, I still wasn't ready to tie Heather to J.J., not yet, not without talking to her to get her side of the story. I'd kept her out of this so far, what was a little longer? I owed her that much for wrecking her life one night five months ago. "Nothing to worry about. I took her there a couple of times. When I was doing errands for Artie or making sure one of the comics hadn't trashed the place. You can cross her off your list of suspects."

"Those errands involve Heather touching the bed frame in the master bedroom? And the bedside lamp and the bathroom vanity and…I could go on." Freeman's voice had hardened. "You know how I feel about bullshit games, Channing."

"Look, Freeman. I don't remember what the errands involved. Maybe she made the bed or something. When I find Heather, I'll ask her."

"Maybe I'll ask her first. Heather Dempsey has now officially become a 'person of interest' to the Fairfax County Police Department. So if you find her, you best let her know I'm looking for her." I heard Freeman draw in a sharp breath and I pictured the scowl on his face. The scowl that had cracked many a scumbag in the interrogation room. "We clear?"

"Crystal," I said. "Crystal."

———

After Freeman's call, I hadn't felt like going to the park to do some work. Tough to think of funny stuff after that conversation. And my gut ached from not being able to tell him the truth about J.J. sleeping with Heather. How could people lie, day in and day out? I'd be riddled with ulcers.

Instead of working, I downed a handful of Tums and fired up the DVD player to watch a couple of flicks I'd bought off Blockbuster's 2-for-1 table. Twenty minutes into the first one, I ditched it and tried the second, only lasting ten minutes before giving it the heave-ho. I guess there was a reason they'd been in the bargain bin. I turned the TV off and reclined on the couch.

Do my laundry or go grocery shopping? My funk had returned and both chores seemed insurmountable. So I sat in the dark and thought about the Dempsey girls, one dead, one missing.

An hour later, Kathleen Dempsey called. She needed to see me, *right away*, could I come over? It was *very, very* important. Although she wasn't my mother-in-law, I knew a command when I heard it, so I told her I'd be there in twenty-five minutes. I made most of the lights, weaving through traffic and negotiating the hilly, winding back roads, past country estates and horse farms with alacrity. I made it to the Dempseys' with three minutes to spare.

Kathleen greeted me at the door and ushered me into the living room, where we'd sat the last time, where William Dempsey had destroyed cherished family keepsakes with his pipe wrench. I wasn't afraid for my well-being; she had assured me over the phone Dempsey wouldn't be around.

Today she looked haggard, as if she'd been digging a garden with her bare hands for the last fifteen hours. No makeup, uncombed hair, wrinkled clothes. It was the first time I could recall that Kathleen Dempsey hadn't seemed 100 percent put together. It disturbed me.

Like last time, I sat on the couch while she perched on the edge of the chair across from me. This time, though, a somber mood hung in the air from the get-go. "Thanks for coming, Channing. I…I appreciate it." She forced a wan smile, but it seemed engulfed by the overarching sense of loss her body exuded.

"Sure. Kathleen." I glanced around. All the photographs seemed in place and there were no signs of busted glass or broken picture frames, as if Dempsey's outburst had never happened. Maybe in her mind it never had.

"Well. I asked you to come over because…" She bowed her head and wrung her hands in her lap. "I didn't feel like I could have this conversation over the phone, so…thanks for coming." She lifted her head and stared at me with glossy eyes.

Had something happened to Heather? I wasn't sure I wanted to know, but I couldn't *not* know. "What's wrong? Have you heard from Heather?"

"No. You?"

I shook my head. "No. But I'm still looking. I'll find her."

Her eyes wouldn't meet mine. Had she given up hope? Or was she embarrassed about her daughter's penchant for putting others through the wringer with her disappearances?

"Is that what you wanted to talk about?" I asked.

"No. It's not that. It's…" She broke off and tried a smile to lighten the mood, but the only thing she accomplished was dragging it further into the mire. "Oh, why is this so hard?" She got up and turned her back on me. I waited for her to get the courage to tell me what she so desperately wanted to, feeling my insides contracting into a tightly wound ball.

Kathleen whirled around and drew herself up, crossing her arms in front of her. Took a breath. "William and I have separated." She held her chin high for a few seconds, then exhaled and her body shrank before me. She dropped into her seat and stared at me, waiting for my reaction.

"Separated? I'm so sorry to hear that." Of course, if Dempsey's recent behavior at home had been anything like the last couple of times I'd seen him, I wasn't sorry in the least. Kathleen was far better off without a madman sharing her bed.

Kathleen leaned forward. "Yes. We've decided to go our separate ways. Lauren's death had cracked an already faltering foundation, and Heather's, uh, disappearance set the whole thing crumbling. It seemed to push him over the edge. Obnoxious, verbally abusive, the whole nine yards." Her voice had gained some strength. Once the floodgates opened, her feelings came pouring out.

"Well, if there's anything I can do, just let—"

"Thank you, Channing. Just so you know, I never blamed you for Lauren's death. I know you loved her very much. She felt the same way about you, too." A wistful smile shone through her tears. "I'm sure you knew that. Lauren wasn't shy in expressing her feelings. In that respect, she was like her father."

I nodded. Neither Lauren nor Dempsey ever shied away from giving someone their opinions. No matter what turmoil might ensue.

Kathleen cleared her throat. "Uh, speaking of William…"

"Yes?"

"I'd steer clear of him for a while," she said, meeting my eyes.

Good advice, but a little late, considering my nighttime parking lot encounter. "Okay. I understand."

"No, I don't think you do. Not exactly. William is a dangerous, vengeful man, willing to blame anyone who's convenient. And he's very protective of his daughters." She paused and pointed at me. "You for instance. Not only does he blame you for Lauren's death, and for Heather's disappearance, he…" Her head dropped and she mumbled something into her lap.

"What?"

"He blames you for our breakup, too." Her head oscillated slowly, to its own cadence.

Yeah, I think I'd make a concerted effort to avoid William Dempsey. "I'm sorry about your difficulties with William. If there's anything I can do, just name it. And thanks for the heads-up. I'll be careful." I rose to leave.

A mask of fright now covered Kathleen's face. "He's unstable, Channing. He's dangerous. I'm afraid he's going to do something terrible." She swallowed hard. "I've changed the locks."

I tried to be as calming as possible, but I wasn't sure I was up to the task, considering I was this lunatic's scapegoat. "If he comes around bothering you, call the police. Let them handle it. Okay?"

She nodded and opened her mouth to speak, but closed it abruptly. Then opened it again. "He took his gun. I looked in his closet this morning and the gun safe was empty. He feels he has nothing left to live for. First Lauren, then Heather, now me." Her features melted into an amorphous blob.

So Dempsey has a gun. Like daughter, like father.

Kathleen started sobbing, slowly at first but gaining speed rapidly. Her shoulders shook and she gasped for breath between the sobs. Stared at me and kept on crying.

It took every once of restraint I possessed to keep from joining her.

———

As I turned into my condo's parking lot, Skip called. "You'd better come down here, man. I got a bad feeling about what Artie's getting ready to do."

The tone of Skip's voice fueled an adrenaline rush. "Where are you?" I executed a quick U-turn in the lot and waited for an opening to shoot back into traffic.

"I'm in my car, a block from Reed's place. Artie's sitting at a little café, two doors down, sipping a coffee, staring at the club. It's like one of those movies about the guy who gets so pissed off, he stalks his prey, captures him, and then pulls out his fingernails, one by one."

"He's just sitting there?" I asked.

"Yeah. But you better hurry. Artie never sits anywhere for long."

I hauled ass on I-66 across the Potomac into the city, then zig-zagged my way along the grid-like D.C. streets, maintaining phone contact with Skip the whole way. Traffic wasn't too bad—on the weekends, it was always much lighter into the city than the bumper-to-bumper workdays. It still took me just under forty minutes to get to Foggy Bottom. When I arrived at Skip's car, there weren't any open spaces, so I pulled up alongside him and rolled down my window.

"Where is he?" I asked.

Skip pointed across the street, a half block up. "Right there. Under the yellow umbrella. He hasn't moved. Just keeps staring at the front doors of the CCC."

Artie sat at a table by himself with his back toward us. "Thanks, man. I've got it from here," I said. "Catch you later." I jammed Rex into reverse and backed up, waiting for Skip to leave so I could take his parking spot.

He roared off, and I parallel-parked, killing the engine. Better to confront Artie now than wait until something ugly erupted. I hopped out, timing the gap in traffic to cross the street. Safely on the sidewalk, I sauntered up to Artie's table and slipped into the chair next to him. "This seat taken?"

Artie didn't even glance at me. "Would it matter if I told you it was?"

"Nope." I stared at the front door of the Capitol Comedy Club. An awning protruded about ten feet over the sidewalk, but it was high up, so you could see the orange door clearly. It was closed.

Artie didn't say anything. Stubborn man.

"So, come here often?"

Stone face.

"There must be a thousand places to get a cup of coffee closer than this one," I said, eyes on the CCC. Maybe if I didn't gaze into his face directly, he wouldn't get spooked. Like some kind of wild animal on the veldt.

"I happen to like their coffee," he said. "Worth the drive."

"Right." I snapped my fingers and raised my voice. "Hey, isn't that Reed's club?"

Artie didn't flinch. "Yes, I believe it is."

"Wow. What a coincidence. You having coffee right here. Who woulda thought?"

My mentor finally turned his head in my direction. "Channing. I'm just an old goat enjoying a hot beverage. Leave me alone, will you? Don't you have a club to run?"

"Don't worry, it's not even one o'clock. Besides, Donna can run that place by herself, in her sleep."

"Then why am I paying you?" Artie asked, focused again on the CCC's front door.

"Because you like my company?"

"Feh," he said, shooing a fly away with his hand. I wasn't sure if he was talking to me or to the fly, but I let it go.

I glanced around for a server, then realized it was one of those walk-up places like Starbucks. I didn't want coffee that badly. More importantly, I didn't want to risk Artie making a kamikaze run at CCC while I ducked inside.

Artie seemed unperturbed by my presence, as if he'd expected it all along. I touched his forearm. "Come on. Let's go. You can't go after Reed. He didn't burn down the condo. And if you were thinking he killed J.J., forget it. Freeman checked and he has an alibi. Reed may be an ass and he may be trying to get his hands on The Last Laff, but you can't go after him for that."

He took a deep breath and let my hand rest on his arm. "We'll see."

"Artie, you can't sit here and—" I broke off my sentence as a tall, curly-haired guy turned the far corner and headed for the Capitol Comedy Club's front door. He strode right to it, pulled the door open, and disappeared inside. I felt my jaw hang open as I turned to speak to Artie. Nothing came out.

"What?" Artie asked, sensing something had caused me to short circuit. "What's going on?"

"That guy who just went into the CCC? He's Ryan Rizzetti, Heather Dempsey's boyfriend."

"So what does that mean?" Artie asked.

I managed a shake of the head. "Fuck if I know."

TWENTY-SEVEN

ARTIE AND I WAITED and watched. About fifteen minutes later, Ryan came bursting through the door as if he'd been launched from a slingshot. He half-jogged, half-skipped back in the direction he'd come from. The way he bolted, it looked as though someone might be chasing him, but no one exploded through the door in hot pursuit.

I considered following him except I didn't want to leave Artie unattended, and I didn't think Ryan would lead me to Heather. I figured he came by to see if Reed knew where she might be. After all, she'd worked there in the past, and according to Nathan, Ryan met her at some kind of party associated with the club. All that happened a long time ago, so either Ryan knew something more than I did, or he was getting as desperate as me. I'd have to talk with him again to see which it was.

"We done here?" I asked Artie, prepared to enumerate the dozens of reasons why he couldn't attack Reed.

He shrugged and turned his cup upside down, allowing a couple drops of joe to *splot* on the table. He swooshed them away with his napkin. "Okay. I've finished my coffee, and it was worth the drive. But I've got something I'd like you to do." He stuffed the napkin into his cup.

"I will not kill Reed for you."

Artie didn't even crack a smile. "I'd like you to go catch the comedy thing at the burger thing. On the Mall."

The Comedy Throwdown at the Burger Battle. "Come on, Artie. We already talked about that. Not a wise use of my time. Not a wise use of anybody's time."

He glared at me. "You never know, my friend. You never know. Reed's probably got his scouts there. Prick." Artie was paranoid about getting scooped by another booker or club owner who found the next comedy superstar at some out-of-the-way dive.

"Seriously?"

His glare intensified.

I sighed. "Okay. You're the boss." Besides, I had nothing better to do this afternoon, except catch up on my sleep and worry about Dempsey finding me and attaching electrodes to my gonads. "But I have a condition."

Artie's right eyebrow rose.

"You need to go directly back to the club and stay out of trouble."

Artie's eyes narrowed. "Where else would I go, anyway?" He rose slowly and pitched his cup into a nearby trashcan, not saying another word. As had become my custom, I walked him to his car and watched him take off.

I hadn't planned to attend this year's Burger Battle, not with everything going on in my life. But after coming into the city to defuse Stalker Artie, I figured I might as well follow orders and check things out. He'd been in this business for a long time, so maybe he knew something I didn't.

Or maybe he wanted me out of his hair for a while.

I called Skip and told him to be on the lookout for Artie's return.

———

When I got to the car, I phoned Ty to see if he wanted to meet me at the burger shindig. He agreed almost before I'd finished my sentence, saying he'd been looking for an excuse to ditch studying, and although I wasn't *l'excuse parfaite*, I'd do in a pinch.

I cruised the side streets near the Museum of Natural History and lucked into a parking space half-hidden between two SUVs. Was this another sign things were turning around for me? One could hope. I locked Rex up, crossed Constitution Avenue, and fell in with a gaggle of tourists until I reached the Mall. Then I turned west, away from the Capitol, and headed toward the Washington Monument.

There were few better places to be in early spring than our nation's capital. Nearby, along the Tidal Basin, the cherry blossoms had peaked a couple weeks ago, their pink buds a harbinger of nature's annual rebirth. And of the crowded tourist season.

Today's warm weather brought scores of picnickers, Frisbee-players, and joggers out on the National Mall to enjoy the fresh air. And in just about any direction you looked, you could spot some monument or statue or historic building, basking in the bright sun. Spring always brought optimism on its scented breeze, and I took a deep breath, inhaling all the optimism my lungs could hold.

As I ascended the long incline to the Washington Monument, the wind whipped the fifty flags surrounding it, and the hardware clanging against the flagpoles reminded me of the time I visited the U.N. Building. I was about seven and my mother wanted to show me where—in her words—peace got made. Although we didn't actually go into the building, just being on the plaza watching the array of international flags had inspired me. Back then, I thought making peace had to be a cinch, especially if all it took was a bunch of diplomats discussing things in a fancy air-conditioned building.

A line of people circled the monument beneath the flags; the kids wore baseball caps and the adults held brochures and cameras and fiddled with backpacks slung across their shoulders. On the other side of the monument, I took a moment to absorb the scene. The World War II Memorial, the Reflecting Pool, and good ol' Abe stretched out before me, as people flew multi-colored kites in the foreground. To my left, tucked away in a small grassy area by a traffic circle, was the tent city marking the Burger Battle.

The annual event, sponsored by a local radio station, was an excuse to eat huge quantities of ground beef and surreptitiously quaff even larger quantities of adult beverages. About thirty of the area's restaurants set up booths, and throngs of people carrying strips of red paper tickets wandered around, trying to decide whose burgers they'd gorge themselves on next. Ostensibly, there was some kind of prize for the burger voted best, but the real prize for the restaurateurs was the increased visibility. I always wondered what kind of in the organizers had to be able to get a permit to host such an example of crass commercialism a mere two hundred yards from the Washington Monument.

Of course, where there was food, there was entertainment. In addition to a slate of musical acts, the Burger Battle sponsored a comedy showcase. The Comedy Throwdown was like a giant-scale open mic night, with a twist. Here, two comics "dueled" on stage, at different mics. One would do his set, followed by the other, leaving the audience to choose a winner. The Throwdown field narrowed—winners facing off against other winners—until all the pretenders were eliminated and a champion crowned. Of course, the biggest difference between a "normal" open mic and the Throwdown were the several hundred people passing judgment on your performance. More than enough to put a hitch in your giddy-up if you froze or got tongue-tied.

I made my way down the hill, watching the plumes of smoke from the grills dance in the breeze. Seeing the smoke made me flash back to the night Artie's condo was torched. I banished the image from my mind, instead concentrating on the mass of humanity enjoying the sunny day.

When I got closer, the smell of charred meat started my stomach growling. Must be chow time. Before I could locate the nearest ticket booth, Ty appeared at my side. I slapped him on his shoulder and it felt like I was hitting a concrete pillar. "Hey. Thanks for meeting me."

"No sweat. Thanks for calling. I was starting to go bonkers. Can too much studying be bad for you?"

"Sure. All work and no play makes Ty a dull boy." I nodded at the row of booths. "Hungry?"

"I'm a vegetarian." No expression on his face.

I couldn't tell if he was kidding, but thinking back, I couldn't recall a time I'd seen him eating meat. I stared at him for a couple seconds and he didn't crack. "Whatever. I'm not. And besides, I don't think I can watch the Throwdown on an empty stomach."

I bought a handful of food tickets and we strolled around, checking out the offerings. Purveyors ranged from the low-joint-on-the-totem-pole Hungry Hectors Burger Emporium to the upper crust steak houses, like Morton's, that served twenty-dollar burgers to the expense-account crowd. Somehow, at the Burger Battle, eating from paper plates with plastic forks had a way of equaling things out.

As we scoped out the main food aisle, many of the people waddling by hardly glanced up from their grease-stained paper plates heaped with burgers and fries. It was a disheartening—and somewhat disgusting—picture of gluttony. Only in America.

I got my burger from the stand with the shortest line, not caring if the masses knew something about the food's quality I didn't. Ty settled for a Sprite and a side of fries. Sufficiently armed, we headed to the end of the "battlegrounds" where the stage had been erected.

A white guy in a dashiki—sporting a wild 'fro—was just beginning his set. "How you all doing, D.C.?" he yelled into the mic, working the stand back and forth, rolling it along small arcs on its circular base. "Doin' all right?" Across the stage, his competitor had his arms folded across his chest, looking down at his shoes. I didn't recognize either of the comics.

The crowd—those who were paying attention—yelled back. I took a bite of my burger, unleashing a stream of warm grease down my chin. I wiped it away with an onion skin-thin napkin.

The comic rolled the mic stand faster. "Great, great. I love this town. And I love this country. Where else can a guy with no discernible skills get to live in the big white house over yonder? In my neighborhood, a guy like that wouldn't even get hired by the local drug dealers, ya know? Not qualified. But here, he gets to be President! No wonder all those illegals want to come here. No skills? That's okay, you get the top job! El Presidente!"

A heckler shouted out something I couldn't make out.

The comic set the mic stand down and turned in the heckler's direction. He raised both hands and pointed at the group gathered right in front of the stage. "Hey. I don't come down to your business and tell you how to flip burgers, do I?"

The crowd groaned. Rule number one of comedy: know your audience. And this audience had quite a few guys and girls in aprons taking a break from their grills. Insulting burger flippers at the Burger Battle might not be the best idea, especially when your advancement to the next round is in their hands. I took another bite of my hamburger.

"What's with you? Don't you know funny? Shut up and let me finish," the comic said, pleading in his voice.

More shouts from the crowd.

Mr. Dashiki sputtered.

The crowd, smelling fresh meat, shouted louder.

The comic emitted what sounded like a growl, then he let fly with the big guns. "Hey, fuck y'all, you douchebags. I don't need this sh—" His mic died, and two burly guys wearing orange Burger Battle T-shirts hopped onto the stage and escorted the man out, one on each side. With families—and children—in the crowd, the organizers had to be vigilant.

The remaining comic bowed once to the crowd, then clasped his hands above his head like a prizefighter. After another bow, he strode off the stage. Winner by default.

About five years ago, I'd entertained the notion of performing here. Luckily, the feeling had passed quickly. Since then, I'd made it to a few Throwdowns as a spectator, and it seemed something like this happened every year. The comic was an idiot. But some small part of me felt sympathy for the guy. First of all, it was tough to do a PG set, and second, once a group of hecklers got started, it was difficult to regain order. Usually the best thing to do was to ignore the barbs. But every comic I knew learned that lesson the hard way. I remembered some of my earliest gigs. Afraid to show weakness, I didn't back down from hecklers, and there were a few times when they got much bigger laughs than I did. *That* was embarrassing. I stuffed the last bite of hamburger into my mouth and folded the paper plate into thirds.

Ty elbowed me. "Artie wanted you to see this? He think you were going to find someone good here?"

I swallowed before speaking. "You know Artie." Even though the talent was substandard, this venue was better than some bowling alley-cum-Chinese restaurant in Outer Hicksburg where he could have sent me trolling for the Next Big Thing.

A guy in white tails—the emcee—came out and told everyone to hang in there for a few minutes while they rounded up the comics for the second round.

I turned to Ty. "How's life treating you? I mean your 'real' life, you know, away from the comedy club."

"Great. Fantastic. As usual." Ty always saw the glass three-quarters full. Nothing halfway about him. "Why?"

I shrugged. "Things have been tough for me. Artie. Just wanted to make sure our craziness hasn't affected you too much." I took a big breath. "And…"

"What?"

"I hate to ask more from you, but I need a favor."

"Just name it." Ty's face opened up.

"I've asked Skip to keep an eye on Artie. Make sure the old guy doesn't get his nose into something he can't get out of," I said, examining Ty to see if he already knew what I was talking about. Hard to read. "He's royally pissed at Reed and I'm afraid he'll let his temper lead him down the wrong path."

"I didn't realize Artie had a temper," he said.

Maybe Ty had a career in stand-up after all. "Yeah, well, Skip can't watch him all the time, so I was wondering…"

Ty pursed his lips, nodding. "Say no more. I'll get with Skip and we'll set up a babysitting schedule. Got to work around my classes, though."

"And, uh, I can't pay you."

"Seeing the appreciation on your face and hearing the gratitude in your voice is thanks enough," Ty said. "Plus, I'll get to find out what Artie really does all day long. Probably sits on his ass reading *Mad* magazine or something."

"Thanks, man. I owe you." I opened my mouth, then closed it.

"What?" Ty asked. "Got something else for me?" Add *perceptive* to Ty's long list of positive attributes.

"There's this guy. Lauren and Heather's father, actually. William Dempsey. He's going through some stuff and he's mad at me. Might want to come down to the club to *express* his anger, if you know what I mean." I described him for Ty, making sure to emphasize the pipe wrench and the handgun. "If you could keep an eye out, you'd be doing a big favor for me. And for my internist."

"Pipe wrench, huh? Don't worry, no angry white guys will get by me. If somebody bad comes sniffing around the club, I'll handle it. That's what I get paid for, right?" He pounded his grapefruit-sized fist into his hand, twice, for effect. Then he flashed me a menacing smile.

"Yeah. Just giving you a heads-up." I smiled back, but I knew the truth behind the tough-guy facade. Unlike many bouncers who went looking for a fight at every opportunity—no matter how trivial—Ty was a pacifist, relying on his appearance as a deterrent. Worked in the Cold War, worked for Ty. Since I'd bought into the club, I'd only seen him get into it once, after some drunk slapped a woman and drew blood. Ty had been so shaken with what he'd done he'd taken a couple days off to gather himself. Of course, if you asked me, the guy deserved every one of those twenty-two stitches.

Ty and I spent most of the next hour wincing as the Burger Battle crowned a Comedy Throwdown champion. With what I saw, I didn't think Artie needed to worry about getting scooped. Not in the least.

It wasn't until I was back in my car, driving west on Interstate 66, that I thought more about seeing Ryan at the CCC. What the hell was going on?

TWENTY-EIGHT

Last night, Otapi killed.

Both shows, he absolutely destroyed, and Artie and I enjoyed ourselves for the first time in a long time. To make things sweeter, it was one of the best Saturday nights—financially—that we'd had in months, almost as good as J.J.'s. Maybe my life would really turn around now.

After last night's rousing success, I was still feeling the buzz. It was weird, really. When those people were laughing and applauding, they weren't showing the love to me—I just owned a part of the club. I hadn't even been the one to book Otapi. With all the shit raining down on my head recently, I should be feeling like an old shoe on the side of the highway. But I wasn't. Maybe my euphoria was only temporary and I'd feel like crap again later, but the vicarious high I felt gave me hope, told me I had a future. Maybe there was a drop of truth to all that "life goes on" and "time heals all wounds" pabulum. Even the gaping hole at my core where Lauren belonged didn't threaten to destroy me as it usually did.

One thing was for sure—I was getting seasick riding this emotional roller coaster.

While downing a bowl of Cap'n Crunch and a pear for breakfast, I thought about my friends. Virtually every one was a comic, or worked in the business in some capacity. Was that normal? I suppose it made sense. We worked together, we played together, and in some cases, we lived together. It was hard to escape the close-knit world of comedy when you lived it twenty-four/seven. If I weren't a comic, I'd probably be hanging around in comedy clubs anyway. At least I got paid to do it.

Although it made sense that my entire life revolved around comedy, sometimes it felt claustrophobic, like the walls were pressing in and I didn't have an escape hatch.

I dumped my cereal bowl in the sink and threw on some sweats. Ventured out into the condo hallway. It was early, especially for night crawlers, but I craved companionship, someone I could share my good feelings with, someone outside the business for a change. Someone halfway sane.

I listened at Erin's door. All quiet. I pressed my ear against the smooth, painted steel and its coolness tickled my skin. No sound, no vibration. I thought about knocking but didn't want to let my selfishness disrupt someone else's life. It wasn't right imposing on others, especially one of the only "normal" friends I had, no matter how needy I felt.

I told myself I'd count to twenty and if I didn't hear anything, I'd forget about it and leave.

Twenty seconds later, I left.

———

About noon, I grabbed the duffel bag of old notebooks and set off for the quiet of the club. I had a few hours before anyone showed up, and I knew I'd be able to get more work done without the temptations of the refrigerator, cable box, Xbox 360, and a shelf full of books I hadn't read yet. The only distracting thing at the club was the mountain of undone chores, but I was sure working on my act—no matter how difficult—would be more enticing than scrubbing the floors or alphabetizing the cleaning supplies in the storage room.

Coming to the club during the middle of the day on a Sunday gave me a different—and probably healthier—perspective on things. An art supply shop, a dry cleaners, an independent pet shop, and Lee's occupied one end of the L-shaped center, while an auto parts store, a bagel café, a dollar store, and a sofa gallery sandwiched us on the other side. Everywhere you looked, "regular" people milled about.

Families, kids, teenagers, old people. People from all demographics had business at the shopping center, in stark contrast to our clientele. Most of our customers were between the ages of twenty-one and forty-five. Sometimes we'd book an act that had been around awhile, and we'd get a smattering of people in their fifties. Otherwise, we seemed to attract a very narrow—and predictable—range of customers.

I sat in my car soaking up the diversity and realized it might do me good to get out more, at least in the light of day. There was so much I was missing. After a few minutes, my yen for diversity gave way to my desire to get some work done. I grabbed the duffel bag, hopped out, locked the car, and merged with the other errand-doers, however briefly, as I crossed the parking lot to the club.

As expected, no one else was there yet. Barely noon, most of the club's employees—the ones not still sleeping—were enjoying family time or off doing *their* errands.

I went directly to the office. Before starting on my material, I had some talent scouting to do, if you weren't too precise about the meaning of "talent." My search of the filing cabinets began with the letter R, for Rizzetti. Twice through the drawer yielded nothing. Evidently, Nathan had been right about him—pie in the sky only.

I shut the bottom drawer and moved to the top one. Dug out Nathan Borghat's DVD and played it. Unlike Skip, Nathan had some game. More polished than most, he had pretty good material and above average timing. He seemed more at ease behind the mic than he did on his back deck, and he displayed the ability to conjure up some mojo with the audience. All pluses. On the minus side, he rushed some lines and laughed a little too much at his own jokes. Both fixable.

I read through his resume. Lots of open mics, a couple of special guest spots a few years ago at some out-of-town clubs I'd never heard of. Hard to tell about the quality of those gigs. These days, everybody and their uncle opened comedy clubs. In bowling alleys, Thai restaurants, car washes. In coffee shops, bookstores, pizza joints, colleges, hospitals, retirement homes. No venue was safe from the comedy juggernaut. Few attracted the quality of comics we hired here, but that didn't stop the hopefuls from putting those so-called clubs on their resumes. Reading between the lines was a crucial skill for bookers and club owners. It only took getting burned a couple times by bogus credits before you learned to be a lot more circumspect.

I once asked Artie what he thought was the most important factor in a young comic's development. He hadn't hesitated: stage time. The bigger the audience the better, but as long as there were at least a few warm bodies, getting stage time, getting *experience*, was the key. And it correlated. If you took two guys the same age with about the same type of material, you could tell who had paid his dues versus the guy whose biggest performance was in front of a bunch of friends at a frat party.

I removed Nathan's DVD from the player and stuck it back in his file, wondering why Artie hadn't bothered to check him out in the flesh.

Enough procrastinating. Time to get to work. I unzipped the duffel bag and flipped it upside down, emptying the contents onto Artie's desk. The notebooks tumbled out in a heap and the racquetball bounced a few times, *thonk, thonk, thonk*. I caught it with my good hand before it rolled off the edge of the desk.

Lowering myself into Artie's chair, I assessed the jumble. On the cover of each notebook, I'd jotted down the starting and ending dates, so I was able to sort and stack them, newest on bottom, older ones on top. Some books spanned as little as a week, while others spanned months. My writing speed depended on how much in the zone I was and what else was going on in my life.

I opened a fresh notebook and flipped to the first page. At the top, I wrote today's date and the title, CHANNING HAYES, ACT II, in big, bold—optimistic—letters. My plan was to copy all the buried gems I found in the old notebooks into a spanking new notebook. From there, I'd work and rework the kernels into something usable. The beginning of a new phase in my comedy career.

I removed the oldest book from the top of the stack and turned to the beginning, eager to be transported into the past. I read the first few sentences anxiously, nervously, hoping the funny would jump off the page and hit me squarely between the eyes. After a few paragraphs, however, my reading slowed. I couldn't recall having written any of this. These were the words of someone else, in a different time, a different place. I mean, the material *seemed* like something I might have written, but I couldn't consciously remember having jotted down a single word.

I paged through the notebook, pausing here and there to read the entries. Some of the material seemed vaguely familiar, but there were no passages that had landed in my act. None I could point to and say, *aha, there's the bit about the crazed cabbie from Tuscaloosa and the midwife*. Most of the stuff I'd written in these notebooks over the years got altered, edited, revised, and massaged a dozen ways to Sunday before it was ready to go, but I was having a tough time identifying anything—even the slightest germ of an idea—that seemed recognizable. Worse, nothing seemed remotely funny to me. Would I really have to start from scratch?

I squeezed the racquetball in my left hand, hoping the familiar action might stimulate me. No sparks. I held it up to my nose and inhaled deeply, counting on the rubbery smell to get me going like it always had in the past. I smelled harder, then squeezed harder, but nothing loosened in my brain.

I stared at the blank notebook.

The moment of truth had arrived and all I could think about was how dry my mouth was. I left the office in search of something to quench my thirst. I grabbed a soda from the refrigerator behind the bar and guzzled half the can in one swig. Cleared my throat. Felt much better. Leaned my elbows on the bar and gazed across the room.

On the far wall, large black plastic letters spelled out *The Last Laff* in stylized script. Below them, a tag line read: *...Is The Best Laff.* A three-foot white Greek comedy mask hung next to the motto. When I'd suggested to Artie that we update things and ditch the creepy face, he said it's been good enough for thousands of years, why mess with it? I didn't recall seeing anything so cheesy at Reed's place.

I turned my attention to the dark stage. Closed my eyes and imagined how the audience would react after my first comeback show. Visualized all the patrons exploding into a standing O.

My eyes popped open. There wouldn't be any ovations—standing or otherwise—unless I got to work. Soda in hand, I started back to the office when something caught my eye. A shadowy figure, darker than the other shadows, seemed to sit in one of the chairs facing the stage. Front row center at the VIP table. I hadn't turned on the houselights when I came in; Artie was always on everyone's case to save money wherever we could. If you squinted right, the shadow looked like a person. "Hello," I called. No answer.

Then it hit me. The shadowy figure was a ventriloquist's dummy. Maybe Trafalgar had left his behind and Artie had found it and set it out, or maybe Artie had booked another ventriloquist for this week. I tried to talk myself into it, but something about the shadow's size and shape unnerved me. "Hello?"

Despite the soda, my mouth felt parched. My pulse hammered at my temples as the sick truth smacked me in the head. No ventriloquist would leave behind his dummy.

I dashed from behind the bar to the light panel, stage right. Hit the houselights and ran across the stage to the big white-taped X on the floor, center stage. There, in the front row, staring up at me with bulging dead eyeballs was Ryan Rizzetti, a second smile carved into his neck and a microphone rammed into his mouth.

I hit my mark, puking all over the X.

TWENTY-NINE

THE COPS DESCENDED ON The Last Laff like a flock of seagulls scrapping for old French fries on the boardwalk. They spent hours analyzing the crime scene from every angle. Meticulous and grim, they barked orders, took names, and drank coffee, plenty of coffee. I must have talked to four or five or ten different people—detectives, CSI-types, technicians, medical examiners. Anyone with a question seemed to seek me out. I lost track of time and of faces, anesthetized by the shock of Ryan's death. Freeman directed traffic, but I got the sense he couldn't run interference for me. I felt utterly alone in my nightmare and held no hope of awakening.

Artie arrived, face already scarlet. He fumed and sputtered, buzzed and fluttered, alighting everywhere in the club not restricted by police tape. Which didn't leave much beyond the front sidewalk. And even there, the rubberneckers—all those regular people taking care of their chores on a Sunday afternoon—gathered and gawked and gossiped, sending Artie into conniptions. Gangland-style slayings weren't good for business.

I had faded into the background, content to watch the stern-faced technicians shuttle back and forth between their vans and the club, when Artie grabbed my shirt and pulled me fifty feet out into the parking lot, past the police cars and evidence vans. "You know who did this, don't you?"

I knew whom he was going to finger, but I shrugged, not wanting to disagree with him and make him angrier. As if you could make a hornet angrier.

"That prick Reed. This Ryan guy goes there yesterday and to-day, wham, bam, thank you ma'am, he's dead. What other explanation is there?" As he spoke, his head swiveled this way and that, as if he were expecting to spot Reed returning to the scene of his crime.

"I don't know, Artie. Doesn't seem quite right to me."

"You kidding? First he kills J.J. after we discussed a long-term with him. Then he burns down my condo. Now he leaves a body in my club, as a giant 'fuck you.' He's after me, all right." Artie kept scanning the parking lot, searching for something or someone. Maybe just hoping the truth would drive up in a Chevy.

"If that's true, why kill Ryan? You didn't even know him," I said.

Artie's head stopped moving. "True. But Heather did. And Heather knows you. And you know me. Ergo." He brushed his hands together, like a baseball player knocking the dirt off. "So it all fits."

Obviously, the stress had affected Artie's powers of logic. I had a slightly different theory. In mine, Heather—more specifically, *screwing* Heather—was the thread tying J.J. and Ryan together. They'd both had sex with her and now they're dead. And who was psycho enough to go after the screwers? William Dempsey, giving new meaning to "overprotective father." I fervently hoped he realized my relationship with Heather was strictly platonic.

"Got nothing to say? Then I guess you agree with me," Artie said. "Tonight's a goner, pardon the wordplay. Hopefully, we'll be able to open soon. Take the night off and we'll regroup tomorrow."

Maybe we should take a month or two off. "Whatever you say. You're calling the shots here."

Artie jerked his head at the club. "I'm going back in. Make sure nothing happens to the liquor." He glowered at me as he left.

A few minutes later, I caught Freeman's eye from afar and waved him over. He stopped in his tracks, shrugged, then came my way. "What do you want?" he asked. A toothpick stuck out of his mouth.

"Got any suspects?" I asked.

He stared at me.

"Got anything?"

His expression remained impassive, except for a nose twitch. "Do I look like I'm holding a press conference?"

I remained silent.

Freeman glanced over his shoulder toward all the activity. Then turned to me and spoke in a low voice. "Little blood means he was killed elsewhere and moved here. Means the killer meant this as some kind of message," he said, tilting his head. "You understand this message?"

I shook my head. "Nope. Sorry." A lot of messages had come my way lately, all indecipherable.

He kept his eyes on mine for a couple of seconds, then continued. "Back door was jimmied. I thought you fixed that after the fire."

Leave it to Artie to try another cut-rate solution. I shrugged.

Freeman continued. "According to your partner, nothing seems to have been taken."

"He would know. He tracks every dollar bill and half-filled, watered-down bottle of scotch."

"Uh-huh. You say you knew Rizzetti?"

"Come on, we've already been through that." I'd told him, and every other cop I'd spoken to, about his relationship to Heather and about my talking to him. And I told him I'd "heard" Ryan visited Reed at the CCC. However, I left out the part about Artie stalking Reed with the intent to disembowel him. No need to bog Freeman down with an abundance of details. "I also told you to check out William Dempsey. He's gone off the deep end, and according to his wife, he's got a gun and he's dangerous."

"Yeah, we're looking for him. You really think he killed his daughter's boyfriend?"

I shrugged. "Isn't that a universal theme? Father kills unworthy suitor."

"Maybe in the Middle Ages." The toothpick danced in his mouth. "What about the condo? Why would Dempsey torch it if all he was after were those who had 'despoiled Heather's honor'?"

"Who knows? Latent anger? Attack on Artie or me for encouraging Heather to do stand-up? He never approved of that 'comedy shit,' as he called it."

Freeman shook his head. "And LaTasha James?"

"Wrong place, wrong time." I exhaled. "Shit. I don't know, Freeman. You're the detective. That's why you get the big bucks."

"Uh-huh." Freeman plucked the toothpick out of his mouth, then repositioned it securely. "J.J. and Heather ever hook up?"

Time to come clean. "You know, I've been thinking about that. And it wouldn't surprise me if they had. In fact, I think I remember J.J. saying something about meeting up with her the night before his first show." My heart pounded.

Freeman stared at me. I didn't think he needed a polygraph to know what was going on. "I should take you in and turn you over to Perlstein. Let him interrogate you. You think *I'm* a hardass?"

I held my palms up. "That was days before J.J. got killed. I'm sure it had absolutely nothing to do with it."

"We're friends. But don't fuck with me. Heather Dempsey is mixed up in this, and we both know it. She might not have killed J.J., but she knows what the hell's going on. Better than we do, that's for sure."

"I guess we can ask her when we find her."

"Uh-huh," he said, eying me as if *I* were a suspect. I sure hoped he was the forgiving type. "One more thing."

"Yeah?"

"Bad things keep happening on your turf. A logical man might think someone had it in for you guys. Watch your back, buddy. Don't want to find the corpse of Channing Hayes decomposing somewhere. Whose balls would I break then?"

———

I swung by Nathan's about eight, hoping he'd had time to recover from the detectives' thorough interrogation. When he answered the door, he looked exhausted, as if he'd just gone twelve rounds with Mike Tyson. At least his ears still seemed intact.

"Shit. What do you want?" He wore khakis and a black T-shirt with the words *Dead Hed* printed in pink.

"Had a few questions I wanted to ask. I tried calling." I'd phoned a dozen times and he'd never answered. If I knew he would have answered his door so willingly, I'd have come over sooner.

"A few questions? I'm all questioned out. Sorry." He started to close the door on me, but I put my palm squarely in the middle of the door and braced my arm. Nathan glanced at my face, saw I wasn't planning on leaving until I talked with him, and his whole body sagged as if he'd been suddenly filleted. "Fuck. Whatever." He stepped back and I stepped in.

Nathan shuffled into the kitchen and flopped into the nearest chair. A couple cans of Pabst rested on the table. He eyed them, but didn't pick one up. "Ask. Ask your questions."

I eased into a chair across from him. "You have any idea who would kill Ryan?"

"No."

"No enemies? No crazy clients? No stiffed bookies?"

"No. No. No." Nathan shook his head once with each no.

"He say anything about Heather's father, William Dempsey? He been around here? Maybe he called?"

Nathan's face puckered. "Huh? You think Heather's father killed Ryan? Oh shit."

"Had he come by looking for Ryan?" I asked.

"Not that I know. I've never met him. Or talked to him. Did Ryan do something to Heather?"

"I don't have any idea." A thousand questions pinballed around in my head. "What did you tell the cops?"

"Nothing." His eyes flitted to the beer cans and back to me. "I mean I just answered their questions."

"When did you last see him?"

He pursed his lips. "Friday. Friday night."

"You didn't see him at all yesterday?"

Nathan shook his head, shot another glance at the beer cans. Moistened his lips. "Nope. Not at all. But I went out last night, so he might have been here. I don't know."

Nobody knew much—that was the problem. Ryan's visit to Reed yesterday didn't exactly jibe with my William Dempsey-as-murderer theory, and the mismatch had lodged in my gut. I needed an explanation that fit. "You have any idea why Ryan went to see Gerry Reed yesterday afternoon?"

"What? Ryan knows Gerry?" Nathan shifted in his chair. A few beads of perspiration appeared on his forehead. "I didn't know that."

"I thought you and Skip took Ryan to a CCC party. Isn't that where he first met Heather? That's what you told me."

Nathan didn't answer. He swallowed hard, and I could practically hear the gears grinding in his head, evaluating lie after lie until he came to one he thought might fly. Finally, a candidate surfaced. "Reed wasn't there. At the party. Reed wasn't there that night."

Lame. "But Ryan still would have known who he was, right? I mean, you knew him and Heather knew him. You said Ryan was thinking about doing stand-up. Reed's name must have come up once or twice."

"Maybe." Nathan squinted as he tried to noodle it through. "So?"

"So why do you think he might have gone to talk to Reed? About his act?"

Nathan snorted. "No fucking way. I told you. The only place Ryan was funny was in his own head. He didn't even have an act. He was just trying to stay close to Heather."

A thought came to me. Ryan seemed pretty hot as he marched into the CCC. And Ambyr had pegged him as the jealous type. "Was Reed sleeping with Heather?"

Nathan flushed. "What? That can't be true. No. Not Heather. No, no, no, no, no. She wasn't like that."

"Like what?" I asked. I'd hit a nerve with the jealousy angle, but it wasn't Ryan's jealousy in play here. Nathan was wrestling with the green monster.

"Heather wouldn't sleep with Reed. He's too…slimy." He made a face a five-year-old might think looked slimy. But there was something behind it. Like maybe he did think Reed was involved somehow.

I leaned closer and spoke softly. "You like Heather, don't you?"

The color on Nathan's face deepened. "No. I mean, sure, but not like that. What, you think this is sixth grade? I told you, we went out once and we didn't really click very well."

"Maybe you were jealous of Ryan. Maybe you thought it would be easier to cozy up to Heather without Ryan in the picture."

Nathan's mouth opened and he stared at me, slack-jawed. Blinked fast. I was just making it up, not believing for a second Nathan had the stones to kill someone. Had I hit on something? "Should I call my detective buddy and let him know what I think? I'm sure he wouldn't mind coming back out here and hauling you in to interrogate you *properly*."

His head moved back and forth, mouth opening and closing like a beached carp. "No. No, don't do that. I…" His eyes closed.

I reached across the table and grabbed his wrist with my good hand. His eyes popped open, filled with confusion. I squeezed once, then eased up. "Tell me what's going on," I said through clenched teeth. I'd stomached enough bullshit and evasion.

"Don't hurt me. Please."

I had no intention of hurting him. But he didn't have to know that. "Tell me what's going on with Heather, goddamnit."

Nathan tried to shake me off, but I held his hand down on the table, applying only as much pressure as I needed to keep his attention. He began to cry, slowly at first, then faster, until the tears began to drip down his cheeks. I released his wrist, but he didn't let up. In a small, thin voice he said, "Okay. Okay. You're right, I haven't told the truth. But *I'm* not going to tell you about Heather. You can ask her yourself."

THIRTY

I DROVE WHILE NATHAN sat shotgun issuing directions. He wouldn't tell me where we were going, preferring to pretend he was Jason Bourne or some other spook on the way to a clandestine rendezvous. For all I knew, maybe this *was* some kind of international spy caper, and I was the unwitting stooge with some microfiche hidden up my ass.

He took me south through Reston, then east on Route 50 into the heart of the City of Fairfax. It was the same Route 50 I had taken to get to Heather's apartment in Chantilly, ten miles west, with the same agglomeration of fast food joints and big box stores and car dealerships. One day, all of Northern Virginia will be overrun with wall-to-wall 7-Elevens and McWendyKings. And everyone will weigh 350 pounds and wobble when they walk.

"Right up ahead," Nathan said, pointing to the driveway beyond a Capital One Bank branch.

I pulled Rex into the lot of the Eastwinds Motel and parked under a large neon sign fashioned in the shape of a captain's wheel.

The sign had been erected in an era when neon was in vogue, and if someone had bothered to maintain it, the twenty-foot art-deco wheel might still have retained some kitsch value. Now it was a tangle of broken metal rods and impotent glass tubes. A roadway eyesore. I killed the engine.

"Heather's here?" A small wooden VACANCY sign hung on rusted metal hooks outside the motel office. From the look of the place, I doubted the motel even owned a NO VACANCY sign.

"Yeah." Nathan's eyes darted around.

"And how do you know this?" Besides mine, there were exactly three cars in the parking lot. None were Heather's. None had been manufactured in this millennium.

"I followed Ryan here."

I maneuvered in my seat to face Nathan head on. "You followed Ryan? Why?"

"He was acting strange. Wasn't that worried about Heather. I figured something was up." Nathan didn't meet my eyes; instead, he stared out the window at the peeling paint on the motel walls.

"When?"

"When did I follow him?"

"Yes," I said, raising my voice. If I thought punching Nathan in the face would have expedited things, I would have.

"Friday night."

"After I talked to you?" I asked. Nathan had been well on his way to oblivion when I'd seen him in the afternoon. I wondered how much more he'd had to drink before he followed Ryan.

Nathan nodded, like a bobblehead doll on busted springs.

"Why didn't you ask Ryan about it?"

Nathan laughed, but it wasn't because I'd amused him. "Ryan wasn't the type to share his life. We were roommates, not friends. Especially after he started dating Heather."

Another round with the green monster. "So you and Ryan and Heather never hung out together?"

A biting laugh. "Hardly."

"Okay. Let's get to it. Come on." We got out of the car. "Which room is hers?"

"Second from the end." Nathan pointed to the right.

We walked across the lot, me leading the way, Nathan trailing a step behind. Probably so he wouldn't have to talk to me. Up close, the motel looked even seedier. When we got to the door, Nathan took up a position two yards behind me, out of the line of fire. Some secret agent man. I banged on the door with my fist. No answer. I banged again. "Heather. It's Channing. Open the door."

I listened for the sound of a TV, for the sound of movement, for the sound of the deadbolt sliding back, but the only noises I heard came from the cars whizzing by on the road behind us. I wasn't expecting a tearful reunion, considering Heather hadn't returned any of my million phone calls. But I was expecting at least an acknowledgment of my concern and an explanation of her disappearance, however crazy and convoluted it might be. I wasn't expecting her to hide in a ramshackle motel room from me while I pounded on the door and pleaded to let me help her.

I pounded again. "Heather. Open up. It's Channing. I'm not leaving until I talk to you, so you might as well open this door." I glanced along the cracked concrete walkway fronting the rooms. Not a sign of life anywhere. What this place lacked in ambience, it made up for in utter desolation.

I turned to Nathan, who hadn't said a word since we'd walked across the parking lot. "Do you think she's in there?"

He shrugged. "Maybe she went out for a bite to eat."

"What, no room service?"

Nathan gave me the dreaded blank stare, not sure if I was serious. I definitely needed to work on my material.

I knocked twenty times and still no one came to the door.

"There's no car here," Nathan said.

He was right; the closest vehicle was twenty yards away. "Come on. Let's talk to the desk clerk."

A bell jingled overhead when I opened the door to the motel office, and a man rose from behind a wood-paneled counter topped with mottled Formica. About sixty years old, he sported a full head of cotton-white hair and wore a three-piece pinstripe suit. The knot of his shiny red-patterned tie bobbed as he spoke. "Good evening, gentlemen. How may I help you?" The slightest trace of an English accent gave the whole scene a surreal quality. Maybe the Ancient Mariner had retired from his life on the seas and was now living out his days in this dive.

"Good evening. We're looking for the woman in the next-to-last unit. Heather Dempsey," I said, hooking my thumb over my shoulder in the vague direction of her room.

"That would be Unit 11." He smiled, displaying a rack of perfect teeth. Must not have grown up in England. "Are you friends of hers?"

"Yes, we are. My name's Channing Hayes. This is Nathan Borghat." I nodded at Nathan, and he took a small step forward, but still hung back, like a three-year-old hiding behind the folds of his mommy's dress.

"Okay. Please wait a moment." The clerk punched in the numbers on the phone, a desk model with a pig's-tail cord. The smile remained on his face while he waited for someone to pick up. After a moment, he stuck the phone back in its cradle. "I'm sorry. There's no answer."

"Did you see her leave?" I asked.

"Actually, I've never seen her at all. My son checked her in on…" He flipped through an old-fashioned guest register on the counter. "Well, that would be last Monday."

"She's been here almost a week and you haven't seen her?"

"My son owns the place. I simply work here on the weekends. And I don't recall seeing anyone come or go from that room, either yesterday or today," he said. His smile didn't falter. "Sorry."

I pulled out my wallet and flipped through some pictures until I came to one of Lauren and Heather together. Set it on the counter so he could see. "She look familiar?"

The old guy bent over and squinted at the photo. "I'm afraid I need my glasses." He reached under the counter and came out with a hard-shell case. Put on his specs and adjusted them on his nose. "Ah. That's better." He bent over the photo again. "My, what attractive women. Are they twins?"

"Sisters. Have you seen her?" With my pinky, I pointed to Heather.

"Hmm. No. I would remember. Most of our guests are… well, they don't look like this." He lifted his head and removed his glasses. "I'm sorry, gentlemen. Shall I leave a message?"

I wasn't going anywhere until I spoke with Heather. "How long will she be, uh, staying with you?" I asked.

The clerk stared at me, perhaps wondering if I was trying to pull some kind of scam. I pasted trustworthy on my face and stood up straighter. He leafed through his logbook again. "What did you say her name was?"

"Heather Dempsey."

He shut the register quickly and his smile vanished. In its place, a pointed scowl took root. "I'm afraid there's been a mistake. We have no Heather Dempsey registered."

I glanced at Nathan, who'd come up beside me. He shrugged. Was he trying to put one over on me? Taking me on some kind of wild goose chase? I turned back to the clerk, making sure I covered all my bases before torturing Nathan for info again. "Maybe she used her married name, Rizzetti." Out of the corner of my eye, I saw Nathan wince.

The clerk's tension eased. "Ah yes, of course. Paid through Wednesday. Cash too, which is unusual in this day and age. A nice change of pace, actually, to see young folk take some fiscal responsibility rather than run up their debts. Commendable."

I started to leave, but threw a shocked expression on my face. "Nathan, I hope Heather remembered to bring enough insulin. You know what happens if she forgets to take it."

Nathan opened his mouth, but I laid it on thicker before he could speak. "Oh my, she might have gone into shock. I tried calling her on her cell phone, but she didn't answer. Oh no." I put panic in my eyes and ramped up my breathing as I crowded the counter. "Maybe we should call 911?"

The flustered clerk's head swiveled around, taking in the small office, me and Nathan, and the parking lot beyond. "Yes, of course, 911." He reached for the phone.

I grabbed his arm. "Unless…"

"Yes?"

"Well, you could open the door. I've got her spare kit right here," I said, patting my pocket. "If she's in shock, we'll have her fixed up in no time."

The clerk blinked twice. "Yes, of course. Straight away."

The three of us hustled to Unit 11. With trembling hands, the clerk unlocked the door and flung it open. He stepped back and I rushed in. The covers on the bed were in a jumble. The dresser drawers were pulled out—empty. I ran to the bathroom. Aside from a couple of damp towels on the floor, it was empty, too.

Once again, Heather had taken her act on the road.

THIRTY-ONE

I DROPPED NATHAN OFF and headed home. When I got there, a newscaster's baritone leaked out into the hallway from Erin's slightly open door. My pulse quickened; I'd had enough surprises lately. "Hello?" I said, knocking and pushing the door open a bit farther. An image flashed into my mind of Erin on the floor, naked and spread-eagled, a pool of blood gathering beneath her charred body. I shook it off and stepped inside her condo. The TV played to an empty room.

From the back of the apartment, Erin called out. "Channing? That you? Just a second."

My whole body relaxed and I started breathing again. "Okay," I called back.

A moment later, she came rushing down the hall and engulfed me in a hug. "Are you okay? I heard about the murder on the news. How awful."

Her hair smelled of lavender and she radiated heat like a red dwarf in a nearby solar system. I backed out of the embrace. "I'm okay. Ryan Rizzetti, however, is not."

Erin picked the remote off the couch and muted the TV. "Did you know him?" Her brown eyes searched mine for the pain she thought I was denying. Oddly, after the initial jolt of finding the body had worn off, I hadn't been that shaken. Yet. I knew it would hit me in a day or two. Maybe after I located Heather and found out what was going on my emotions would cut loose.

"Yeah, I knew him. He was dating Heather."

For a second, Erin seemed blank. Then a spark of recognition ignited. "Lauren's sister, right? Oh, that's so horrible. Have you spoken to her? How is she taking it?" She sunk to the couch and nodded to the space next to her. I dragged a chair from the dining table so I could face her while we talked.

"I … uh, I haven't spoken to her." I swallowed and my blood flushed cold for a second. "She's been missing for a week or so." I launched into the details of my search for the elusive Heather, answering Erin's questions along the way. When finished, I leaned back in the chair and crossed my arms. My exhaustion was catching up to me.

"Wow. I can see why you're upset. This isn't fair, Channing. Not one bit." She sounded a little like Lauren. Not the voice, but the compassion behind the words.

"Like my dear mother used to say, 'life isn't a-fair, it's more like a-circus.'" I waited a beat for Erin to stop wincing. "As you can imagine, everyone at the club's terrified. First J.J.'s killed. Then someone burns down Artie's townhouse. And now this."

"Sounds like someone's got it in for you and Artie. Make any enemies lately?"

I explained about Reed's attempts to sign J.J. and buy us out. On the surface, everything pointed to Reed. But I still wasn't buying it.

"What do you think?" She cocked her head to the side, as if she were listening to some unspoken dialogue below the surface.

"I think Dempsey's involved somehow. Going after Heather's lovers. Making some kind of statement or sending some kind of message. Power, control, leave my daughter alone. Maybe he's trying to tell her something."

"Like what?"

"I have no freaking clue." I glanced around and noticed a few books open on the coffee table. Had they been there all along? "Am I interrupting you? Were you working?"

"Yes and yes. But it's okay," she said. "I know how rough this must be and I want you to know you can interrupt me any time you need to talk. Friend to friend. Okay?"

I found myself nodding. "Okay. Thanks. That means a lot to me."

"What are friends for?" She held my eyes for a few seconds, then broke away. "What are you going to do now?"

"Keep looking for Heather. Stay away from Heather's father."

A look of fear passed over Erin's face. "You and Heather?"

I held up a hand. "No, no. We weren't 'dating.' I've been helping her with her act. Ever since Lauren…since the accident, she's had to develop a solo act. I've been her coach, that's all."

"Heather's father should be grateful for that," she said.

"You don't know him. He blames me for Lauren's death."

This time, it wasn't fear on Erin's face, it was anger. "How dare he? It wasn't your fault. Some nutjob ran you guys off the road. That's who he should be pursuing. Not you."

"Yeah, well, the cops investigated and their conclusions were 'inconclusive.' No one really knows what happened that night," I said. "But I'll be sure to tell William Dempsey who he should be gunning for the next time I see him."

Erin's eyes flashed for a second, then her head dropped.

"Sorry. Didn't mean to be flip. It's just hard to talk about sometimes. Frustrating not remembering, you know?"

Her head bobbed up and there was something in her face. "Forget it. Just make sure nothing happens to you, okay?"

"Trust me, I'll do my best." I yawned and hoisted myself out of my chair.

We said our goodnights and I crossed the hallway to my condo, Erin's deadbolt clicking shut behind me.

I peeled off my clothes and flopped into bed, but couldn't find deep sleep. Too many unpleasant thoughts and unformed theories clattering around in my fatigued brain, like dirty, jagged stones in a rock tumbler.

I drifted in and out. During each period of wakefulness, I tried to connect the dots using the information I knew, hoping the resulting vector would lead me in the right direction. J.J. and Ryan had both been murdered. Ever since I'd found Ryan's body, I'd been going on the assumption that Heather was the common link. Her disappearance roughly coincided with the beginning of all the trouble, and she'd slept with both victims. Plus, she'd gotten a gun. But what if Heather wasn't the link, what if she were one of the data points? What if J.J, Ryan, and Heather had all been targeted because of their stand-up comedy?

Technically, Ryan wasn't a stand-up comic. But according to Nathan, he held aspirations, however ephemeral. Of course, this "theory" begat a slew of questions: Who wanted to kill comics? Why? And were other comics in danger? I tried to wrap my head around these questions and come up with a more detailed explanation, at least one that made sense. Unfortunately, nothing popped out at me. The more I thought about it, the more I thought I was weaving fantastic tales from the whole cloth of speculation.

After two hours of fitful sleep, I slipped out of bed and padded to the living room. Retrieved a photo album from the bookcase and returned to bed.

I folded my pillow and jammed it under my neck. Got comfortable. Lauren had arranged this album, merging our pictures. Two lives becoming one. Some were from my childhood, some were from hers, and there were some from our lives together. A "hers, mine, and ours" theme. I flipped it open to the first two facing pages. A baby picture of me "smiled" at a baby picture of Lauren.

I paged through the album. My mother and me in front of some theater in New York. Lauren, Justin, and Heather at her family's mountain cabin—where Lauren and I spent a great weekend once—holding fishing poles. Lauren and me downtown, horsing around on the Capitol steps. Until recently, I'd never believed someone could feel so happy and so sad at the same time.

I gently closed the album and turned off the light, praying Lauren would visit me in my dreams.

THIRTY-TWO

THE RINGING TELEPHONE SNAPPED my slumber like a dry twig, and I awoke, eyes drawn to the photo album on my night table. A shot of disappointment hit me as I realized I hadn't dreamt of Lauren. I ran my hand across my face trying to dislodge the cobwebs, wondering what fresh hell was breaking loose now.

"Yeah?" I mumbled into the phone. Not all the cobwebs had dissolved.

"Channing? It's Skip. I need to talk to you, man." Skip wasn't half the morning man I was. If he was already awake, something big must be brewing.

"Okay. Shoot." I dug my elbows into the bed and raised myself into a sitting position.

"Can we do this in person? I...I...think th-th-that would be better."

Shit. "Okay. Where are you?"

"Don't worry. I made it convenient for you. I'm at the Juice & Java right down the block from your place."

"See you in five." I hung up and wiped my face again. When this was all over, I needed a vacation.

I took a leak, threw on some clothes, ran a comb through my hair, and banged through the door. Arrived at the coffee shop almost before Skip had hung up his phone. He leaned against the wall out front, sipping something from a neon yellow cup, and greeted me with a wiggly-fingered wave. "Morning, dude," he said. "Sorry to roust you out of bed so early."

I shrugged. "No sweat. Ty watching Artie?"

"Yeah. I've got the evening shift," Skip said, small smile on his lips.

"Good. So what's the problem?"

He nodded at the door. "Want to get something first? Go on, I'll get us a table."

I went inside and ordered a small plain coffee, regular roast, black, and survived the barista's reproachful look without giving her any lip. Coffee in hand, I found Skip sitting at a table inspecting its metalwork lattice. He seemed pretty tense, but sometimes it was hard to tell what was going on in his spastic mind.

"Okay. We've got our coffees. We're talking in person. Now what's the big deal?" I asked, taking a sip. The coffee was worth putting up with the surly help. Maybe I should go back in and get a muffin to quiet my growling stomach.

"Nathan called me last night. He's a total, complete mess." Skip glanced around the outdoor seating area. People occupied some of the other tables, but no one seemed interested in our conversation.

"I would be too, considering what happened."

Skip swallowed some of his brew. "Yeah, I guess. But he wasn't just sad. He said he felt guilty."

"Guilty? About what?" I thought I'd cornered the market on guilt.

"You name it. He spouted off for about an hour. Rambling, crying. Like I said, it wasn't pretty."

I swallowed a mouthful of coffee. "Details. I need some details." Skip had a habit of glossing over salient facts. I'd been trying to get him to put more details into his act to help the audiences relate better.

"Oh, right. Sorry." A sheepish grin. "He feels guilty about Heather's disappearance. He told me about following Ryan to the motel and taking you there. He thinks that if he'd told you sooner, you would have been able to talk with her. Get her to stop running around. He's worried something bad might have happened to her and it's his fault."

"That thought crossed my mind, too. But I didn't say anything to him about it."

Skip shrugged. "He also feels guilty about Ryan's death for the same reason. If he'd confronted him about keeping Heather's whereabouts a secret, the whole thing would have been exposed and maybe he'd still be alive."

I nodded and sipped some more coffee. Or maybe Dempsey just would have gotten to him sooner. Who knew? Did logic really apply with lunatics? "How well do you know Nathan?"

Skip stared off into the distance. Across the street, a couple men in business suits, carrying identical briefcases, walked in lock-step away from us. He watched them for a moment, then turned back to me. "We were closer before I started at your place. When we hung around the CCC, we'd see each other every two or three days. Go to shows at other places some. He was a 'comedy buddy.'"

Another rookie to pal around with, try new stuff on. You know how it is. A bunch of young, struggling guys who all thought we were the next Chris Rock."

I knew. The comedy scene reminded me of an aquarium. A bunch of fish thrown together where only the strongest, most cunning, fastest, or most adaptable survived. Those who did got a chance to swim in progressively bigger tanks. "Heather hang out with you guys, too? Nathan told me he went out with her once. That sound about right?"

Skip squinted. "Yeah. She wasn't interested in anything more. And boy, he kept trying. Was always coming on to her, asking her out. She was polite turning him down, usually made some kind of joke about it. Hell, we all wanted to go out with Heather. I mean, who wouldn't? Hot, funny, bubbly. Friendly." He stopped abruptly, glanced at me, then swallowed. "Hey, you know how it is among comics, r-r-right?"

"I thought she was dating Brooks Spellman back then."

Skip nodded. "Yeah, she was. I didn't say we all asked her out, I'm saying we all *wanted* to."

"Who all?"

"I don't know. Nathan. Ryan. This guy named Augustin. Couple other guys. Me, I guess, although I never would ask her. Didn't think Brooks would find it too cool."

"And he didn't mind when Nathan asked her out?"

Skip shrugged. "She only went out once with Nathan. Brooks probably didn't even know. And then there was the accident." The way he said the word "accident" made it sound like it had affected him somehow.

"What about 'the accident'?" An edge crept into my voice.

He played with his cup, turning it in circles. "You know, we were all at Spanky's that night. At the show. Celebrating Heather and Lauren's success, right along with them and everyone else. Drinking and toasting and carrying on. You don't remember any of it, do you?"

I shook my head. Thankfully, my memory of that night had been taken from me.

"They absolutely killed. I remembered Heather being so excited about their future prospects. She told me a booker from New York had been in the audience and handed her his card after the show. Wanted her to tell him when their first New York show was so he could make sure to attend."

I hadn't heard any of this before. Then, I would have been so proud. Now, I guess it didn't really matter.

"After the accident, Heather seemed different. Totally understandable. Losing your sister like that…" He chewed on his upper lip for a second. "She stopped hanging out with us. Stopped going to other clubs. Sort of dropped out of the scene for a while. Of course…"

"What?"

"All of us kind of went our separate ways. I came to work for you guys, and Artie practically forbade me to ever go back there. Brooks went out west, Nathan took a 'break' for a while—which he's still on, by the way. I never heard from Augustin again. It was almost like that accident ended a chapter in our lives. I guess we all realized our mortality through the accident, or something. Kinda weird, huh?"

I didn't answer him, gazed off into the distance. The accident had been the most disastrous event of my life, sending me into a downward spiral I might never escape from. To think it had affected others profoundly, aside from the Dempseys and me, was hard to grasp. I sipped coffee and struggled to keep my feelings in check. After a few minutes, it was time to get to the crux of the matter and find out why Skip was so torqued.

"I understand Nathan's upset. But why are you telling me this? And so early in the morning, too."

Skip's eyes grew large. "I've never seen him like this and I'm worried. He's upset about Ryan. And he feels guilty about him and Heather. To top it all off, he's afraid."

"Of what?" Did Dempsey have some reason to go after him? Had he been fooling around with Heather behind his roommate's back?

"You, boss. He's afraid of you."

"What? Why should he be afraid of me?" Maybe I hadn't treated him very well, but I never threatened him.

"He thinks you're mad at him."

I rolled my eyes. "I am. He's a little twerp. But I'd never hurt him."

"Yeah. I think he knows you wouldn't ever hurt him physically. I think he's worried about you screwing with his career to get back at him for what he did."

"Who does he think I am, the second coming of Swifty Lazar? How could I screw with his career, even if I wanted to?" I pointed at Skip. "Which I don't by the way."

Skip held up his hands. "I know, I know. I told him you weren't like that, but he's flipped out. Not listening to reason. He thinks you're going to blackball him around town. I told him it doesn't work that way. He just cussed a blue streak."

"What do you want me to do? It doesn't sound like me talking to him is a good idea."

Skip took a couple of quick breaths. "There's something else. He asked me if I knew Reed had been sleeping with Heather."

"What?" I tried to keep my voice down, but failed.

He looked puzzled. "Nathan said *you* told him Reed and Heather were sleeping together."

"I never said that. I asked him if *he thought* they were sleeping together. I have no idea who Heather's been sleeping with." Except for J.J. and Ryan, that is.

Skip leaned in and whispered. "Here's the thing, boss. I think they might have been. Right after she broke up with Brooks. I got some weird vibes. In fact, Reed might have been the reason they broke up."

I ran my good hand through my hair. "Christ. Did you tell that to Nathan?"

He swallowed, then nodded. "Not in so many words, but I didn't deny it either. I thought you confirmed it for him. You got to know Heather pretty good. I figured if you told him, it must be true."

I closed my eyes. The thought of Heather and Reed together turned my stomach, and it wasn't so much the fact he was about thirty-five years older. It was the fact he was a smarmy backstabber who had it in for Artie. I opened my eyes and caught Skip staring at me. "You really think they were doing it?" I asked.

"Yeah. Maybe. I don't know." He held his palms up and shrugged. "What matters is that Nathan thinks it happened. And he thinks it might still be going on. He said something about going to see Reed and it didn't sound like he was in a talkative mood."

Skip tapped his cup on the table as he spoke. "If he loses his temper there, Reed will squash him like a beetle. Nathan's not the sturdiest of guys. You've got to help save him from himself. Please?"

I exhaled. Things just kept getting better and better. Had my conversation with Nathan sent him down the path of his own destruction? Shit and double shit. "Okay. I'll talk to Reed. Give him a heads-up." I rose and crushed the cup in my hand. "Don't tell Artie where I've gone. I don't think he'd like me helping his sworn enemy. Not one bit."

THIRTY-THREE

AFTER CIRCLING THE BLOCK four times, I found a parking spot with a view of the Capitol Comedy Club's garish front door and settled in to wait. I'd called the club and the recording said the business office opened at noon. I figured Reed would be along shortly thereafter. Prick or not, he had the reputation of being a hard worker.

I'd stopped and picked up a meatball sub for brunch and ate it in the car. Washed it down with a lukewarm Sprite left over from who knows when. I could still detect a trace of carbonation, so it couldn't have been rolling around on the floorboards for more than a year or two. People strolled by the club, but no one stopped. Most turned into the café where Artie had been conducting *his* stakeout the other day.

Several times, I'd picked up my phone to call Freeman and fill him in on my adventure with Nathan and catching a whiff of Heather's trail, but each time I hung up before dialing. After I talked to Reed, I hoped to be able to give him more. Much more.

I had the feeling everything was going to fall into place, and I'd be able to deliver the perpetrator of this mess to Freeman all wrapped up in a bow. And if wishes were horses, beggars would ride.

I finished my sub, balled the wrapper up, and tossed it into the back. One of these days, I'd either clean Rex out or trade him in for a newer—or at least cleaner—model. Yeah, right. I wouldn't get rid of Rex until the last mechanic familiar with a rotary engine died.

I brushed a few crumbs from my shirt and pictured Heather and Reed naked, doing the dirty deed. I forced the image from my mind quickly—I wanted my food to stay down. I knew what she saw in him. Power, wealth, experience. Things she probably wasn't finding dating within her own demographic. Maybe that's why she went after J.J. He possessed those things, with a little fame thrown in as a bonus. Very enticing to an ambitious doe-eyed comic.

I wondered if Lauren would have done the same, if she hadn't fallen in love with me. It only took me a nanosecond to arrive at my conclusion: no way. Though they were sisters and bore an uncanny physical resemblance to each other, inside they were made of different stuff. Heather was insecure and flighty, Lauren confident and solid. Made you think about the whole nature-nurture debate. What had happened to Heather that she turned out so unlike her sister? Lauren often wondered about it, wishing she could have done something to even the score for Heather. But real life isn't like that; you can't decide to give your sister a few ounces of your self-control in exchange for a teaspoon of her ditziness.

Reed's arrival interrupted my philosophical musings. He strode past the café and, after a fleeting glance over his shoulder, yanked open the orange door and entered his club. I gave him a few minutes to get settled, then hopped out of my car and followed him in. There was no bouncer or ticket taker to stop me, no receptionist screening visitors. I followed a professionally lettered sign—Business Office, with an arrow—down a long corridor, running shoes silent on the carpeted floor. I'd almost reached his office when I heard him say hello to someone on the phone.

I slowed, then changed my mind and picked up speed. Burst through the open door and stood before his desk, hands on hips. His eyes went wide and he barked into the phone, "Gotta run. Call you back in a few." He set the phone down and a shit-eating grin grew on his face. "Well, well, well. Mr. Hayes. Finally come to talk turkey." He motioned with his hand. "Have a seat. *Mi casa es su casa.*"

I nodded and lowered myself into his visitor chair. "Morning, Reed. I was in the neighborhood, thought I'd drop by." He seemed at ease, as if he had people barging in on him all the time.

Reed kept the smile fueled. "I've got no beef with you. In fact, I hear you're a stand-up guy, no pun intended. It's your partner who rubs me the wrong way. Has for many years now."

"What is it with you guys anyhow? Seems a little…childish."

He shook his head and waved his hand in the air. *Never mind.* "Did he send you to tell me he's decided to reconsider my offer?"

I laughed. "No, not quite."

"Well, he should. It makes perfect sense. I just bought Laughs-A-Go-Go in College Park. And Improv Central in Annapolis. Got my eyes on something in Germantown. I've got a growing thing here, and I don't have to tell you what that means, as far as establishing a brand. Cutting costs. Getting more bang from my promotional buck." He paused, opened a desk drawer, and pulled out a nail file. Began working on the fingers of his left hand. The scraping sound irritated my nerve endings. "I'm not sure you understood my full proposal. Despite the spate of, uh, bad luck you've experienced lately, I still want to buy you out."

"Yeah, you've made that clear."

His eyes twinkled. "Yes, but what you don't understand is I'd keep you on to run the place."

"Like employees?" I asked. "Or more like indentured servants?"

Reed chuckled under his breath. "More like partners, I'm thinking. You'd be doing the same thing you're doing now, except without all the stress and risk. You guys are doing a pretty good job out there, but it can be taken to the next level. With the proper executive management and critical mass that Capitol Comedy can provide, The Last Laff would flourish." He stopped filing and eyed me. "And the price was a good one, despite what Artie thinks. I'm a hard-charging guy, but I'm fair."

I stared at him, not sure whether to make nice or tear him a new one.

"So what do you say?" he asked, predatory smile nudged aside by a smarmy look.

"Frankly, I didn't come here to talk about your offer."

Reed's brow furrowed. "Really? Then why *are* you here?"

"Nathan Borghat and Heather Dempsey," I said, in a voice void of inflection.

His face tightened. "What about them?"

"Nathan been by?"

"I haven't seen him in months. Why?" Reed examined me, as if he thought I was pulling a fast one. I ignored his question.

"What about Heather? Seen her lately?"

"No. She involved with Ryan's death?" he asked.

I locked eyes with him, trying to bore deep within to read the truth, the unfiltered truth. "Don't know. She's missing. What do *you* know about Ryan's death?"

His head jerked back. "Nothing. Told the cops the same thing. I know just what was in the news. He got killed at your place. Nasty, I bet."

"What did he want the other day?" My tone had intensified.

Reed tilted his head. "What do you mean?"

"He came to see you. What about?"

"How'd you find out? Cops tell you?" He stared at me.

I didn't answer. No need to tell Reed about Artie's stalking. World War III could wait.

Reed eyed me, head tilted as he fiddled with his nail file. "No, I bet it wasn't the cops. Must have been Ryan."

"What did he want?" I asked.

"Nothing. Wanted to know about some of Heather's friends. From back when she hung out here. That's all." His eyes flitted about, finally settling on a mug of pens on his desk.

"What did you tell him?"

He faced me. Sighed. "I used to tease Heather about her gaggle of admirers. She was the only woman in a group of stand-up wannabes, losers mostly. She—"

"What about Lauren?"

Reed took a deep breath. "Lauren kept to herself. She did her act with Heather, but never really hung out here—the only time I ever saw her was on stage, and truthfully, the sisters only performed for me a few times. I guess she was off with you most of her free time. On the other hand, Heather seemed to live here.

248

She loved dishing it out with the other guys, but she was different. She had talent, capital T, that raw, unteachable gift. The essential ingredient. The others were mostly dreamers and grinders." He closed his eyes for a second, lost in the past, then opened them. "Anyway, she had them all eating out of her hand. Gorgeous, talented, vivacious. The whole package. Why she didn't set her sights higher had me stumped. I kept telling her to leave them all behind, but she didn't want to."

"Who was in this little group?" I asked.

He tilted his head back and consulted the ceiling. "Let's see. Nathan. Skip Gold. Brooks Spellman, who she dated for a while. It got pretty hot and heavy there, but she came to her senses eventually. And there was Augie Something-or-Other, and a set of twins from Southeast, and a couple other guys. They'd come and go, dead leaves on the wind. There are a lot of wannabes in this biz, as I'm sure you know."

"Did Ryan say why he wanted to know all this? I mean, couldn't he have just gotten the info from Heather?"

"I asked him that and he made a weird face. Didn't answer me directly but I got the feeling Heather didn't want to tell him for some reason. He was plenty pissed about something, that's for sure." Reed shrugged, expression *too* innocent. He might have been a good comic in his day, but Artie was right, he was a bad liar now.

"You ever sleep with Heather?"

Reed blanched. "What? No. She's just a kid." His rapidly blinking eyes and wavering voice betrayed his words.

"You disgust me," I said, shaking my head. "And you're right. Compared to you, she is just a kid."

He opened his mouth to speak, blew his breath out. "After she dated Spellman, she was very down. Needy. She initiated it." He held his palms up and grinned. I felt like reaching across the desk and slapping the smirk off his face into the trashcan. "What was I supposed to do? Beautiful, passionate girl shows some interest in me. I went with the flow. Two consenting adults and all that. No one got hurt. In fact, I think she enjoyed it as much as I did. Maybe more." Then he turned serious. "A week or so later, she—and you—got into that accident. She wasn't the same after that. Pity."

"You still sleeping with her?"

Reed's Adam's apple danced. "No. No, I'm not. But I don't think I'd tell you if I was."

"Uh-huh. Well, it seems Nathan just found out. He had a thing for Heather and…I don't know. Maybe he thinks you had something to do with his roommate's death."

"Ryan and Nathan lived together?"

I nodded. "You didn't know that? If he comes around, watch out." I wondered if Skip had interpreted Nathan's comments correctly. It was hard to believe he had the balls to confront someone, although maybe he did have the right idea. "You tell Ryan you slept with Heather?"

Reed shook his head quickly. "No. Like I said, he was agitated coming in. I'm not stupid."

"What was he angry about?"

"I'm telling you, he wasn't making much sense. He was too pissed to even sit down, kept pacing back and forth."

"He must have said something about what he was after."

"I think he mentioned something about someone threatening Heather. But he was ranting, so I don't know for sure. Really. I wish I could help you more." Reed gave me a look he believed was sincere, but was halfway around the world from sincere.

"Threatening her about what?"

"Didn't say. I told him if it was that serious, he should go to the cops. He just laughed. Said he was going to handle things himself. Guess that didn't go so well, did it?"

"No, guess not. What were you doing at Artie's townhouse?"

Reed licked his lips, thought for a moment. "What, it's a crime to go visit someone? I went over there to talk to J.J."

"About what?"

"This and that. Doesn't matter now, does it?"

"If it doesn't matter, why not tell me? Satisfy my curiosity. The sooner I know, the sooner I can get out of your hair."

Reed stared at me.

"I wonder what Artie would do if he found out you were in his condo. Probably go berserk. Do something rash. You know Artie."

He blew out some air. "Aw, hell. Nothing was going on, I was just trying to find out what it would take to get him to ditch you guys and play my club. Exclusively."

"When did you see him?"

He tilted his head back. "I think it was a Wednesday. Yeah, day before he opened up at your place."

"And how did it go?"

"Not too well, actually. He didn't feel right leaving you guys in the lurch. Said he owed Artie. No accounting for taste, I guess."

Artie would be happy to hear about J.J.'s loyalty. "Bet that pissed you off."

Reed fiddled with his nail file, didn't answer. But I could tell he was steaming.

251

Usually, sore losers bugged me, but I was enjoying this. "You get high with him?" I figured I might as well ask all the questions I could think of. Worst he could do was refuse to answer. And that would be an answer itself.

"No. No drugs. Unless you consider beer a drug. Had a beer, talked, then left. That's it."

"You tell the cops any of this?"

"The cops already asked about me being at the townhouse. I told them just what I told you. The truth."

"You tell them the truth about sleeping with Heather?"

Reed did his statue impression for a moment. "No. Not yet. Didn't see what it could have to do with Ryan's death. Not at first. But talking to you, I think it might be a good thing. Don't you?"

"Yeah, I think you should tell them. And anything else that's pertinent, too. I'd hate to see you thrown in jail for obstructing justice." I rose. "By the way, did you happen to tell your wife about sleeping with Heather?"

Reed's eyes narrowed and I thought I detected a puff of steam coming out of his ears.

"You might want to rethink your takeover plans. Tell the esteemed Mr. Hamilton that you've changed your position *vis à vis* making an offer for The Last Laff. I'm sure if I had a little talk with your wife, she'd agree with me."

Now the steam was clearly visible.

"One more thing. Artie's right about you. You *are* a giant prick."

THIRTY-FOUR

SOMEONE WAS THREATENING HEATHER. That explained a lot. Why she ran, why she'd kept running. Why she wanted a gun. What it didn't explain, at least not that I could figure, was J.J.'s death, or the arson, or Ryan's death. Although Ryan's death certainly could have something to do with it. I mean, what better way to threaten Heather than to kill her boyfriend?

But why would someone want to threaten Heather? What had she done serious enough to get someone killed?

After leaving Reed, I'd driven to The Last Laff. Now I sat in the parking lot deciding what to do next. I needed to find Heather before whoever was after her did. But I had no scent to follow and I was pretty sure Heather hadn't left me a trail of breadcrumbs. I pulled out my phone and called her. Hung up after hearing the same mailbox-full message I'd been hearing for days.

Punched in Freeman's number and waited a couple of rings. "Easter."

"Hey, it's Channing."

A snort. "Well, well. To what do I owe the pleasure?"

I explained about my conversation with Reed, emphasizing Reed's sexual relationship with Heather.

Freeman said, "I guess I need to pay yet *another* visit to the slimy Mr. Reed. Don't worry, I'll try to remain impartial." I knew Reed didn't stand a chance. "By the way, there was no sign of struggle on Rizzetti's part. Nothing under the fingertips, no defensive wounds. Like someone snuck up on him from behind. We still don't know where it was done. You'd think someone would have noticed a large pool of blood, wouldn't you?"

"Any more on the fingerprints from Artie's townhouse?" I asked. "You found Reed's there, you know."

"Thanks for the reminder. What would I do without you? Why, I'd probably be directing traffic somewhere," Freeman said. I could almost see his eyes rolling. "You think he killed Ryan? Why?"

"Shit. I don't know what to believe. You talked to Nathan, Ryan's roommate, yesterday?"

"Of course. Why?"

"What was your impression?" I asked.

"Seemed pretty torn up over it. Cried a little. I'll ask again, why?"

I told Freeman about my conversation with Nathan and about him following Ryan to the motel. I also told him about my trip to the Eastwinds. When I finished, I held my breath.

"Goddamnit, Channing. When were you going to tell me that? Shit, can't you let me be the detective, here? I'm a hell of a lot better at it than you. I don't get on the stage and tell jokes, do I?"

"Not funny ones, anyway," I said, to complete silence. "Give me a break, will you? I was going to tell you. But it was late when I got back last night and then I got involved with Reed first thing this morning. I'm telling you now."

Freeman clicked off without saying goodbye.

———

As soon as I got to the club, I dragged Artie back to the office. Closed the door behind us. "I need to talk to you."

He stared at me.

"It's serious."

He exhaled and sat. Nodded to my chair. "Have a seat. Take a deep breath first. Then I'm all ears."

I did what I was told, except I took several deep breaths. "Something serious is going on with Heather. She didn't run away because she was scared of going on stage. And I don't think she ran away because she was bored, or looking for attention, or yearning for some kind of adventure, like she'd done in the past." Artie paid rapt attention, not even fiddling with his cigar or a paper clip or anything. "I think someone has threatened her and she doesn't know what else to do except run and hide."

"I know what to do. Call the police. Get Freeman in on this."

"I'm way ahead of you. And he's looking for her."

"You think she's mixed up in J.J.'s death and the fire and the dead hooker, too?" He swallowed. "You don't think she killed her boyfriend, do you? Slashed his throat like that? That's ruthless."

"No way. She didn't do *any* of those things. But whoever's threatening her might have. That's why I think she's in such danger."

Artie nodded and seemed to be formulating something in his head. "Let me get this straight. Whoever's after Heather killed J.J., the hooker, torched my townhouse, and killed Ryan?" His mouth stayed open.

"Yeah. That's what I'm thinking."

"Holy shit," Artie said.

I nodded. "That's what I'm thinking, too."

"And we're suffering the collateral damage in all this. We better get our shit together. Time to circle the wagons closer. Come on."

I followed Artie out onto the floor. He directed me to a table and told me to stay put, not to move a muscle. A minute later, he reappeared with Donna and Ty at his side. "Sit," he said. Donna and Ty took their chairs with barely a nod in my direction.

"What now, Artie?" Donna said, clearly perturbed. "We've got work to do. *Real* work."

Artie stared her down and then glanced away. Donna could take anyone in a staring contest. I started to speak, but Artie steamrolled me before any sound came out of my mouth.

"Listen up. We need to talk about whether we should open tonight. In the wake of what's going on around here."

"What *is* going on around here?" Donna asked. "Exactly?"

Artie gave a quick recap, glossing over some of the finer points. When he finished, he pointed at me. "Got anything to add?"

I licked my lips. "Unfortunately, I do. William Dempsey, Lauren and Heather's father, has gone around the bend, as they say. If he shows up here, don't confront him. Call the cops pronto." I nodded at Ty. "You too, big guy. He may be armed, so be careful."

Ty said, "Don't worry. I could use a little exercise."

"Shit," Donna said. "Crazy guys and guns do not go together."

Artie started to say something, but I interrupted. "Uh, I got another thing. A guy named Nathan Borghat—one of Skip's friends actually—is pissed at me. So if he shows up, tell him I'm not around. Tell him I've quit. Or better yet, tell him I've left the country on a one-way ticket. I don't think he's dangerous, though, so you don't have to call the cops. Just show him the door." I stopped talking, but no one moved.

"You got anyone else pissed at you?" Donna asked me.

I could think of a few more people but kept my mouth shut.

Artie cleared his throat and everyone's eyes turned toward him. "So what do you guys think we should do?" he asked.

"Full speed ahead," Donna said. "Nobody scares me off."

Artie nodded, shifted to Ty. "How about you? What do you think?"

"Since when do you ask my opinion about things, you slave driver?" He asked in a menacing voice. Then he unleashed his dimples. "Whatever you think is good with me. You know that. I can handle any malcontent who walks through our doors. Efficiently, and with a smile on my face." He kept on chuckling to himself. Nice to know at least one person was amused.

Artie shook his head, turned my way. "And you?"

"I'm with Donna." I said. "What's the point in waiting? We've got to reopen sooner or later. Might as well be tonight."

Artie nodded. "That's what I like to hear. Everyone in agreement, everyone anxious to put this terrible thing behind us. But…" He raised one arm and pointed to the sky, like some colonial orator denouncing taxation. "…We have our work cut out for us and we need to be prepared."

"Prepared for what?" I asked.

"You found a body here yesterday," Artie said. "Right over there." He pointed to an empty spot on the floor, directly in front of center stage. Where the table I'd found Ryan used to be. After the police were finished with it, Artie had broken its legs off and thrown all the debris into the Dumpster out back. Chair, too. "It's awful, but people are going to be curious. That's human nature. And judging from all the calls we've gotten so far—from the press and otherwise—tonight will be a madhouse. We need to stick together, get all hands on deck, and circle the wagons. Remember, there's no 'I' in team."

"What are you talking about?" Donna asked. She had the least patience for Artie's semi-coherent rabble rousing.

"Reporters. Video crews. Paparazzi. Nutjobs. Sickos." Artie ticked them off like items on a grocery list. "All asking questions and taking pictures and disrupting business at our humble comedy club. It's going to be insane."

"You're confusing me, Artie. Do you want to open, or do you want to wait until things blow over?" Donna asked. "Can't you just cut to the chase for once?"

"I don't want to do anything that puts anyone's safety in question," Artie said. "Better to err on the side of—"

I rapped on the table with my knuckles. "Artie. We're all behind you. And it's settled. We open tonight." I didn't want to put the entire burden of the decision on Artie. If something went wrong, I wanted to shoulder some of the blame, too. I took a page from his motivational playbook. "If we stick together, we'll survive. Watch each other's backs and take care of our own business. Just don't toss any reporters out on their asses. We got enough bad press having someone dump a body here. We don't need any more."

I looked up and found Artie admiring me, small smile on his face. "I couldn't have said it better myself."

"Done?" Donna asked, one eyebrow raised. "I got stuff to do."

"Almost," he said, as he drew himself up to his full five feet seven inches. "Remember, we run the best damn comedy club in the world. And we're a family. Don't ever forget that. And be careful." He waved at Donna and Ty with the back of his hand. "Okay, you can get back to work now."

Artie waited until we were alone before speaking. "I know Skip and Ty have been following me. Making sure I don't go postal and try something with Reed."

My mouth fell open. "What? I don't know what—"

He waved me off. "Stow it. I know they've had a tag-team thing going on, and I know they didn't come up with that idea on their own." Artie looked at me like he had when he'd first taken me under his wing five years ago. "Thanks, Channing. I appreciate your concern. It means a lot to me." No sarcasm, no anger. He seemed genuinely grateful, but I wasn't positive. He wasn't grateful often enough for me to be able to read it well.

"Sure," I said, waiting for the cartoon anvil to drop on my head. *How dare you follow me? What, you think I'm a loose cannon? Get out of here. Go on, git! Take the horse you rode in on and never come back!*

Artie simply nodded. "I know you're worried. But I'd never do anything to jeopardize this club or hurt you or your career. That includes getting thrown in jail for assaulting that prick Reed." He made two fists, jabbing the air a couple times before finishing with an uppercut. "As much as I'd enjoy it."

So Artie wasn't a potentially homicidal maniac after all. Good to know. "I'll tell Skip and Ty to knock it off. They were worried about you too."

He puckered his face. "Yeah, sure they were. They were worried about their paychecks stopping." He shot his thumb and forefinger at me.

"Artie, I don't think—"

He held up his hand. "This is what you need to do. Right now." He paused to make sure I was hanging on his words. "You need to get your ass out of here and look for Heather. Forget me, forget the club. Go find Heather. Make sure she's safe. That's the only thing Channing Hayes needs to concentrate on right now. Heather Dempsey."

I gave him a blank stare. "I've been looking and come up empty. I don't think I'd know where to look next."

Artie rolled his eyes and laid into me. "You knew her pretty well, right? You should be able to find her faster than the creep who's threatening her. And faster than Freeman, too. Think about it. You're a smart guy. You'll find her." He tapped his temple with his forefinger. "Think hard."

"But what about the club tonight? All hands on deck, and circle the wagons, and all that togetherness crap?"

Artie snorted. "Please. You think you actually do anything around here? Things'll run a hell of a lot smoother with you out of the way." He waved me out the door, as if he were shooing flies. "Get going. Scram. We'll be fine here. Go find Heather."

THIRTY-FIVE

F<small>IND</small> H<small>EATHER</small>.

But where to look?

I figured I might as well start at the last place she'd been seen, try to pick up her tepid trail. Maybe somebody at the Eastwinds Motel remembered something about Heather's stay. On my drive over there, I decided to work the phones and make sure Heather hadn't somehow doubled back on me. My first call went to her mother, Kathleen. I figured she'd be hunkered down in her bunker trying to protect herself from Dempsey. The phone rang six times before the answering machine kicked in. *Hello, this is the Dempseys. Please leave a message. And have a great day!* The voice of a chipper Kathleen. Must have been recorded many months ago, before their lives—and marriage—had tumbled into the shredder.

I tried Justin's, hoping Heather had taken refuge with her brother like she had the night after she'd slept with J.J. His wife, Bertie, answered the phone and told me Justin was at work. Bertie and I had never hit it off, but there was no animosity between us.

Just two people with absolutely nothing in common, aside from the love of a Dempsey. Although she didn't know Heather's whereabouts, she was pretty sure Heather wasn't staying in their guest room. An infant cried plaintively in the background as I asked for Justin's work number. After a long silence, Bertie forked it over. I thanked her and hung up.

I got transferred twice before Justin picked up. "Yeah?" he said, impatient. Must be real busy at the lab. Probably mapping a new genome or curing cancer or something.

"It's Channing. Have you heard from Heather?"

"No. Not a peep. Still can't find her?" he asked.

I detected a trace of concern in his voice and wondered if Heather realized how many people cared about her. If she had, maybe she wouldn't have taken off without telling anyone. "Not for lack of trying, that's for sure. You'll call me if you hear from her, won't you?"

"Yeah," Justin said. "Uh, listen, Heather's, uh…I'm sure she's all right. This is her m.o. Disappears, then resurfaces like nothing happened. She'll do the same here, you'll see."

"I hope so." I didn't feel like arguing.

"Okay, then. I've got to go, I'm swamped. Good luck."

I said goodbye and clicked off. I guess there was caring and then there was *caring*.

Nathan was last on my list, but he didn't answer his home phone or his cell. Must be out searching for Heather, too. Or for Ryan's killer. Or for Reed. I hope he found *something* he was hunting for, as long as it wasn't me. Maybe he was simply looking for a little peace of mind.

This time when I got to the Eastwinds, I parked in a space marked, "Ten minutes, check-in only," right outside the manager's office. There were a few more cars in the lot and the neon sign didn't look so bad from this angle, but the motel still fell a couple stars shy of making Fairfax's Top Ten Destinations list.

The smell of onions and tuna fish accosted me as I entered the office. Behind the counter, a younger, more disheveled version of the clerk I'd met on my last visit was watching Oprah on a small television. No three-piece suit, just a shabby T-shirt painted with a slogan I couldn't make out. "Help you?" he asked, one bloodshot eye on me, the other glued to the tube. He didn't bother getting up off his ass.

"Yeah. Got a few questions."

"This about the chick whose boyfriend got killed?" he asked.

"Yeah it is, as a matter of fact." Now I had about seventy percent of his attention.

"Cool," he said, and he stood to face me, beer gut stretching out the old T-shirt so I could make out the distorted slogan: *If nature's so great, why don't Hummers grow on trees?* Under the words, there was an orchard of Hummer trees, with several tiny Hummers growing like apples.

"So what can you tell me?" I asked.

He turned off the TV, leaving Oprah in the dust. I guess some real-life sensationalism in your front yard trumped Oprah's distant brand. "Cops called a few minutes ago. They're on their way."

"Oh?" Freeman had jumped right on my tip, not that I had any doubt he would.

"Yeah. They asked if we cleaned the room yet. Ain't Friday, is it?" The clerk emitted a raspy, phlegm-filled laugh. Then his eyes narrowed at me. "What do you want, anyhow? You a reporter?"

I held up my good hand. "Oh no. Just a friend. Trying to locate her." I leaned in and lowered my voice. "I'm not sure she's even heard what happened to Ryan." Which was true. Part of me hoped she was in Tahiti, enjoying the sun and the mai tais, far from this madness.

His eyes opened wide for a second. "You come by with another guy. With some insulin?"

"Uh, yeah. That's right. How did you know?"

"You spoke to my father. He gave me a report," he said. "Hope she's okay."

"Yeah, thanks. She didn't come back, did she?"

The clerk cleared his throat. "Nope. Sorry."

"You checked her in, right?"

"Sure did." He looked at me for a sign to continue. I nodded eagerly. "She and her boyfriend checked in a week ago. Paid for ten days, in cash, which I happen to really appreciate. Gave 'em a deal, too. I didn't see much of her during the week. A couple of times alone. A couple of times with him. Seemed to get along pretty good, I guess." Now he leaned toward me and lowered his voice. "You think she killed him?"

"No. She did not kill him."

The clerk nodded, as if I'd told him watermelons rained from the sky every third Wednesday. "Okay, you say so."

Jerkoff. "You know anything I might find useful?"

The clerk glanced around. Raised an eyebrow. "There is something." He glanced around again and did a double take. The local stars of community theater had nothing to fear. "I got some info. Might be helpful to somebody."

"Okay. I'm listening."

He gazed out the window as he rubbed his thumb and forefinger together. "As I said before, I'm a big fan of cash." He kept his face averted while he shook me down. Must have seen it done that way in some 1970s private dick flick.

"How much is this info worth, do you suppose?" I asked, wondering if this guy were related to Heather's landlady. Probably just watched the same cliché-infested movies.

"Dunno. Watcha thinking?"

As he watched out of the corner of his eyes, I made a big show of peering into my wallet. Gave him a couple of big sighs. "How's ten bucks?" I removed a ten-spot and held it up in my mangled hand.

His head swiveled around and he focused on the bill in my hand. Something flickered behind his eyes, a look I'd begun to grow accustomed to. I guess it's hard not to act even a little surprised when you see a two-fingered hand, up close and in the misshapen flesh.

He recovered fast enough, plucking the money from my hand carefully, as if he'd get cooties if he touched me. "Deal."

The clerk reached under the counter and produced a scrap of paper. Unfolded it. "My father left this. It says that someone else came by asking about your friend. Wanted me to tell you, just in case you stopped by again." He tilted his head at me. "Guess he got a good read on you."

"What did the guy look like?"

"Note don't say."

"What else *does* it say?"

"Nothing much." The clerk handed me the note so I could see for myself.

I read the neat cursive. A guy had come by asking about Heather an hour after Nathan and I had. No physical description. No mention of a vehicle. Nothing about the guy wielding a pipe wrench. "Shit," I said aloud.

The clerk shrugged. "Sorry."

"Can I talk with him? Your father?"

He shook his head. "He's on the road. Driving to Connecticut. And he refuses to get a cell phone, the old dinosaur."

Double shit. Dempsey was right behind me. He'd tracked Heather here, and for all I knew, he'd been able to figure out where she'd gone next. It was possible—probable, even—that now I was the one lagging behind. "Did you see anything unusual last week? Anything that seemed out of place?"

He gazed out the front window. "Hmm. Not that I can remember. Got plenty of other guests to attend to, though. So I might not have seen everything going on."

I didn't know what his definition of "plenty" was, but I was pretty sure Webster wouldn't be printing it in any of his future editions. "No suspicious characters lurking about?"

His eyes glowed at the mention of suspicious characters, more gossip to tell his wife over their pork and beans dinner. "Nope. Just the regular customers. Of course, most of them are suspicious enough." He laughed again, but it quickly morphed into a full-fledged coughing attack.

I left before the cops arrived.

THIRTY-SIX

Life's funny sometimes.

One moment I didn't have a clue where Heather might be. The next moment, I had a strong suspicion. I didn't remember anything particular happening as I climbed into Rex outside the motel office. No bolt of lightning or blow to the head or wind whispering secrets in my ear. It was one of those inductive leaps made by the subconscious, wholly without effort on my part. I got in the car and I knew.

Of course, I wasn't *sure* I knew where she was. But I had the same sense of being right I used to get when I was in college and got stumped by a problem, went to sleep, and awoke knowing the answer. I just *knew* I knew.

A sense of calm washed over me. In a few hours, I'd either find her or I wouldn't, but at least—for now—I could stop wondering and worrying. I had a destination, a goal I could achieve. For the first time since Heather disappeared, I felt hopeful about locating her.

I started up the engine, strapped myself in, and adjusted the seat for the long ride.

Fifteen minutes later I was pointed west on I-66, keeping up with the commuter traffic heading home after a long day in the salt mines. I set the cruise control to maintain a steady speed. Ever since the accident, I found myself steering with both hands or with my right hand, but never with my left hand for any extended period of time. I didn't think it was because I was uncomfortable—physically—doing it. After all, I could hook my thumb and forefinger around the wheel and steer just fine. No, it was a mental thing, not wanting to acknowledge my deformity. Because of the memories it triggered. I knew I was being foolish—how could I ever forget what happened? I didn't need a few missing fingers or an ugly scar to jog my memory.

In the world of stand-up, the prevailing wisdom says a comic should hit the audience up front with any visible quirks, "calling the moment." If you're 450 pounds, you'd better mention that fact first, or the audience will be too busy wondering if you're aware you're fat to laugh at your jokes. Ditto for a long beard, bald head, or big nose. I knew what the prevailing wisdom would say about my scar and missing fingers. Lay it on the line from the outset. Call the moment.

Good evening, everyone, I'm the Seven-Fingered Comic. You can call me a freak, or better yet, you can call me Freakenstein's Monster. But whatever you do, just don't call me late for dinner. Ba da bing.

But I wasn't sure I could open my act that way. I was afraid my talking about it in front of a cold room might bring back the painful emptiness. And no one laughs if the comic's crying for real. I'd thought of a bunch of ways I could keep my "quirks" hidden. Stuff my hand in my pocket and keep the right side of my face to the audience the whole night. Wear gloves and a ski mask, or put a paper bag over my head like the old Unknown Comic. But that shtick had been done already and screamed of desperation. Besides, too many people in the business already knew me.

You know what sucks about having only seven fingers? Much harder to be a two-fisted drinker. Hey bartender, I sure could use three more fingers of scotch, hold the scotch. Ba da bump.

Working on the edge and baring your soul in front of strangers took guts, something every comic learned quickly. Far too many funny people never made it because they were afraid. Afraid to look squarely in the mirror, recognize the warts and blemishes, and bare them to the harsh light of the audience, never realizing it was exactly those imperfections that sired good comedy.

And the imperfections had to be genuine, because in the end, a comic must be true to his material. Audiences can sense when a comic's just making it up, phoning it in. It never works for a guy to get on stage and start riffing on the difficulty with relationships when he's been in a solid marriage for years. Or for someone to do a bit on drugs who's never even smoked a doobie. The audience can see right through him, like dogs smell fear.

The traffic in my lane slowed as a car carrier ahead ground its gears up a long incline. I waited for a gap in the left lane, then zipped into it. Glanced at my watch. I was making good time. If things kept up, I'd be there well before dusk.

I recalled some of the best comics I'd ever seen, live, taped, or on TV. Bruce, Cosby, Carlin. Pryor. Seinfeld. DeGeneres. They all drew from within, turning the everyday into the unique, sharing their warped version of reality with their audiences. Connecting with them on some unseen level. Few can do it. Fewer still can do it well enough to keep everybody in stitches for an hour.

But being funny wasn't always easy on the soul. Many comics faced a whole different set of demons than normal people. Always second-guessing, always unsure of themselves. What if my stuff isn't funny? What if I'm the only guy on the planet who sees the humor in my ping-pong ball collection? That's why flameouts are so common in the comedy business. Mercurial performers catch an updraft and ride it perilously, fearlessly surfing the thermals. No nets, no security blankets. When they come crashing down, many aren't itching to fly again.

You know what else sucks about missing three fingers on one hand? I can't flip anybody off while I'm driving, at least not without taking my own life into my one and two-fifths hands.

A sign for my exit appeared and I changed lanes. In a mile, I'd exit onto I-81 North.

At least Heather had held it together as she prepared to get back on stage. The accident had turned me into a washout, a quivering blob of Jell-O, whenever I thought about getting back on the horse. I'd called Sammi and told her I was coming back, but I now knew it for what it was—a motivational device only, and a fragile one at that. I had no real confidence I could get the job done. Strictly hope and a prayer. Looking back at the few attempts I'd made to work on my act over the past ten days, I realized that I'd bailed out before I could even get a good premise down on paper. What did that say about me? Chickenshit? Or still in recovery mode? Would I be in recovery for the rest of my life?

The neurologist who saw me right after the accident said victims who'd sustained head trauma sometimes experienced altered personalities. That some people "changed" after a severe accident. I remembered a guy from high school who wrapped his car around a tree late one Saturday night. He'd gone from being the class clown to a funeral director's straight man. Had I lost my sense of humor? Would I ever summon the courage to find out?

Okay, all together now. Everybody in the back, too. Don't be shy. Does that hideous scar on your face hurt? No? It's killing me!

I popped a CD in and listened to Nirvana for forty-five minutes, every so often touching the hard, ridged patch of skin on my face. It *was* killing me.

I exited the highway and negotiated the bumpy country roads, catching glimpses of the scenery as I concentrated on staying out of the ditches. Rolling hills, wooded valleys, long stretches without a fast food restaurant in sight. On another day, I'm sure I would have enjoyed the ride. Now I had a singular purpose in mind. Finding Heather.

And I was betting she was at her family's old vacation cabin.

THIRTY-SEVEN

LAUREN AND I HAD spent a weekend there once, when it had been between rentals. As a kid, her family vacationed there every summer for a week or two, and she always talked about how much fun she'd had hiking and exploring and doing all sorts of outdoor activities I'd never had the chance to try growing up in the city. Whenever she recalled those halcyon days, her eyes lit up like fireflies.

According to Lauren, by the time all the Dempsey kids reached high school, spending time with the family came in a distant second to hanging out with friends, and her father had turned the property over to a management company to rent. Dempsey still owned the cabin but as an investment only, and I got the sense it didn't attract business like it once had. Lauren told me her mother had wanted to sell it, but her father refused, saying the cabin held too many fond memories for him to just "abandon" it. So he kept it and paid some guy to maintain it, and would still invite his kids to use it whenever they wanted. To Lauren's knowledge, neither of her siblings had ever taken him up on his offer.

If I was wrong about Heather being there, what was the harm? Four or five hours wasted. After all the time I'd spent looking for her, it was a no-brainer to come here and see for myself. Besides, the drive up had cleared my head.

I followed signs until I found the main road nearest the cabin. From there I figured I'd remember the rest—I'd always been good with directions, remembering things in pictures, patterns, and spatial relationships instead of relying solely on written words.

Two miles along, I passed the Fantastic Fruits Orchard where Lauren and I had stopped to pick apples, and I smiled. The motel desk clerk's Hummer orchard T-shirt might have been the catalyst that jostled my memory of the Dempsey cabin. Funny what triggers things.

About a mile later, I found what I was looking for—Little Hawk Lane. I turned onto the rutted gravel road and crept along, searching for the cabin's driveway as Rex bounced on the uneven terrain. Thick woods bordered both sides of the road, and I was sure more animals used this path than vehicles. I kept my eyes peeled for the driveway; when Lauren and I came, we'd passed right by it on our first several tries. I slowed to about five miles per hour, which also had the benefit of not kicking up so much dust.

It didn't take long to find the place. Fifty yards down the lane on my right, a wooden sign with the name Dempsey burned into it marked the drive. I didn't remember the sign from my previous visit, but I guess stuff changes in two years. The rental company probably put it up, tired of complaints from lost renters.

I headed up the narrow driveway. The cabin sat on a hill in a small clearing, but the long, steep driveway wound through the trees, and if it were dark or slippery, the driveway would be a bitch.

Today though, I had no trouble climbing the half-dozen switchbacks through the woods, even if I had to keep my speed at a pace just a hair faster than PARK.

When the driveway broke through into the clearing, my breath caught. The cabin, fifty yards away, looked exactly like it had on my earlier visit, with one notable exception. This time, two vehicles were parked in front of it. Heather's Jeep and Dempsey's black Mercedes SL350.

I hit the brakes, thoughts racing. Somehow, I didn't think this was just a father-daughter vacation. Kathleen had been terrified of Dempsey, and what he might do with his gun. And he certainly had seemed unstable when he'd accosted me. He'd gone off the deep end, and I had the feeling he was looking for someone he could take out his frustrations on.

It didn't make sense that he'd found Heather and kidnapped her, not if both cars were here. It was more likely that he'd tracked her to the cabin as I had. Could he be holding her hostage? Would he really harm his daughter?

I thought about turning around and going for help, but if he'd seen or heard me, he'd bolt before I could get back. And who knew what he might do to Heather in the process.

I backed my car down the driveway until it was hidden from the house. Then I hopped out and flipped my cell phone open. Waited a minute. No signal. I was on my own. If I was wrong and Dempsey and Heather were here, communing peacefully with nature, then I'd come across as an ass, barging in on them. That didn't bother me one bit, as long as Heather was safe. On the other hand, if Heather was in trouble, I needed to help her. Pronto.

A large grassy front lawn sloped to my right. Across the clearing, more woods. I worried about Dempsey's gun, but I was pretty far from the cabin. Still, I didn't think it wise to show my face, so instead of cutting across the clearing, I darted back along the driveway and cut into the trees. Staying beyond the tree line for cover, I circled the lawn to my right, picking my way through the underbrush, weaving through saplings and bushes, tree trunks and vines gone wild, trying to be as quiet as possible. Daniel Boone I wasn't, but unless he was listening for me specifically, I didn't think Dempsey could hear me with the doors and windows closed.

In a few minutes, I'd gone one-hundred-eighty degrees and now faced the rear of the cabin. A door led out back, from the kitchen—if I remembered correctly—flanked by a pair of windows on one side and a single window on the other. No sign of movement. Was it too much to hope that Dempsey had gone on a hike and left Heather in the cabin by herself?

I retraced my path until I had a direct line from the woods to the back corner of the house. The window closest to the corner belonged to the bedroom. It seemed the least likely spot where someone might be looking out.

I took a deep breath and exhaled. Then I made a beeline for the corner, keeping as low as I could. When I reached the cabin, I flattened myself against the wall, trying to blend in with the siding. Staying hidden from anyone who might be looking out the window. I held my breath and waited. Waited for Dempsey to come flying around one of the corners, gun blazing. Shooting first, asking questions later. Nothing happened and gradually—very gradually—I began breathing again.

When my pulse slowed enough for me to move without fear of trembling, I inched along the wall toward the closest window. I scrunched down and peeked into the lower left-hand corner. The room was dark. My recollection had been on the money—a bedroom—but with the sun glaring off the glass, it was hard to tell if it was occupied. I duckwalked under the sill to peer into the next window. A hallway leading to the kitchen, only the refrigerator visible. I canted one ear toward the glass and listened, hoping to hear voices—people, radio, TV—but all I heard were the chirrups of crickets in the woods behind me.

I proceeded to the next window and looked in. Kathleen Dempsey stood by the fireplace talking to Heather, who sat on the couch facing her. I rapped on the window, and when Heather saw me, her eyes went wide with surprise. Kathleen's head whipped toward me. It took a moment for her to recognize me, but then she waved me around to the front door.

Ten day's worth of tension drained from my body as I walked around to the front. Kathleen had come in the Mercedes, not Dempsey. She and Heather had gone to ground to hide from their respective stalkers. Pretty smart, at least in the short term. I guess Dempsey would think to look here at some point, just as I had, but hopefully Freeman would corral him first. I climbed onto the porch and before I could rap on the door, Kathleen stuck her head out. "Hello, Channing." Her trademark smile seemed plastic and forced. "Come in." She opened the door just enough to let me in and closed it behind me.

It took a moment for my eyes to adjust to the darkness inside the cabin. When they did, Heather hadn't moved; she sat on the couch with her legs drawn up under her, the same way Lauren used to sit. The expression on her face unnerved me. I'd expected gratitude or joy or at least some semblance of happiness. After all, we'd been working closely together for months and had developed a friendship. Right now, I saw fear.

"Join the party," a deep voice intoned. "Join the fucking party."

THIRTY-EIGHT

I SPUN AROUND. DEMPSEY sat at a table, bottle of booze in one hand, gun in the other.

"Throw the deadbolt, *dear*," he said to Kathleen. She locked the door, then went to sit next to Heather on the couch. Dempsey addressed me. "I wasn't sure you'd ever track Heather down. Took you long enough."

"I don't know what you're—" I stammered.

"Oh, where are my manners? Have a seat, *Channing*. Take a load off." He pointed to a chair across the table. "Want something to drink?" He held up his bottle for a second, waved it in the air, then brought it down on the table with a *thud*, keeping the gun trained on me. Behind him on the kitchen counter, the remnants of a telephone lay scattered. Someone had busted it into three or four pieces and yanked the cord from the wall. *Someone*.

I eased into the chair, one eye on Dempsey, one eye on Heather. She didn't look in my direction, instead keeping her attention on the dark fireplace.

Kathleen spoke first. "Don't worry about William, Channing. It's me he's after. Never was good at taking rejection." She sneered at him. Not wise to sneer at the guy with the gun, especially if he was unbalanced.

Dempsey waved his gun in the air. "Hey, I'm not holding you against your will or anything." An evil smile accompanied his words. "Go on. Leave. Just don't take the car. It's in my name."

Across the room, Kathleen's eyes pierced holes in Dempsey. "You're a bastard, William. I should have dumped you years ago. You were a bastard then, too, just not as overt about it."

"*Bastard*? You had no trouble letting a bastard support you for years. Then you just kicked him out of the house when things got rough. Hah. You call *me* a bastard?" Dempsey took a sip from the bottle of booze and wiped his mouth with his sleeve. His chest heaved as he tried to control his breathing.

Freeman always used to say domestic disputes were the nastiest. I could see why. A temporary lull gave me an opening. "Heather, are you okay?"

Across the room, Heather nodded, a single bob of the head. Not very convincing.

I spoke to her, trying hard to shut the others out. "What's going on?"

Kathleen put an arm around her daughter, whispered something in her ear.

Dempsey laughed it off. "Go on, Heather, tell him what's going on if you want to. If you feel *comfortable* doing it, that is." He turned to me. "Won't tell me *shit*."

Heather nodded at her mother. "Mom?"

Dempsey cackled. "That's priceless. You women can't do anything for yourselves. Go on, puppetmaster, you tell him then. You always managed to turn the girls against me, anyhow."

Kathleen's face glowed crimson. "Fuck you, William." Then she spoke to me, as if Dempsey wasn't there. "Channing, it's been a terrible ordeal for Heather. An old boyfriend's been hounding her. Trying to get her to see him again. She's told him—repeatedly—that she doesn't want to get back together, but he won't take no for an answer," she said, glancing over at Heather for confirmation.

"Who are you talking about?" I directed my question at Heather.

"A boy named Brooks Spellman," Kathleen said. As she said his name, Heather's eyes flickered.

"Brooks Spellman? He's the one who's been after you?" When I'd talked to him after his open mic performance at the CCC, he seemed down, not obsessed or angry. Had I mistakenly attributed his glumness to his bombed set, instead of to his pursuit of Heather?

Kathleen nodded. "Yes. It got so bad that Heather came here to get away. She called—right after I spoke with you last—and I drove up to keep her company. Thought it might be good for me to get away for a bit, too." Her eyes narrowed and she glowered at Dempsey. "Needless to say, he wasn't invited."

I wondered if Heather knew her father had killed J.J. and Ryan. I didn't think now was the right time to confront Dempsey about it, though. I wasn't too keen on joining that short list.

"Thought you could hide from me, did you?" Dempsey said, then turned his bleary eyes toward me. "Neighbor who watches the place for me called, said a couple of *broads* had shown up. 'Course I knew who they were. So I came up, parked at his place, and tromped through the woods to visit my *broads*." He cackled again. "They say they hate me, but they don't mind coming here, to my house, sponging off me."

Kathleen turned to me. "Channing, when I found out Heather was here, safe, I should have called to let you know before I drove up. But Heather begged me not to. I'm so sorry you're mixed up in this."

I didn't respond to Kathleen. Instead, I spoke to Heather, trying to connect. "Why didn't *you* call and tell me what was going on? At the very beginning? I could have gotten Spellman off your back." I struggled to keep my voice calm, my anger in check. At least until I got the whole story. Then I'd allow myself to explode.

This time, Heather spoke for herself. "I was embarrassed. About running out on you and Artie at the club. And I didn't want to drag you into my stupid personal affairs. You've been so nice helping me with my act, I didn't want to take advantage, and I didn't want Brooks hassling you either. I'm sorry. I should have called."

Something wasn't right here. "If Spellman was bothering you so much, why didn't you call the police?"

At the mention of the police, Dempsey shifted in his chair, and his grip on the gun tightened.

Heather fidgeted on the couch. "What could they do? My word against his. And even if I got a restraining order, those things never work. He'd still call me and follow me around."

"You could have told me, honey," Dempsey said. Heather flinched at his use of the word *honey*. "I would have taken care of it."

"You can't kill someone for that, William. For Pete's sake, come back to reality," Kathleen said, her voice full of venom.

"Death is too good for some people," Dempsey said, staring at me.

My chest constricted and breathing became more difficult. A million thoughts ran through my mind, none of them pleasant.

"What now, William?" Kathleen asked. Her arm still encircled Heather, but her tone had become defiant. A mother bear protecting her cub.

Dempsey cocked his head and glared at me. "Now?" He glanced at his wife and daughter to make sure they were paying attention. "I don't know. I wasn't *really* planning for Lauren's murderer to show up."

"What are you talking about?" Kathleen asked. Her lower lip trembled.

"Channing here killed our Lauren. We all know that. Wouldn't you like to see justice carried out?"

"Stop it. Channing's not guilty of anything. He's a victim. It was all a horrible, horrible accident. That's all," Kathleen said. "You're a victim, too, William. And me. And Heather. We're all victims. But you've got to get past this. You can't blame everyone around you. Your hate is destroying you, can't you see that?"

"Will you all just *stop*?" Heather jumped off the couch. "Channing's not guilty. He didn't kill Lauren. Please don't hurt him, Daddy." Tears flowed down her face.

Dempsey didn't say a word but kept the gun aimed my way.

Heather raised her voice. "I lied. I lied about Brooks. He doesn't want to *get back together* with me," she said. "He wants to kill me."

THIRTY-NINE

"WHAT? WHY WOULD HE want to kill you?" I asked. I wanted to get up and go to her, embrace her, console her, just like I'd done for Lauren a thousand times. But I didn't want to ignite Dempsey so I stayed put.

Heather paced the room. In her pink T-shirt and gray sweatpants, she looked like any other twenty-something girl, just kicking back. But from her jittery movements and uneven tone, you knew something serious was going on. Ten days on edge, and it was a wonder she could still function at all. While we waited for her to explain, Heather paced, lips moving without sound. Finally, she spoke. "No. No. Forget it. Let's all just forget about this. Get on with our lives. Trust me, it's the best thing."

"Like hell we will," Dempsey said. "Give it to me straight, girl."

Heather walked in my direction and stopped three feet away, gazing at me with her deep dark eyes. In that instant, I saw both Heather and Lauren, melded together in some kind of mind-blowing optical illusion. In those eyes, she carried enough pain for everyone.

"I'm sorry, Channing. I killed Lauren," she said, her voice a whisper.

"Jesus Christ, Heather. If anyone's responsible for her death, it's me," I said. "If I hadn't been drinking, I'd have been driving. And I would have kept the car on the road." I'd been shouldering the guilt and wasn't prepared to share it. It had been my excuse, my crutch, for why I hadn't been able to move on. I'd relinquish it on my own terms.

"No, you don't understand. It was all my fault. I killed her, Channing. I'm sorry." Her tears flowed freely.

"What the hell are you talking about?" Dempsey said. Kathleen had come up behind Heather and grasped her shoulders. We *all* wanted to know what she was talking about.

Heather swallowed great gulps of air. Tried to calm herself. Kathleen attempted to hug her, but Heather shrugged her mother's arms away. "Oh God, oh God, oh God. Brooks was so mad at me. For breaking up with him, for seeing someone else. He couldn't take no for an answer. He came to Spanky's that night to see our act, and he had a few. More than a few. He was really wasted. He followed us from the club and was playing highway chicken with Lauren. He ran into us on purpose, trying to run us off the road. Lauren couldn't control it and we spun around. Flipped over. Hit the pole. Rolled into the ditch. All that blood…"

The walls of the cabin closed in on me. My frame of vision slowly contracted until I couldn't make out any shapes, only colors and movement, brightness and shadows. Brooks Spellman ran us off the road. On purpose. He killed Lauren. Playing a fucked-up game of chicken because Heather *broke up* with him? Some asshole gets dumped and he destroys people's lives? *My* life? Brilliant red soaked into the crevices within my brain. Part of me felt like tearing through the cabin, upending furniture and bashing windows, screaming at the top of my lungs. A bigger part of me felt like crawling into a hole and dying.

Kathleen held Heather, whose shoulders heaved as she sobbed.

"Why didn't you tell the police when it happened?" Dempsey asked.

Heather kept on crying.

"Goddamnit. Answer me." Dempsey banged the table with the butt of his gun.

Heather's crying slowed to a sniffle. "I didn't know then. My memory has come back slowly. First a few snatches, then more and more."

Once again, I prayed my memories of that night would never return.

Heather continued. "At first, I didn't know if what I was remembering was true. I had so many bad dreams, it was hard to tell what was real and what wasn't." Her eyes darted around, settling on nothing. "I didn't know for sure until Brooks showed up, in person. Said he'd just come back from L.A. and he wanted to look me up. See how I was doing. Get back together. As soon as I saw his face, I knew the truth about that night. I was sure. It was like the fog had lifted. I knew he'd been the one who forced us off the road. But it was all my fault. If I hadn't gotten mixed up with Brooks in the first place, Lauren would still be alive."

Dempsey squinted. "So once you remembered, why didn't you tell someone? Me. Or the cops."

"When he asked me about that night, I was so scared, so confused. I think he was trying to find out what I knew, see if I was going to turn him in or blackmail him or something. I told him I didn't remember a thing—which was exactly what I'd told the police right after the accident. I was in such a panic, I couldn't believe I actually got the words out."

"You should have told me. I would have set him straight," Dempsey said, and from his tone, there was no doubt in my mind he would have.

"I told him I'd go out with him the next night, just so he'd leave me alone. He said no problem, and I thought I'd pulled it off, but he called me the next morning, told me he didn't believe me. Asked me what I really saw that night. I tried lying again, but he threatened to kill me if I went to the police with some kind of 'wild story' that he was involved in the accident."

"I would have protected you," Dempsey said, waving his gun in the air.

"He said he'd kill you and Mom, too," Heather said. "And Ryan. He said he'd kill you if I told, and it wouldn't be pretty." She turned to me. "That's why I left The Last Laff before my set. I was afraid Brooks would be in the audience. I ran out. I didn't know where I could go that Brooks wouldn't find me. Went to see J.J. at the comedy condo. Then I bounced around, trying to keep away from Brooks. Finally, Ryan put me up in a motel." She pointed at me. "I didn't want to tell you and get you dragged into this. Put you in danger. Please forgive me, Channing. Please." She seemed like she was twelve years old.

A terrible thought occurred to me. Had Dempsey killed J.J. and Ryan because he thought they'd harmed or even abducted Heather, when in fact they'd been *helping* her? I eyed Dempsey, trying to spot some sign of remorse on his face. But I sensed nothing. Was he that cold?

"Where is Spellman now?" Dempsey asked.

"I don't know," Heather said, between sobs. "I don't know."

I snapped out of my daze. "I'll call Freeman. Tell him—"

"Who's Freeman?" Dempsey asked.

"Police detective. Friend of mine. He can pick Brooks up." I pulled my cell phone from my pocket, and opened it up. Zero bars. "Shit."

Dempsey said, "Signal comes and goes. Mostly goes." He pointed to the remains of the phone on the counter behind him. "Landline's not working too well either." After a long moment of deliberation, he rose slowly. "Come on, let's go find a good cell. Figure this goddamn mess out."

"Heather and I will wait here," Kathleen said.

Dempsey's eyes narrowed to slits. He pursed his lips. "No. Don't think so."

"Why not?"

A sick laugh emanated from Dempsey. "How many stories has our little girl told over the years? Tales of misfortune. Excuses. Complete fabrications. She's a pro. I'm not sure she's telling the truth now."

Kathleen stepped up, got right in Dempsey's face and hissed at him. "You think she made up the fact she feels guilty for killing her own sister? You are a sick fuck. I should have left you years ago. I was too weak then. But I'm not weak now."

He brought the gun up and aimed it at her chest.

I launched myself at Dempsey, catching him by surprise. My momentum knocked him backward and he tipped over in his chair. I heard a loud thump as his head hit the wall of the counter behind him.

"Come on, let's go." I grabbed Heather's hand and dragged her toward the door, Kathleen on her heels. I fumbled with the deadbolt, finally throwing it open. Behind us, Dempsey groaned and cussed. I flung the door open and pushed Heather through, then grabbed Kathleen and did the same. "Go, go. Run. My car's down the drive."

I glanced over my shoulder and saw Dempsey pick up his gun. I slammed the door behind me as I raced to catch up to Heather and her mom. All three of us sprinted toward freedom. We flew down the drive, letting gravity help propel us. After twenty yards or so, I'd pulled even with Heather. "Hurry, hurry, he's right behind us." Another glance over my shoulder confirmed it—Dempsey had emerged from the cabin and was chasing us, waving his gun in the air.

We closed in on my car—thirty more yards to go. Next to me, both Heather and Kathleen were pumping as fast as they could, their breath sounding like twin diesel engines. "Almost there. Keep it up. Go, go, go."

Behind us, Dempsey started hollering. "Stop. I'll shoot, goddamnit. You better stop."

Up ahead, the drive curved and disappeared into the woods. As we negotiated the bend toward Rex, Heather stopped short. "Oh my God." Her hand pointed at my front tire.

It was flat.

A hunting knife had been plunged into Rex's sidewall.

FORTY

I FROZE. SOMEONE ELSE was here in the woods with us. And our visitor wasn't too friendly.

Dempsey came lumbering up. "Nobody move. I don't want to shoot, but I will, you run off again." He struggled to catch his breath and it took him a moment to notice the deflated tire. "What the hell?"

A shot rang out and Dempsey crumpled to the ground. I hit the dirt, pulling Heather down with me. Together we rolled behind my car. The report rang in my ears.

Kathleen knelt next to Dempsey's body, wailing.

"Get down. Over here," I yelled to her as I scanned the tree line across the clearing. Best I could tell, the shot had come from the far side, halfway along the arc I'd taken earlier on my romp through the woods. "Kathleen!"

Her head slowly swung in my direction. "Get down. Get over here."

She glanced over her shoulder, then back at me. Snapped out of it and scrambled over. No one fired at her.

The three of us huddled together behind Rex, breathing heavily. Kathleen kept repeating the words, "Oh my God." The fright in Heather's face sent me shivering. I pulled out my cell, still no signal. I closed the phone and listened. No more gunfire, no sounds at all, save for the crickets. Ten feet away, Dempsey was dead or dying, and there was nothing we could do about it. Not without risking our own lives, at least.

I tried to collect my thoughts, willed myself to remain calm and consider our options. While I was thinking, a voice called out. "Come on out. The coast is clear."

I felt Heather tense next to me. "It's him. Brooks. He's here. He's trying to sucker us." Heather's fingernails dug into the flesh on my arm so tightly I thought she'd draw blood.

"Come out. It's okay. I got the guy who shot your friend," Spellman said.

Heather screamed at him. "Fuck you, Brooks. Fuck you."

"Heather. Get your ass out here. We've got to talk," Spellman yelled, giving up the ruse. If we were back home, a thousand people would have heard the commotion and gathered around to see what was happening. Up here, the only ones within earshot were the squirrels.

"No way," Heather yelled back. "No fucking way."

Another shot rang out. Above us, a bullet thwacked into a tree, sending a few leaves fluttering down to earth. "That was a warning. Next time, it's for real," Spellman called out.

Heather started sobbing quietly beside me. I pried her fingers from my arm, scooted to the front of the car, and craned my head around the bumper keeping as close to the ground as I could. No sign of Spellman across the clearing. He'd hidden himself away in the woods waiting to ambush us. He'd succeeded.

"No!" I heard Kathleen scream. I whipped my head around in time to see Heather dashing down the driveway. Across the clearing, I heard Spellman yell something, followed by a flurry of rustling leaves and breaking branches. He'd set off in pursuit of Heather.

"Stay here," I told Kathleen. "Find a hiding place and keep trying 911 on the cell." I tossed her my phone and scrambled toward where Dempsey had fallen. A quick look at his lifeless face told me what I needed to know. I grabbed his gun and took off.

I raced down the curving driveway, careful not to lose my footing on the gravel. I kept close to the edge, ready to dive off the path if Spellman came bursting from the woods in a surprise attack. He'd been on my left, and I figured he'd stay there as he headed down the hill in a more-or-less direct line, aiming to cut off Heather as she descended the hilly driveway switchbacks.

Through the trees, I spied a glimpse of pink race by. Heather's T-shirt. "Heather. Stop. He's chasing you," I screamed, but the pink blur kept on going, didn't even slow down. My pulse pounded in my ears and the sound of the gravel below my feet was surely giving away my position. Would I even be able to hear Spellman if he sprang from the woods right on top of me?

I skidded to a stop and dropped to one knee. Squinted and listened. Dusk had fallen, and the shadows were deepening quickly. Off to my left, something crashed through the woods, about forty yards away. I slipped into the forest and headed for the noises as silently as I could.

Branches clawed at my face as I pushed through the dense undergrowth. In some spots you could see twenty yards ahead, in others you couldn't see a Winnebago ten feet in front of you. As I plowed deeper, I slowed my pace, picking carefully through the trees, hoping to catch a glimpse of Brooks or Heather between tree trunks.

Voices up ahead brought me to a halt. I hunched down, listening. Brooks was talking. I couldn't make out the words, but the tone seemed soothing, the lilting patter you'd use with a toddler to get him to pick up his toys. I shifted to my right, trying to get a bead on him. His voice came from about eleven o'clock, so I moved counterclockwise, slowly, careful to avoid stumbling or tripping, knowing any noise would betray me. A frontiersman, tracking his prey.

Then I spotted him, crouching behind a tree, holding the gun by his side. Every few seconds, he'd raise his head, look around, then duck down again.

I crept up on him from behind, at a slight angle, closing the gap to about forty feet. His words became clearer. "You'd better show your face. Else I'm coming after you."

"I told you, I've got a gun," Heather said, voice strong and defiant, like her mother's had been facing up to Dempsey.

"Bullshit. Where'd you get a gun?"

"When you threatened me, Ryan bought me one. Taught me how to use it, too," she said. "Why don't you come over? I'd love to show you how good a shot I am. Come on, fucker."

If she were telling the truth, wouldn't she have used the gun to escape her father? Of course, maybe my arrival on the scene had

messed up her plans somehow. With Heather, you never really knew.

Spellman stayed in position behind his tree, tapping the barrel of the gun against the bark in a steady rhythm. I couldn't see Heather—too much brush between us—but she sounded like she was another fifteen yards beyond Brooks. Hopefully, she'd hidden herself well behind a large trunk or in a dense thicket. And if she did have a gun, I hoped she *had* practiced with it. A lot.

"Heather, Heather, Heather. Ryan's dead. I gutted him like a fish. Come out. I'll treat you right."

"You killed Ryan?" Heather's voice cracked.

"J.J., too. Assholes. Told you I'd kill everybody you cared about. Besides, they weren't good enough for you. And I got a chance to screw Artie and that chump Channing while I was at it. Not giving me a shot. Hell, I'm better than half the no-talent shits they hire." Brooks shifted position and I sensed he was getting impatient. "Now get your tight ass out here, bitch. If I have to come in there, it'll get painful."

"Fuck you, Brooks. Come over here, I'll shoot your balls off. If I can find 'em, that is."

I inched closer, hefting Dempsey's pistol in my good hand. I'd fired a friend's gun a few times at a range once. Turned out to be a decent shot, but I'd had two good hands to aim the pistol. Spellman had taken that away from me, too. I continued my stealthy approach.

"Heather. This is your last chance." Brooks stood and pressed himself against the tree. Getting ready for his assault.

I picked up my pace, risking more noise. I needed to get closer before he attacked Heather.

"Fuck you, Brooks. You're a dead man," Heather said.

Twenty feet away from me, Brooks shook his head and pushed himself off the tree trunk. Seemed to take a deep breath, preparing to make his move.

I dropped into a shooter's stance and wrapped my left thumb and forefinger around my shooting hand to steady my aim. Hollered at him. "Brooks. Drop the gun."

He spun around, firing wildly, frantically trying to locate my voice. I aimed for his chest and pulled the trigger. He yelped as the impact knocked him off his feet. His gun flew into the bushes. In the background, Heather screamed.

I dashed over to Spellman, who lay on his back in agony, hand pressing on his shoulder. "You shot me, you motherfucker." He made no move to get up.

"It was you that night? Ran us off the road." I spoke in a calm monotone.

A surge of panic showed on his face. "What? No. No. Who told you that?"

"Don't mess with me. Now's the time to come clean. Before…"

Spellman's eyes filled with terror as he realized he was facing his judge, jury, and executioner. "No. No. You've got it wrong. All wrong."

I raised my left hand. "You took my hand from me." I pointed to the scar on my face. "You left me with deeper wounds than this. You killed Lauren."

He stared at me, mouth open, no sound coming out.

"You took my life from me."

He scrambled backwards, propelling himself by digging his heels into the dirt and pushing, skittering along like a crazed crab

until his head bumped up against the tree he'd been hiding behind. I took a few steps toward him. Brandished the gun.

I loomed over Spellman for fifteen seconds, or maybe it was fifteen minutes, I'd lost track. On the ground below, his face pleaded with me. For mercy, for life. His screams mixed with Heather's to form a macabre chorus.

I took a deep breath and aimed the gun down and pulled the trigger, my finger trembling against the hard metal. I pulled and pulled and pulled until my finger ached and the bullets came no more.

The blasts echoed in the woods, echoed in my ears.

Echoed in my soul.

FORTY-ONE

Ten after one in my therapist's office. I took a deep breath and reclined on the couch, wiped out after recounting my harrowing experience in the woods. I realized I'd avoided asking the question I most wanted an answer to. Had I omitted it on purpose, so I couldn't get the answer I dreaded? If there's one thing I've learned in these sessions, it didn't pay to be coy. I leaned forward and the question sprang from my lips. "Did I do the right thing?"

An enigmatic smile. "What do you think?"

"I don't know. If I knew, I wouldn't have to ask." I shook my head. If I wanted evasion and bullshit, I knew dozens of other places I could get them for free.

"Society says you did the right thing sparing Spellman's life." A pause. "Is that what you want to hear?"

I shrugged. I didn't know what I wanted to hear. I guess I wanted to believe letting Brooks live and go on trial for murder was "better" than gunning him down in cold blood in the dark woods. I wanted somebody to stand up and tell me that—in so many precise and

296

well-articulated words—rather than hiding one's true beliefs in a miasma of political correctness. Was I asking too much?

"Channing. When you get down to it, it only matters what *you* think. Do *you* think you did the right thing?"

I swallowed and considered the question for the gazillionth time. "Yeah, I guess." Here on the couch, the idea of taking some-one else's life seemed reprehensible. I wasn't a murderer. But I wasn't sure I'd done the right thing, not really. In the woods, in the heat of the moment, I'd wanted to blast Spellman's brains out. Make him pay for what he did. Something deep within me had moved my hand two feet to the side. Was it my "true self," or had I been a coward? Who knew? I never would. Now, the idea of Brooks Spellman breathing air or watching TV or reading books while he sat in a cell made me want to retch.

"Feeling guilty?"

"About what?" I asked, stifling a laugh. What *didn't* I feel guilty about?

"Not 'taking care' of Lauren's murderer? Do you think that's why you need affirmation you did the right thing? To help assuage your guilt?"

There's no hiding in therapy. "Yes. You're right, of course. I *do* feel guilty. I *am* guilty."

"Two overwhelming drives—not to kill another human, aveng-ing Lauren's death—in opposition. I think whatever you decided would have left you with enormous guilt. A sort of 'damned if you do, damned if you don't' scenario. Don't be too hard on yourself, Channing. We're only human. Every one of us."

———

Artie forbade me to return to the club for at least a week. But after seven days of forced sabbatical, I made sure to get to The Last Laff before anyone else on my first day back. I let myself in and took my time wandering around the empty place, running my hand over the bar, rummaging through the refrigerator in the kitchen, walking out on stage in front of an imaginary—and appreciative—audience.

I missed it terribly. All of it.

I waited in the office for Heather. She'd called last night, wanting to meet me, and I told her to come by the club around one. She refused to say why on the phone, even after some persistent questioning. I'd let it go, coming up with my own list of possibilities, ranging from profuse thanks, to telling me off in no uncertain terms, to pulling a gun and shooting me like *I* was Brooks Spellman. You never could tell with Heather.

Since the incident, I'd seen her exactly once, at her father's funeral. I'd stayed in the background and didn't speak to her beyond a single expression of condolence. We'd been through a lot together, and unfortunately, the memorable times were mostly unpleasant. Who wanted to be reminded of that?

At one-thirty, I heard the outer door open and Heather call out.

"Back here," I shouted.

In a moment, her head appeared in the office doorway. She took a tentative step forward. "Hi, Channing."

"Come on in." I rose and hugged her, but the embrace was stiff, perfunctory. She may have looked like Lauren and shared many of her mannerisms, but she lacked any of Lauren's depth and warmth. Sort of a washed-out replica, like the one-hundredth Xerox copy of a copy. "How you doing?" I asked, as we broke apart. Neither of us sat. This was going to be a short conversation.

"Okay, I guess," she said, twirling her hair around one finger.

"How's your mom?"

Heather made a little face. "She'll be okay. She'll have a tough time coming to grips with all that happened, but she's stronger than she looks."

"Good," I said, pausing for a second. I had a question I wanted to ask, though I didn't want to seem insensitive. But I needed to know. "Would you have shot Brooks if he'd gotten close enough in the woods?"

Heather shook her head. "Didn't have a gun. I was bluffing."

"But Ambyr said she'd overheard you talking about it. On the phone."

"Yeah. Ryan and I discussed it. I wanted one, but he talked me out of it. Didn't want anyone to get hurt accidentally."

I nodded, unsure of what I could say to ease her pain.

She cleared her throat. "I'm going to Denver. To visit a friend. I just wanted to…" She averted her eyes.

"Denver, huh? Going to try some clubs there?" I asked, but I knew the answer. Heather wasn't ready for the emotional challenge of performing in front of an audience, not yet. She needed to get herself together first.

"I dunno. Maybe." Her hair twirled tighter.

I snapped my fingers. "Hey, almost forgot." I reached under my card table desk into my duffel bag and pulled out Heather's Dumbo towel. Held it out to her. She stared at it but didn't take it, a wistful smile on her lips.

"Thanks," she said. "But why don't you keep it? Maybe you'll have better luck with it."

"Okay." I tossed it onto the table. I'd wait until Heather was gone before I threw it into the round file. Didn't want to appear rude, but I knew it wouldn't bring me any luck either.

Heather swallowed and gazed at me with those dark brown eyes, same as Lauren's. "Channing, I just wanted to say thanks. For everything. I know I screwed up and I'm sorry. Can you ever forgive me?"

"I'll work on it," I said with a wink. "Take care of yourself, Heather."

She nodded, eyes glossy.

"Come on, I'll walk you out."

———

After Heather left, I stayed outside to soak in some fresh air. Sat on the curb and closed my eyes, conjuring images of warm tropical breezes and majestic mountain peaks. The endless procession of undulating waves crashing on the beach. Tried to get centered, tried to take all the bad things and lock them in a box in the back of my mind. Wasn't too successful.

Ten minutes later, a cool shadow fell over me. I cracked open my eyes.

"Hey there, Channing. Vacation over?" Artie said, slight grin on his face. "I didn't wake you, did I?"

"No. Just thinking."

"Oh, then I'm not interrupting anything important. Come on," he said, jerking his head for me to follow.

Nobody spoke until we reached the office.

"Why don't you sit at the desk?" Artie said. Before I could protest, he'd settled down into my folding chair. "What'd you do this past week?"

"Nothing much." Aside from a few long talks with Erin, moping around the condo hadn't been very captivating. I was glad to be back at the club, at work, in my element.

"Hell of a thing, huh?"

"Yeah." It hadn't taken long for Freeman to put together the evidence, once we gave him Brooks Spellman. Brooks had hired a call girl to murder J.J. with tainted coke, trying to warn Heather that if she talked about the "accident," the same fate might befall her. When the hooker chickened out the first time, Brooks lured her back to try again by doubling her pay, and, unfortunately for J.J., she was successful. Then, to cover his tracks, Brooks killed her and burned down Artie's townhouse in a lame attempt to eliminate all the evidence in one fell swoop. Freeman also found blood evidence in the trunk of Brooks's car linking him to Ryan's murder. Another—more personal—message to Heather to keep her mouth shut. After that, Brooks ended up tailing me, counting on my relationship with Heather to lead him to her. It worked.

"You sure you're okay? You spaced out there for a minute." Artie said, concern on his face.

"I'll be fine."

"Good. Hey, listen. Reed's turning tail. He's withdrawn his offer, said he's going to concentrate on developing his recent acquisitions rather than expanding his empire into Northern Virginia," Artie said, rolling his unlit cigar around in his mouth. "I think he's afraid of us. I kind of hope he changes his mind and tries to compete with us here. We'll knock his block off." He jabbed the air in front of him, then eyed me, hoping I'd reflect his spunk. I'm sure my face was flat.

"That's good," I said, half listening.

"You don't look so hot. You *sure* you feel okay?"

"Yeah, yeah, I'm fine."

Artie took out his cigar and pointed it at me. "I'm here to support you, pal. You need more time off, okay. You want to keep things like they are now, that's okay. You want to get back on the road, that's okay too. Life's far too short to be stuck in a place you don't want to be. Laughter's great medicine, but for those of us who have to deliver it, comedy's hard work. That's why they call it show *business*, not show *playtime*."

"Thanks, Artie," I said. He was right, life's too short. And I needed to get on with mine. Heartache or not, angry or not, guilty or not, time didn't wait. If I wanted to be true to myself, if I wanted to be true to Lauren, I needed to forge ahead. Maybe it was time to call my uber-agent Sammi and get back on stage.

———

Three weeks later, I was the opening act at a small club in Leesburg. It had been a struggle to get fifteen minutes of new material ready in time, but I made it.

And, man, I killed.

THE END